SHADOWS
ON THE
WALL

❦————❧

The Dark Tales of
MARY E. WILKINS FREEMAN

SHADOWS
ON THE
WALL

The Dark Tales of
MARY E. WILKINS FREEMAN

Edited by
MIKE ASHLEY

This edition published 2022 by
The British Library
96 Euston Road
London NW1 2DB

Selection, introduction and notes © 2022 Mike Ashley

Dates attributed to each story relate to first publication.

Cataloguing in Publication Data
A catalogue record for this publication is available from the British Library

ISBN 978 0 7123 5406 6
e-ISBN 978 0 7123 6744 8

Frontispiece illustration from the front cover of the first UK edition of
The Wind in the Rose-Bush, John Murray, 1903. Illustration on page 303
is by Peter Newell, included in the same John Murray edition.

Cover design by Mauricio Villamayor with illustration by Sandra Gómez
Text design and typesetting by Tetragon, London
Printed in England by CPI Group (UK) Ltd, Croydon, CRO 4YY

CONTENTS

INTRODUCTION

Escaping the Chains

Mary E. Wilkins Freeman, or Mary E. Wilkins as she was known for the first forty-nine years of her life before her marriage to Dr. Charles Freeman, was renowned as one of the leading regional writers in the United States. Her stories were set mostly in Massachusetts, and later New Jersey, and were popular because of their realism in both their characterization and settings. More than one critic noted how her keen observation of people's ways of life, their views and relationships made her fiction come alive.

This is just as true of her supernatural stories, where you feel you can enter the minds of the characters and experience the strangeness developing around them. Yet, realism does not seem an obvious companion to the supernatural. Wilkins managed to create a bedrock of reality whilst introducing strange, uncertain events through the thoughts and actions of her characters.

It was a process that Wilkins developed gradually over the years. She had a fascination for the mystical and unusual but was not sure all of her strait-laced, often elderly readers would appreciate it, so she was careful. It was not until she was nearly fifty, at around the time of her marriage, that she let rip and produced a half-dozen strong supernatural stories for her one notable collection of such stories, *The Wind in the Rose-Bush*, published in 1903. Although other of her works have been reprinted in recent years, in the near century since her death her name was kept alive by enthusiasts of the supernatural because of that one volume. Critic Everett F. Bleiler, who was always sparing with his praise, went so far as to call them "among the best from the American Edwardian period" in his *Guide to Supernatural Fiction*, whilst S. T. Joshi, in his two-volume history of horror fiction, *Unutterable Horror*, remarked that her stories "occasionally generate substantial power."

Because of the power of *The Wind in the Rose-Bush*, the book has stood on its own and the rest of Wilkins's weird tales have been largely overlooked, lost amongst her significant output of children's and regional fiction. Yet she was interested in the weird and unusual from the very start and that interest was stimulated by her upbringing.

Mary Ella Wilkins, as she was christened—she changed her middle name to Eleanor after her mother's death—was born in Randolph, near Boston, Massachusetts on Hallowe'en, 31 October 1852. She came from a long line of Puritan families. Her father, Warren, was descended from Bray Wilkins who had emigrated from Wales to Massachusetts in about 1630. He became involved in the notorious witch trials in Salem in 1692 and it had been his testimony that had contributed to the conviction of his grand-daughter's husband, John Willard, and his subsequent execution. That Puritan streak remained strong in the Wilkins household and was one of several factors that caused young Mary to feel repressed, and unable to express herself. Witchcraft features in several of her historical stories and is an element in "Silence", included here.

Young Mary was further repressed by the over protectiveness of her mother, Eleanor. The couple had already lost a child before Mary was born. A second son, Edward, was born when Mary was two but he died three years later. A daughter, Anna, came along the following year, 1859, and though she survived infancy, she died in 1876, leaving Mary the only child. Even though Mary was by then twenty-four, she had been so under the thumb of her parents that she felt as if she had never been allowed to mature into adulthood. Her father expected religious obedience, her mother expected her to undertake all the household duties, but all Mary wanted to do was read and write.

At this time the family were also in financial distress. Her father, who was an accomplished carpenter and furniture builder, had set up in business in Brattleboro, Vermont, in 1867, but his hope to build a substantial house never came to fruition, and the family lived in a cramped cottage whilst their income dwindled and fortune failed. Mary's father also despaired that she would ever marry. It seems that Mary had a brief romantic fling with Hanson Tyler, the son of a local vicar into whose home the family had moved, but he did not return the feelings and, as a naval ensign, he was seldom at home. Thereafter she seemed to show no interest in men and spent all her time, when not doing the household chores, curled up in a chair, reading. Needing to contribute to the family finances, Mary also worked as a music teacher at a local girls' school.

All this shaped Mary's views on life. Although by her early twenties she was, to a large degree, conditioned by her upbringing, she did not like the Puritanical repression and she could not accept a patriarchal society. In her experience, although men, and in particular fathers and husbands, wielded the dictatorial authority, they did not necessarily possess the wisdom. In her New England surroundings, young Mary became all too aware, even comforted by the significant presence of middle-aged and elderly women who understood how the world ticked and could advise, and in some cases, prompt men in their actions.

Mary's mother died unexpectedly in 1880 and her father, with failing health, moved to Florida, leaving Mary alone in Brattleboro. It was now, with relative freedom, and the need to earn an income, that Mary turned her thoughts to writing. At first, she sold several poems to the children's magazine *Wide Awake* which was published by Daniel Lothrop—a distant relative of her mother—in Boston. The first, "The Beggar King", published in March 1881, earned her a cheque for $10, which is close to $270 or about £200 in today's purchasing power. She was soon selling *Wide Awake* and its rival *St. Nicholas* one or two poems or short stories a month, which she continued for the next decade, providing a significant income to help her move back to Randolph after her father died in April 1883.

She moved in with her only close childhood friend, Mary Wales. Despite suggestions that they might have had a lesbian relationship there is no overt evidence in the surviving correspondence. Rather they appear to have been close friends, and Mary Wales was able to provide the degree of motherhood and sisterhood that Mary Wilkins had lost.

The stability with Mary Wales allowed Mary Wilkins the freedom to continue with her writing. In fact, Wilkins later recalled that her friend would confine her to her study until she had written a set quota of words each day. Before she had a typewriter, Wilkins tried to achieve a thousand words a day but once she acquired a typewriter this shot up to three or four thousand.

Although her children's poetry and stories provided a basic income, and resulted in her first two books, *Decorative Plaques*

(1883) and *The Adventures of Ann* (1886), Wilkins was determined to sell to the adult market. In November 1881, while still living in Vermont, she had submitted an entry to a story contest run by the *Boston Sunday Budget* and was astonished to win the first prize of $50—around £1000 today. She later reported that after buying herself some essentials and a few knick-knacks she gave the rest away. The story, long believed lost, was rediscovered amongst reprints in other local newspapers. Called "Her Shadow Family", it shows her predilection for the uncanny, and almost certainly drew upon her failed relationship with Hanson Tyler. It tells of a spinster in her forties who had been engaged to a sailor but he had gone away to sea and not returned. In her imagination, though, he has come home and they have a family, which exists about her like ghosts—in fact she once recalled the title of the story as "A Ghost Family". She later grew unhappy with the story and never included it in any collection and it lacks the strength to include here, but it shows that from the start Wilkins liked to explore lives both in the real world and our minds.

Later that year Wilkins sold her first true adult story to a major magazine, *Harper's Bazar*, where "Two Old Lovers" appeared on 31 March 1883. It again drew upon unrequited love where a middle-aged couple enjoy each other's company but never marry. There is no mystical element in the story. The editor of *Harper's Bazar*, Mary Booth, almost rejected it because it was written in a rather childish scrawl, betraying Wilkins's restricted upbringing. It was this story that opened Wilkins's career. Booth encouraged her to explore her potential for creating local colour and realism and she was soon selling regularly to both *Harper's Bazar* and its elder sister, *Harper's New Monthly Magazine*. These stories were collected in her first two adult books, *A Humble Romance* (1887) and *A New England Nun* (1891) which proved extremely popular and established her as a writer of merit.

It is amongst these early collections that her first supernatural stories appeared. "A Symphony in Lavender" (1883) is often listed as her earliest supernatural story, but it's really only a tale of a dream, again about unrequited love. More significant, and the first included in this collection, is "A Far-Away Melody", also published in *Harper's Bazar* a month later, with its portent of death. Her first true ghost story, however, was "A Gentle Ghost", published in 1889, which drew upon the death of her sister thirteen years before. Anna had been a happy, outgoing girl, unlike Mary, but as her health failed she became a forlorn figure and that "forlorn little girl" haunted Mary's memories, becoming the centre of "A Gentle Ghost".

Forlorn, abandoned children continued to feature in her more outré tales such as "The Little Maid at the Door" (1892), not included here, and "The School-Teacher's Story" (1894) which is included. During the 1890s, Wilkins turned to historical fiction where she also drew upon her ancestral heritage in stories like "The White Witch" (1893) and in particular "Silence" (1893), the longest story included here, and her darkest and most violent.

In 1892 she learned that the man she had thought she might wed, Hanson Tyler, had married, and any hopes she might have had in that direction were dashed. At around the same time she met Charles Freeman. Although a qualified physician, Freeman never practised but instead managed his father's profitable wood and coal business. He lived a rather excessive life and drank too much, becoming an alcoholic, but Mary found herself attracted to his unconventional lifestyle. Even so she was wary of marriage, as she still lived happily with her friend Mary. It was eight years before Wilkins agreed to marriage, becoming engaged in October 1900, but it was still not until New Year's Day, 1902, that they married.

During that period Mary wrote "The Prism" (1901), which will be found in my British Library anthology *Doorway to Dilemma* (2019). It tells of Wilkins's fear of the potential loss of her past, her freedom and an age of almost perpetual childhood.

Mary's decade of dilemma over whether to marry Dr. Freeman now inspired a series of weird tales. Wilkins chose the supernatural because she could express herself in a form that would mask her fears but still allow her to explore and perhaps conquer them. It was not just the loss of independence and having to give in to a patriarchal authority that she had deplored in her youth, it was also the recognition that she was beyond child-bearing age and that she would be a wife but not a mother. That provoked another sense of loss which becomes all the more powerful in "The Wind in the Rose-Bush" and "The Lost Ghost", both of which are haunted by the spirits of children that Mary never had. Of equal potency is "The Shadows on the Wall" where Wilkins portrays a loss of self and a situation in which souls pass through a form of death in order to join their kindred spirits.

Mary's marriage to Charles was not happy. She could find some escape in her association with Charles's sisters and mother, a family circle that provided Mary with comfort and support. Charles was a notorious womanizer and his alcoholism increased during their relationship, made worse by his failure to secure the mayorship of his town. Mary's success as a writer, which Charles had originally championed, now emphasized his own shortcomings. In 1909 he was sent to a sanatorium but matters did not improve. He was eventually committed to the New

Jersey State Hospital for the Insane in 1921. The following year the couple became legally separated and Charles died in 1923. He left virtually nothing to Mary, bequeathing his remaining fortune to his chauffeur. But Mary's writing success had long made her financially independent. Nevertheless, one wonders how much being shackled to Freeman led Mary to write "The Jade Bracelet" (*The Forum*, April 1918), one of her last weird tales. This is an untypical story for Mary, especially in its portrayal of a Chinese business owner (using the word "Chinaman", which was typical for that period) as a victim and revenger and its imagery of Chinese mysticism, but it further emphasizes Mary's estrangement at that time.

In 1915 Mary learned that her long-time friend Mary Wales had terminal cancer. This, and other thoughts about old age, probably prompted Wilkins to write "Sweet-Flowering Perennial" (*Harper's Monthly*, July 1915), a wonderful evocation of how old friendships can rejuvenate life. It's a surprisingly overlooked strange tale and has not been reprinted in the company of her other weird stories until now.

Throughout her career Mary had won literary prizes and awards, and in 1926 she was presented with the William Dean Howells Gold Medal for Fiction by the American Academy of Arts and Letters. She was also elected to membership of the National Institute of Arts and Letters.

Mary Wilkins Freeman died at her home in Metuchen, New Jersey, on 13 March 1930, aged 77. Amongst her papers was found an unpublished weird tale, "The White Shawl". She had been undecided about the ending, providing two alternatives. That story is included here with what I think is the most suitable conclusion.

In recent years several of Mary's novels have been reprinted, notably *Pembroke*, *Madelon* and *The Shoulders of Atlas*, all of which explore her anguish in life amongst her New England surroundings, but it is in her weird tales that the true spirit of Mary Wilkins Freeman emerges. It is in these tales that she expresses her soul, her fears and at times her desperation. You can read any of her books, but you will not acquire a complete understanding of her outlook on life until you have encountered her ghosts.

MIKE ASHLEY

A NOTE FROM THE PUBLISHER

The original short stories reprinted in the British Library Tales of the Weird series were written and published in a period ranging across the nineteenth and twentieth centuries. There are many elements of these stories which continue to entertain modern readers; however, in some cases there are also uses of language, instances of stereotyping and some attitudes expressed by narrators or characters which may not be endorsed by the publishing standards of today. We acknowledge therefore that some elements in the stories selected for reprinting may continue to make uncomfortable reading for some of our audience. With this series British Library Publishing aims to offer a new readership a chance to read some of the rare material of the British Library's collections in an affordable paperback format, to enjoy their merits and to look back into the worlds of the past two centuries as portrayed by their writers. It is not possible to separate these stories from the history of their writing and as such the following stories are presented as they were originally published with minor edits only, made for consistency of style and sense. We welcome feedback from our readers, which can be sent to the following address:

British Library Publishing
The British Library
96 Euston Road
London, NWI 2DB
United Kingdom

IN THE MARSH-LAND

ar over in the east is the marsh-land. Naught passes through it but the wind—the wind bent on strange ends—or a bird winged and swift, like a soul; but there are no souls in the marsh-land.

No foot of man sounds the deep pools; no boat cleaves the thick grasses. The pools gleam red; the grass is coarse and thick as the hair of a goat; it is flung here and there in shaggy fleeces tinged with red, as if from slaughter. Over in the east the sun stands low; his red rays color the mist like wine. The flags threaten in the wind like spears, but no heroes wield them.

There is no man in the marsh-land, in whose deep pools could be found death, whose thick grasses could moor a boat forever. It is a lonely place, and only my thought is there, striving to possess it all with wide vision.

Over the marsh-land stray odors from border flowers, but there is no sense to harbor them. Over the marsh-land the sound-waves float, but there is no tongue to awaken them to speech and no ear to receive them. In the marsh-land is God, without the souls in which alone He shines unto His own vision; in the marsh-land is God, a light without His own darkness.

The marsh-land is a lonely place; there is no man there. Only my thought is there, holding what it can encompass of God.

A FAR-AWAY MELODY

he clothes-line was wound securely around the trunks of four gnarled, crooked old apple-trees, which stood promiscuously about the yard back of the cottage. It was tree-blossoming time, but these were too aged and sapless to blossom freely, and there was only a white bough here and there shaking itself triumphantly from among the rest, which had only their new green leaves. There was a branch occasionally which had not even these, but pierced the tender green and the flossy white in hard, gray nakedness. All over the yard, the grass was young and green and short, and had not yet gotten any feathery heads. Once in a while there was a dandelion set closely down among it.

The cottage was low, of a dark-red color, with white facings around the windows, which had no blinds, only green paper curtains.

The back door was in the center of the house, and opened directly into the green yard, with hardly a pretense of a step, only a flat oval stone before it.

Through this door, stepping cautiously on the stone, came presently two tall, lank women in chocolate-colored calico gowns, with a basket of clothes between them. They set the basket underneath the line on the grass, with a little clothes-pin bag beside it, and then proceeded methodically to hang out the clothes. Everything of a kind went together, and the best things on the outside line, which could be seen from the street in front of the cottage.

The two women were curiously alike. They were about the same height, and moved in the same way. Even their faces were so similar in feature and expression that it might have been a difficult matter to distinguish between them. All the difference, and that would have been scarcely apparent to an ordinary observer, was a difference of degree, if it might be so expressed. In one face the features were both bolder and sharper in outline, the eyes were a trifle larger and brighter, and the whole expression more animated and decided than in the other.

One woman's scanty drab hair was a shade darker than the other's, and the negative fairness of complexion, which generally accompanies drab hair, was in one relieved by a slight tinge of warm red on the cheeks.

This slightly intensified woman had been commonly considered the more attractive of the two, although in reality there was very little to choose between the personal appearance of these twin sisters, Priscilla and Mary Brown. They moved about the clothes-line, pinning the sweet white linen on securely, their thick, white-stockinged ankles showing beneath their limp calicoes as they stepped, and their large feet in cloth slippers flattening down the short, green grass. Their sleeves were rolled up, displaying their long, thin, muscular arms, which were sharply pointed at the elbows.

They were homely women; they were fifty and over now, but they never could have been pretty in their 'teens, their features were too irredeemably irregular for that. No youthful freshness of complexion or expression could have possibly done away with the impression that they gave. Their plainness had probably only been enhanced by the contrast, and these women, to people generally, seemed better-looking than when they were young. There was an honesty and patience in both faces that showed all the plainer for their homeliness.

One, the sister with the darker hair, moved a little quicker than the other, and lifted the wet clothes from the basket to the line more frequently. She was the first to speak, too, after they had been hanging out the clothes for some little time in silence. She stopped as she did so, with a wet pillow-case in her hand, and looked up reflectively at the flowering apple-boughs overhead, and the blue sky showing between, while the sweet spring wind ruffled her scanty hair a little.

"I wonder, Mary," said she, "if it would seem so very queer to die a mornin' like this, say. Don't you believe there's apple branches a-hangin' over them walls made out of precious stones, like these, only there ain't any dead limbs among 'em, an' they're all covered thick with flowers? An' I wonder if it would seem such an awful change to go from this air into the air of the New Jerusalem." Just then a robin hidden somewhere in the trees began to sing. "I s'pose," she went on, "that there's angels instead of robins, though, and they don't roost up in trees to sing, but stand on the ground, with lilies growin' round their feet, may be, up to their knees, or on the gold stones in the street, an' play on their harps to go with the singin'."

The other sister gave a scared, awed look at her. "Lor, don't talk that way, sister," said she. "What has got into you lately? You make me crawl all over, talkin' so much about dyin'. You feel well, don't you?"

"Lor, yes," replied the other, laughing, and picking up a clothes-pin for her pillow-case; "I feel well enough, an' I don't know what has got me to talkin' so much about dyin' lately, or thinkin' about it. I guess it's the spring weather. P'r'aps flowers growin' make anybody think of wings sproutin' kinder naterally. I won't talk so much about it if it bothers you, an' I don't know but it's sorter natural it should. Did you get the potatoes before we came out, sister?"—with an awkward and kindly effort to change the subject.

"No," replied the other, stooping over the clothes-basket. There was such a film of tears in her dull blue eyes that she could not distinguish one article from another.

"Well, I guess you had better go in an' get 'em, then; they ain't worth anything, this time of year, unless they soak a while, an' I'll finish hangin' out the clothes while you do it."

"Well, p'r'aps I'd better," the other woman replied, straightening herself up from the clothes-basket. Then she went into the house without another word; but down in the damp cellar, a minute later, she sobbed over the potato barrel as if her heart would break. Her sister's remarks had filled her with a vague apprehension and grief which she could not throw off. And there was something a little singular about it. Both these women had always been of a deeply religious cast of mind. They had studied the Bible faithfully, if not understandingly, and their religion had strongly tinctured their daily life. They knew almost as much about the Old Testament prophets as they did about their neighbors; and that was saying a good deal of two single women in a New England country town. Still this religious element in their natures could hardly have been termed spirituality. It deviated from that as much as anything of religion—which is in one way spirituality itself—could.

Both sisters were eminently practical in all affairs of life, down to their very dreams, and Priscilla especially so. She had dealt in religion with the bare facts of sin and repentance, future punishment and reward. She had dwelt very little, probably, upon the poetic splendors of the Eternal City, and talked about them still less. Indeed, she had always been reticent about her religious convictions, and had said very little about them even to her sister.

The two women, with God in their thoughts every moment, seldom had spoken his name to each other. For Priscilla to talk in the strain that she had today, and for a week or two previous, off and on, was, from its extreme deviation from her usual custom, certainly startling.

Poor Mary, sobbing over the potato barrel, thought it was a sign of approaching death. She had a few superstitious-like grafts upon her practical, commonplace character.

She wiped her eyes finally, and went upstairs with her tin basin of potatoes, which were carefully washed and put to soak by the time her sister came in with the empty basket.

At twelve exactly the two sat down to dinner in the clean kitchen, which was one of the two rooms the cottage boasted. The narrow entry ran from the front door to the back. On one side was the kitchen and living-room; on the other, the room where the sisters slept. There were two small unfinished lofts overhead, reached by a step-ladder through a little scuttle in the entry ceiling: and that was all. The sisters had earned the cottage and paid for it years before, by working as tailoresses. They had, besides, quite a snug little sum in the bank, which they had saved out of their hard earnings. There was no need for Priscilla and Mary to work so hard, people said; but work hard they did, and work hard they would as long as they lived. The mere habit of work had become as necessary to them as breathing.

Just as soon as they had finished their meal and cleared away the dishes, they put on some clean starched purple prints, which were their afternoon dresses, and seated themselves with their work at the two front windows; the house faced south-west, so the sunlight streamed through both. It was a very warm day for the season, and the windows were open. Close to them in the yard outside stood great clumps of lilac bushes. They grew on the other side of the front door too; a little later the low cottage would look half-buried in them. The shadows of their leaves made a dancing network over the freshly washed yellow floor.

The two sisters sat there and sewed on some coarse vests all the afternoon. Neither made a remark often. The room, with its glossy little cooking-stove, its eight-day clock on the mantel, its chintz-cushioned rocking-chairs, and the dancing shadows of the lilac leaves on its yellow floor, looked pleasant and peaceful.

Just before six o'clock a neighbor dropped in with her cream pitcher to borrow some milk for tea, and she sat down for a minute's chat after she had got it filled. They had been talking a few moments on neighborhood topics, when all of a sudden Priscilla let her work fall and raised her hand. "Hush!" whispered she.

The other two stopped talking, and listened, staring at her wonderingly, but they could hear nothing.

"What is it, Miss Priscilla?" asked the neighbor, with round blue eyes. She was a pretty young thing, who had not been married long.

"Hush! Don't speak. Don't you hear that beautiful music?" Her ear was inclined towards the open window, her hand still raised warningly, and her eyes fixed on the opposite wall beyond them.

Mary turned visibly paler than her usual dull paleness, and shuddered. "I don't hear any music," she said. "Do you, Miss Moore?"

"No-o," replied the caller, her simple little face beginning to put on a scared look, from a vague sense of a mystery she could not fathom. Mary Brown rose and went to the door, and looked eagerly up and down the street. "There ain't no organ-man in sight anywhere," said she, returning, "an' I can't hear any music, an' Miss Moore can't, an' we're both sharp enough o' hearin'. You're jest imaginin' it, sister."

"I never imagined anything in my life," returned the other, "an' it ain't likely I'm goin' to begin now. It's the beautifulest music. It comes from over the orchard there. Can't you hear it? But it seems to me it's growin' a little fainter like now. I guess it's movin' off, perhaps."

Mary Brown set her lips hard. The grief and anxiety she had felt lately turned suddenly to unreasoning anger against the cause of it; through her very love she fired with quick wrath at the beloved object. Still she did not say much, only, "I guess it must be movin' off," with a laugh, which had an unpleasant ring in it.

After the neighbor had gone, however, she said more, standing before her sister with her arms folded squarely across her bosom. "Now, Priscilla Brown," she exclaimed, "I think it's about time to put a stop to this. I've heard about enough of it. What do you s'pose Miss Moore thought of you? Next thing it'll be all over town that you're gettin' spiritual notions. Today it's music that nobody else can hear, an' yesterday you smelled roses, and there ain't one in blossom this time o' year, and all the time you're talkin' about dyin'. For my part, I don't see why you ain't as likely to live as I am. You're uncommon hearty on vittles. You ate a pretty good dinner today for a dyin' person."

"I didn't say I was goin' to die," replied Priscilla meekly: the two sisters seemed suddenly to have changed natures. "An' I'll try not to talk so, if it plagues you. I told you I wouldn't this mornin', but the music kinder took me by surprise like, an' I thought may be you an' Miss Moore could hear it. I can jest hear it a little bit now, like the dyin' away of a bell."

"There you go agin!" cried the other sharply. "Do, for mercy's sake, stop, Priscilla. There ain't no music."

"Well, I won't talk any more about it," she answered patiently; and she rose and began setting the table for tea, while Mary sat down and resumed her sewing, drawing the thread through the cloth with quick, uneven jerks.

That night the pretty girl neighbor was aroused from her first sleep by a distressed voice at her bedroom window, crying, "Miss Moore! Miss Moore!"

She spoke to her husband, who opened the window. "What's wanted?" he asked, peering out into the darkness.

"Priscilla's sick," moaned the distressed voice; "awful sick. She's fainted, an' I can't bring her to. Go for the doctor—quick! quick! *quick!*" The voice ended in a shriek on the last word, and the speaker turned and ran back to the cottage, where, on the bed, lay a pale, gaunt woman, who had not stirred since she left it. Immovable through all her sister's agony, she lay there, her features shaping themselves out more and more from the shadows, the bed-clothes that covered her limbs taking on an awful rigidity.

"She must have died in her sleep," the doctor said, when he came, "without a struggle."

When Mary Brown really understood that her sister was dead, she left her to the kindly ministrations of the good women who are always ready at such times in a country place, and went and sat by the kitchen window in the chair which her sister had occupied that afternoon.

There the women found her when the last offices had been done for the dead.

"Come home with me tonight," one said; "Miss Green will stay with *her*," with a turn of her head towards the opposite room, and an emphasis on the pronoun which distinguished it at once from one applied to a living person.

"No," said Mary Brown; "I'm a-goin' to set here an' listen." She had the window wide open, leaning her head out into the chilly night air.

The women looked at each other; one tapped her head, another nodded hers. "Poor thing!" said a third.

"You see," went on Mary Brown, still speaking with her head leaned out of the window, "I was cross with her this afternoon because she talked about hearin' music. I was cross, an' spoke up sharp to her, because I loved her, but I don't think she knew. I didn't want to think she was goin' to die, but she was. An' she heard the music. It was true. An' now I'm a-goin' to set here an' listen till I hear it too, an' then I'll know she ain't laid up what I said agin me, an' that I'm a-goin' to die too."

They found it impossible to reason with her; there she sat till morning, with a pitying woman beside her, listening all in vain for unearthly melody.

Next day they sent for a widowed niece of the sisters, who came at once, bringing her little boy with her. She was a kindly young woman, and took up her abode in the little cottage, and did the best she could for her poor aunt, who, it soon became evident, would never be quite herself again. There she would sit at the kitchen window and listen day after day. She took a great fancy to her niece's little boy, and used often to hold him in her lap as she sat there. Once in a while she would ask him if he heard any music. "An innocent little thing like him might hear quicker than a hard, unbelievin' old woman like me," she told his mother once.

She lived so for nearly a year after her sister died. It was evident that she failed gradually and surely, though there was no apparent disease. It seemed to trouble her exceedingly that she never heard the music she listened for. She had an idea that she could not die unless she did, and her whole soul seemed filled with longing to join her beloved twin sister, and be assured of her forgiveness. This sister-love was all she had ever felt, besides her love of God, in any strong degree; all the passion of devotion of which this homely, commonplace woman was capable was centered in that, and the unsatisfied strength of it was killing her. The weaker she grew, the more earnestly she listened. She was too feeble to sit up, but she would not consent to lie in bed, and made them bolster her up with pillows in a rocking-chair by the window. At last she died, in the spring, a week or two before her sister had the preceding year. The season was a little more advanced this year, and the apple-trees were blossomed out further than they were then. She died about ten o'clock in the morning. The day before her niece had been called into the room by a shrill cry of rapture from her: "I've heard it! I've heard it!" she cried. "A faint sound o' music, like the dyin' away of a bell."

A GENTLE GHOST

ut in front of the cemetery stood a white horse and a covered wagon. The horse was not tied, but she stood quite still, her four feet widely and ponderously planted, her meek white head hanging. Shadows of leaves danced on her back. There were many trees about the cemetery, and the foliage was unusually luxuriant for May. The four women who had come in the covered wagon remarked it. "I never saw the trees so forward as they are this year, seems to me," said one, gazing up at some magnificent gold-green branches over her head.

"I was sayin' so to Mary this mornin'," rejoined another. "They're uncommon forward, I think."

They loitered along the narrow lanes between the lots: four homely, middle-aged women, with decorous and subdued enjoyment in their worn faces. They read with peaceful curiosity and interest the inscriptions on the stones; they turned aside to look at the tender, newly blossomed spring bushes—the flowering almonds and the bridal wreaths. Once in a while they came to a new stone, which they immediately surrounded with eager criticism. There was a solemn hush when they reached a lot where some relatives of one of the party were buried. She put a bunch of flowers on a grave, then she stood looking at it with red eyes. The others grouped themselves deferentially aloof.

They did not meet any one in the cemetery until just before they left. When they had reached the rear and oldest portion of the yard, and were thinking of retracing their steps, they became suddenly aware of a child sitting in a lot at their right. The lot held seven old, leaning stones, dark and mossy, their inscriptions dimly traceable. The child sat close to one, and she looked up at the staring knot of women with a kind of innocent keenness, like a baby. Her face was small and fair and pinched. The women stood eying her.

"What's your name, little girl?" asked one. She had a bright flower in her bonnet and a smart lift to her chin, and seemed the natural spokeswoman of the party. Her name was Holmes. The child turned her head sideways and murmured something.

"What? We can't hear. Speak up; don't be afraid! What's your name?" The woman nodded the bright flower over her, and spoke with sharp pleasantness.

"Nancy Wren," said the child, with a timid catch of her breath.

"Wren?"

The child nodded. She kept her little pink, curving mouth parted.

"It's nobody I know," remarked the questioner, reflectively. "I guess she comes from—over there." She made a significant motion of her head towards the right. "Where do you live, Nancy?" she asked.

The child also motioned towards the right.

"I thought so," said the woman. "How old are you?"

"Ten."

The women exchanged glances. "Are you sure you're tellin' the truth?"

The child nodded.

"I never saw a girl so small for her age if she is," said one woman to another.

"Yes," said Mrs. Holmes, looking at her critically; "she is dreadful small. She's considerable smaller than my Mary was. Is there any of your folks buried in this lot?" said she, fairly hovering with affability and determined graciousness.

The child's upturned face suddenly kindled. She began speaking with a soft volubility that was an odd contrast to her previous hesitation.

"That's mother," said she, pointing to one of the stones, "an' that's father, an' there's John, an' Marg'ret, an' Mary, an' Susan, an' the baby, and here's—Jane."

The women stared at her in amazement. "Was it your—" began Mrs. Holmes; but another woman stepped forward, stoutly impetuous.

"Land! it's the Blake lot!" said she. "This child can't be any relation to 'em. You hadn't ought to talk so, Nancy."

"It's so," said the child, shyly persistent. She evidently hardly grasped the force of the woman's remark.

They eyed her with increased bewilderment. "It can't be," said the woman to the others. "Every one of them Blakes died years ago."

"I've seen Jane," volunteered the child, with a candid smile in their faces.

Then the stout woman sank down on her knees beside Jane's stone, and peered hard at it.

"She died forty year ago this May," said she, with a gasp. "I used to know her when I was a child. She was ten years old when she died. You ain't ever seen her. You hadn't ought to tell such stories."

"I ain't seen her for a long time," said the little girl.

"What made you say you'd seen her at all?" said Mrs. Holmes, sharply, thinking this was capitulation.

"I did use to see her a long time ago, an' she used to wear a white dress, an' a wreath on her head. She used to come here an' play with me."

The women looked at each other with pale, shocked faces; one nervous; one shivered. "She ain't quite right," she whispered. "Let's go." The women began filing away. Mrs. Holmes, who came last, stood about for a parting word to the child.

"You can't have seen her," said she, severely, "an' you are a wicked girl to tell such stories. You mustn't do it again, remember."

Nancy stood with her hand on Jane's stone, looking at her. "She did," she repeated, with mild obstinacy.

"There's somethin' wrong about her, I guess," whispered Mrs. Holmes, rustling on after the others.

"I see she looked kind of queer the minute I set eyes on her," said the nervous woman.

When the four reached the front of the cemetery they sat down to rest for a few minutes. It was warm, and they had still quite a walk, nearly the whole width of the yard, to the other front corner where the horse and wagon were.

They sat down in a row on a bank; the stout woman wiped her face; Mrs. Holmes straightened her bonnet. Directly opposite across the street stood two houses, so close to each other that their walls almost touched. One was a large square building, glossily white, with green blinds; the other was low, with a facing of whitewashed stonework reaching to its lower windows, which somehow gave it a disgraced and menial air; there were, moreover, no blinds.

At the side of the low building stretched a wide plowed field, where several halting old figures were moving about planting. There was none of the brave hope of the sower about them.

Even across the road one could see the feeble stiffness of their attitudes, the half-palsied fling of their arms.

"I declare I shouldn't think them old men over there would ever get that field planted," said Mrs. Holmes, energetically watchful. In the front door of the square white house sat a girl with bright hair. The yard was full of green light from two tall maple-trees, and the girl's hair made a brilliant spot of color in the midst of it.

"That's Flora Dunn over there on the door-step, ain't it?" said the stout woman.

"Yes. I should think you could tell her by her red hair."

"I knew it. I should have thought Mr. Dunn would have hated to have had their house so near the poor-house. I declare I should!"

"Oh, he wouldn't mind," said Mrs. Holmes; "he's as easy as old Tilly. It wouldn't have troubled him any if they'd set it right in his front yard. But I guess *she* minded some. I heard she did. John said there wa'n't any need of it. The town wouldn't have set it so near, if Mr. Dunn had set his foot down he wouldn't have it there. I s'pose they wanted to keep that big field on the side clear; but they would have moved it along a little if he'd made a fuss. I tell you what 'tis, I've 'bout made up my mind—I dun know as it's Scripture, but I can't help it—if folks don't make a fuss they won't get their rights in this world. If you jest lay still an' don't rise up, you're goin' to get stepped on. If people like to be, they can; I don't."

"I should have thought he'd have hated to have the poor-house quite so close," murmured the stout woman.

Suddenly Mrs. Holmes leaned forward and poked her head among the other three. She sat on the end of the row. "Say," said she, in a mysterious whisper, "I want to know if you've heard the stories 'bout the Dunn house?"

"No; what?" chorused the other women, eagerly. They bent over towards her till the four faces were in a knot.

"Well," said Mrs. Holmes, cautiously, with a glance at the bright-headed girl across the way—"I heard it pretty straight—they say the house is haunted."

The stout woman sniffed and straightened herself. "Haunted!" repeated she.

"They say that ever since Jenny died there's been queer noises 'round the house that they can't account for. You see that front chamber over there, the one next to the poor-house; well, that's the room, they say."

The women all turned and looked at the chamber windows, where some ruffled white curtains were fluttering.

"That's the chamber where Jenny used to sleep, you know," Mrs. Holmes went on; "an' she died there. Well, they said that before Jenny died, Flora had always slept there with her, but she felt kind of bad about goin' back there, so she thought she'd take another room. Well, there was the awfulest moanin' an' takin' on up in Jenny's room, when she did, that Flora went back there to sleep."

"I shouldn't thought she could," whispered the nervous woman, who was quite pale.

"The moanin' stopped jest as soon as she got in there with a light. You see Jenny was always terrible timid an' afraid to sleep alone, an' had a lamp burnin' all night, an' it seemed to them jest as if it really was her, I s'pose."

"I don't believe one word of it," said the stout woman, getting up. "It makes me all out of patience to hear people talk such stuff, jest because the Dunns happen to live opposite a graveyard."

"I told it jest as I heard it," said Mrs. Holmes, stiffly.

"Oh, I ain't blamin' you; it's the folks that start such stories that I ain't got any patience with. Think of that dear, pretty little sixteen-year-old girl hauntin' a house!"

"Well, I've told it jest as I heard it," repeated Mrs. Holmes, still in a tone of slight umbrage. "I don't ever take much stock in such things myself."

The four women strolled along to the covered wagon and climbed in. "I declare," said the stout woman, conciliatingly, "I dun know when I've had such an outin'. I feel as if it had done me good. I've been wantin' to come down to the cemetery for a long time, but it's most more'n I want to walk. I feel real obliged to you, Mis' Holmes."

The others climbed in. Mrs. Holmes disclaimed all obligations gracefully, established herself on the front seat, and shook the reins over the white horse. Then the party jogged along the road to the village, past outlying farmhouses and rich green meadows, all freckled gold with dandelions. Dandelions were in their height; the buttercups had not yet come.

Flora Dunn, the girl on the door-step, glanced up when they started down the street; then she turned her eyes on her work; she was sewing with nervous haste.

"Who were those folks, did you see, Flora?" called her mother, out of the sitting-room.

"I didn't notice," replied Flora, absently.

Just then the girl whom the women had met came lingeringly out of the cemetery and crossed the street.

"There's that poor little Wren girl," remarked the voice in the sitting-room.

"Yes," assented Flora. After a while she got up and entered

36

the house. Her mother looked anxiously at her when she came into the room.

"I'm all out of patience with you, Flora," said she. "You're jest as white as a sheet. You'll make yourself sick. You're actin' dreadful foolish."

Flora sank into a chair and sat staring straight ahead with a strained, pitiful gaze. "I can't help it; I can't do any different," said she. "I shouldn't think you'd scold me, mother."

"Scold you; I ain't scoldin' you, child; but there ain't any sense in your doin' so. You'll make yourself sick, an' you're all I've got left. I can't have anything happen to you, Flora." Suddenly Mrs. Dunn burst out in a low wail, hiding her face in her hands.

"I don't see as you're much better yourself, mother," said Flora, heavily.

"I don't know as I am," sobbed her mother; "but I've got you to worry about besides—everything else. Oh, dear! oh, dear, dear!"

"I don't see any need of your worrying about me." Flora did not cry, but her face seemed to darken visibly with a gathering melancholy like a cloud. Her hair was beautiful, and she had a charming delicacy of complexion; but she was not handsome, her features were too sharp, her expression too intense and nervous. Her mother looked like her as to the expression; the features were widely different. It was as if both had passed through one corroding element which had given them the similarity of scars. Certainly a stranger would at once have noticed the strong resemblance between Mrs. Dunn's large, heavy-featured face and her daughter's thin, delicately outlined one—a resemblance which three months ago had not been perceptible.

"I see, if you don't," returned the mother. "I ain't blind."

"I don't see what you are blaming me for."

"I ain't blamin' you, but it seems to me that you might jest as well let me go up there an' sleep as you."

Suddenly the girl also broke out into a wild cry. "I ain't going to leave her. Poor little Jenny! poor little Jenny! You needn't try to make me, mother; I won't!"

"Flora, don't!"

"I won't! I won't! I won't! Poor little Jenny! Oh, dear! oh, dear!"

"What if it is so? What if it is—*her*? Ain't she got me as well as you? Can't her mother go to her?"

"I won't leave her. I won't! I won't!"

Suddenly Mrs. Dunn's calmness seemed to come uppermost, raised in the scale by the weighty impetus of the other's distress. "Flora," said she, with mournful solemnity, "you mustn't do so; it's wrong. You mustn't wear yourself all out over something that maybe you'll find out wasn't so some time or other."

"Mother, don't you think it is—don't you?"

"I don't know what to think, Flora." Just then a door shut somewhere in the back part of the house. "There's father," said Mrs. Dunn, getting up; "an' the fire ain't made."

Flora rose also, and went about helping her mother to get supper. Both suddenly settled into a rigidity of composure; their eyes were red, but their lips were steady. There was a resolute vein in their characters; they managed themselves with wrenches, and could be hard even with their grief. They got tea ready for Mr. Dunn and his two hired men; then cleared it away, and sat down in the front room with their needlework. Mr. Dunn, a kindly, dull old man, was in there too, over his newspaper. Mrs. Dunn and Flora sewed intently, never taking their eyes from their work. Out in the next room stood a tall clock, which ticked loudly;

just before it struck the hours it made always a curious grating noise. When it announced in this way the striking of nine, Mrs. Dunn and Flora exchanged glances; the girl was pale, and her eyes looked larger. She began folding up her work. Suddenly a low moaning cry sounded through the house, seemingly from the room overhead. "There it is!" shrieked Flora. She caught up a lamp and ran. Mrs. Dunn was following, when her husband, sitting near the door, caught hold of her dress with a bewildered air; he had been dozing. "What's the matter?" said he, vaguely.

"Don't you hear it? Didn't you hear it, father?"

The old man let go of her dress suddenly. "I didn't hear nothin'," said he.

"Hark!"

But the cry, in fact, had ceased. Flora could be heard moving about in the room overhead, and that was all. In a moment Mrs. Dunn ran upstairs after her. The old man sat staring. "It's all dum foolishness," he muttered, under his breath. Presently he fell to dozing again, and his vacantly smiling face lopped forward. Mr. Dunn, slow-brained, patient, and unimaginative, had had his evening naps interrupted after this manner for the last three months, and there was as yet no cessation of his bewilderment. He dealt with the simple, broad lights of life; the shadows were beyond his speculation. For his consciousness his daughter Jenny had died and gone to heaven; he was not capable of listening for her ghostly moans in her little chamber overhead, much less of hearing them with any credulity.

When his wife came downstairs finally she looked at him, sleeping there, with a bitter feeling. She felt as if set about by an icy wind of loneliness. Her daughter, who was after her own kind, was all the one to whom she could look for sympathy and understanding in this subtle perplexity which had come upon her. And she would rather have dispensed with that sympathy, and heard alone those piteous, uncanny cries, for she was wild with anxiety about Flora. The girl had never been very strong. She looked at her distressfully when she came down the next morning.

"Did you sleep any last night?" said she.

"Some," answered Flora.

Soon after breakfast they noticed the little Wren girl stealing across the road to the cemetery again. "She goes over there all the time," remarked Mrs. Dunn. "I b'lieve she runs away. See her look behind her."

"Yes," said Flora, apathetically.

It was nearly noon when they heard a voice from the next house calling, "Nancy! Nancy! Nancy Wren!" The voice was loud and imperious, but slow and evenly modulated. It indicated well its owner. A woman who could regulate her own angry voice could regulate other people. Mrs. Dunn and Flora heard it understandingly.

"That poor little thing will catch it when she gets home," said Mrs. Dunn.

"Nancy! Nancy! Nancy Wren!" called the voice again.

"I pity the child if Mrs. Gregg has to go after her. Mebbe she's fell asleep over there. Flora, why don't you run over there an' get her?"

The voice rang out again. Flora got her hat and stole across the street a little below the house, so the calling woman should not see her. When she got into the cemetery she called in her turn, letting out her thin sweet voice cautiously. Finally she came directly upon the child. She was in the Blake lot, her little slender body, in its dingy cotton dress, curled up on the ground close to one of the graves. No one but Nature tended those old graves now, and she seemed to be lapsing them gently back to her own lines, at her own will. Of the garden shrubs which had been planted about them not one was left but an old low-spraying white rose-bush, which had just gotten its new leaves. The Blake lot was at the very rear of the yard, where it verged upon a light wood, which was silently stealing its way over its own proper boundaries. At the back of the lot stood a thicket of little thin trees, with silvery twinkling leaves. The ground was quite blue with houstonias.

The child raised her little fair head and stared at Flora, as if just awakened from sleep. She held her little pink mouth open, her innocent blue eyes had a surprised look, as if she were suddenly gazing upon a new scene.

"Where's she gone?" asked she, in her sweet, feeble pipe.

"Where's who gone?"

"Jane."

"I don't know what you mean. Come, Nancy, you must go home now."

"Didn't you see her?"

"I didn't see anybody," answered Flora, impatiently. "Come!"

"She was right here."

"What *do* you mean?"

"Jane was standin' right here. An' she had her white dress on, an' her wreath."

Flora shivered, and looked around her fearfully. The fancy of the child was overlapping her own nature. "There wasn't a soul here. You've been dreaming, child. Come!"

"No, I wasn't. I've seen them blue flowers an' the leaves winkin' all the time. Jane stood right there." The child pointed with her tiny finger to a spot at her side. "She hadn't come for a long time before," she added. "She's stayed down there." She pointed at the grave nearest her.

"You mustn't talk so," said Flora, with tremulous severity. "You must get right up and come home. Mrs. Gregg has been calling you and calling you. She won't like it."

Nancy turned quite pale around her little mouth, and sprang to her feet. "Is Mis' Gregg comin'?"

"She will come if you don't hurry."

The child said not another word. She flew along ahead through the narrow paths, and was in the almshouse door before Flora crossed the street.

"She's terrible afraid of Mrs. Gregg," she told her mother when she got home. Nancy had disturbed her own brooding a little, and she spoke more like herself.

"Poor little thing! I pity her," said Mrs. Dunn. Mrs. Dunn did not like Mrs. Gregg.

Flora rarely told a story until she had ruminated awhile over it herself. It was afternoon, and the two were in the front room at their sewing, before she told her mother about "Jane."

"Of course she must have been dreaming," Flora said.

"She must have been," rejoined her mother.

But the two looked at each other, and their eyes said more than their tongues. Here was a new marvel, new evidence of a kind which they had heretofore scented at, these two rigidly walking New England souls; yet walking, after all, upon narrow paths through dark meadows of mysticism. If they never lost their footing, the steaming damp of the meadows might come in their faces.

This fancy, delusion, superstition, whichever one might name it, of theirs had lasted now three months—ever since young Jenny

42

Dunn had died. There was apparently no reason why it should not last much longer, if delusion it were; the temperaments of these two women, naturally nervous and imaginative, overwrought now by long care and sorrow, would perpetuate it.

If it were not delusion, pray what exorcism, what spell of book and bell, could lay the ghost of a little timid child who was afraid alone in the dark?

The days went on, and Flora still hurried up to her chamber at the stroke of nine. If she were a moment late, sometimes if she were not, that pitiful low wail sounded through the house.

The strange story spread gradually through the village. Mrs. Dunn and Flora were silent about it, but Gossip is herself of a ghostly nature, and minds not keys nor bars.

There was quite an excitement over it. People affected with morbid curiosity and sympathy came to the house. One afternoon the minister came and offered a prayer. Mrs. Dunn and Flora received them all with a certain reticence; they did not concur in their wishes to remain and hear the mysterious noises for themselves. People called them "dreadful close." They got more satisfaction out of Mr. Dunn, who was perfectly ready to impart all the information in his power and his own theories in the matter.

"I never heard a thing but once," said he, "an' then it sounded more like a cat to me than anything. I guess mother and Flora air kinder nervous."

The spring was waxing late when Flora went upstairs one night with the oil low in her lamp. She had neglected filling it that day. She did not notice it until she was undressed; then she thought to herself that she must blow it out. She always kept a lamp burning all night, as she had in timid little Jenny's day. Flora herself was timid now.

43

So she blew the light out. She had barely laid her head upon the pillow when the low moaning wail sounded through the room. Flora sat up in bed and listened, her hands clinched. The moan gathered strength and volume; little broken words and sentences, the piteous ejaculations of terror and distress, began to shape themselves out of it.

Flora sprang out of bed, and stumbled towards her west window—the one on the almshouse side. She leaned her head out, listening a moment. Then she called her mother with wild vehemence. But her mother was already at the door with a lamp. When she entered, the moans ceased.

"Mother," shrieked Flora, "it ain't Jenny. It's somebody over there—at the poor-house. Put the lamp out in the entry, and come back here and listen."

Mrs. Dunn set out the lamp and came back, closing the door. It was a few minutes first, but presently the cries recommenced.

"I'm goin' right over there," said Mrs. Dunn. "I'm goin' to dress myself an' go over there. I'm goin' to have this affair sifted now."

"I'm going too," said Flora.

It was only half-past nine when the two stole into the almshouse yard. The light was not out in the room on the ground-floor, which the overseer's family used for a sitting-room. When they entered, the overseer was there asleep in his chair, his wife sewing at the table, and an old woman in a pink cotton dress, apparently doing nothing. They all started, and stared at the intruders.

"Good-evenin'," said Mrs. Dunn, trying to speak composedly. "We thought we'd come in; we got kind of started. Oh, there 'tis now! What is it, Mis' Gregg?"

In fact, at that moment, the wail, louder and more distinct, was heard.

"Why, it's Nancy," replied Mrs. Gregg, with dignified surprise. She was a large woman, with a masterly placidity about her. "I heard her a few minutes ago," she went on; "an' I was goin' up there to see to her if she hadn't stopped."

Mr. Gregg, a heavy, saturnine old man, with a broad bristling face, sat staring stupidly. The old woman in pink calico surveyed them all with an impersonal grin.

"Nancy!" repeated Mrs. Dunn, looking at Mrs. Gregg. She had not fancied this woman very much, and the two had not fraternized, although they were such near neighbors. Indeed, Mrs. Gregg was not of a sociable nature, and associated very little with anything but her own duties.

"Yes; Nancy Wren," she said, with gathering amazement. "She cries out this way 'most every night. She's ten years old, but she's as afraid of the dark as a baby. She's a queer child. I guess mebbe she's nervous. I don't know but she's got notions into her head, stayin' over in the graveyard so much. She runs away over there every chance she can get, an' she goes over a queer rigmarole about playin' with Jane, and her bein' dressed in white an' a wreath. I found out she meant Jane Blake, that's buried in the Blake lot. I knew there wa'n't any children round here, an' I thought I'd look into it. You know it says 'Our Father,' an' 'Our Mother,' on the old folks' stones. An' there she was, callin' them father an' mother. You'd thought they was right there. I've got 'most out o' patience with the child. I don't know nothin' about such kind of folks." The wail continued. "I'll go right up there," said Mrs. Gregg, determinately, taking a lamp.

Mrs. Dunn and Flora followed. When they entered the chamber to which she led them they saw little Nancy sitting up in bed, her face pale and convulsed, her blue eyes streaming with tears, her little pink mouth quivering.

"Nancy—" began Mrs. Gregg, in a weighty tone. But Mrs. Dunn sprang forward and threw her arms around the child.

"You got frightened, didn't you?" whispered she; and Nancy clung to her as if for life.

A great wave of joyful tenderness rolled up in the heart of the bereaved woman. It was not, after all, the lonely and fearfully wandering little spirit of her dear Jenny; she was peaceful and blessed, beyond all her girlish tumults and terrors; but it was this little living girl. She saw it all plainly now. Afterwards it seemed to her that any one but a woman with her nerves strained, and her imagination unhealthily keen through watching and sorrow, would have seen it before.

She held Nancy tight, and soothed her. She felt almost as if she held her own Jenny. "I guess I'll take her home with me, if you don't care," she said to Mrs. Gregg.

"Why, I don't know as I've got any objections, if you want to," answered Mrs. Gregg, with cold stateliness. "Nancy Wren has had everything done for her that I was able to do," she added, when Mrs. Dunn had wrapped up the child, and they were all on the stairs. "I ain't coaxed an' cuddled her, because it ain't my way. I never did with my own children."

"Oh, I know you've done all you could," said Mrs. Dunn, with abstracted apology. "I jest thought I'd like to take her home tonight. Don't you think I'm blamin' you, Mis' Gregg." She bent down and kissed the little tearful face on her shoulder: she was carrying Nancy like a baby. Flora had hold of one of her little dangling hands.

"You shall go right upstairs an' sleep with Flora," Mrs. Dunn whispered in the child's ear, when they were going across the yard; "an' you shall have the lamp burnin' all night, an' I'll give you a piece of cake before you go."

It was the custom of the Dunns to visit the cemetery and carry flowers to Jenny's grave every Sunday afternoon. Next Sunday little Nancy went with them. She followed happily along, and did not seem to think of the Blake lot. That pitiful fancy, if fancy it were, which had peopled her empty childish world with ghostly kindred, which had led into it an angel playmate in white robe and crown, might lie at rest now. There was no more need for it. She had found her place in a nest of living hearts, and she was getting her natural food of human love.

They had dressed Nancy in one of the little white frocks which Jenny had worn in her childhood, and her hat was trimmed with some ribbon and rose-buds which had adorned one of the dead young girl's years before.

It was a beautiful Sunday. After they left the cemetery they strolled a little way down the road. The road lay between deep green meadows and cottage yards. It was not quite time for the roses, and the lilacs were turning gray. The buttercups in the meadows had blossomed out, but the dandelions had lost their yellow crowns, and their filmy skulls appeared. They stood like ghosts among crowds of golden buttercups; but none of the family thought of that; their ghosts were laid in peace.

SILENCE

At dusk Silence went down the Deerfield street to Ensign John Sheldon's house. She wore her red blanket over her head, pinned closely under her chin, and her white profile showed whiter between the scarlet folds. She had been spinning all day, and shreds of wool still clung to her indigo petticoat; now and then one floated off on the north wind. It was bitter cold, and the snow was four feet deep. Silence's breath went before her in a cloud; the snow creaked under her feet. All over the village the crust was so firm that men could walk upon it. The houses were half sunken in sharp, rigid drifts of snow; their roofs were laden with it; icicles hung from the eaves. All the elms were white with snow frozen to them so strongly that it was not shaken off when they were lashed by the fierce wind.

There was an odor of boiling meal in the air; the housewives were preparing supper. Silence had eaten hers; she and her aunt, Widow Eunice Bishop, supped early. She had not far to go to Ensign Sheldon's. She was nearly there when she heard quick footsteps on the creaking snow behind her. Her heart beat quickly, but she did not look around. "Silence," said a voice. Then she paused, and waited, with her eyes cast down and her mouth grave, until David Walcott reached her. "What do you out this cold night, sweetheart?" he said.

"I am going down to Goodwife Sheldon's," replied Silence. Then suddenly she cried out, wildly: "Oh, David, what is that on your cloak? What is it?"

David looked curiously at his cloak. "I see naught on my cloak save old weather stains," said he. "What mean you, Silence?"

Silence quieted down suddenly. "It is gone now," said she, in a subdued voice.

"What did you see, Silence?"

Silence turned towards him; her face quivered convulsively. "I saw a blotch of blood," she cried. "I have been seeing them everywhere all day. I have seen them on the snow as I came along."

David Walcott looked down at her in a bewildered way. He carried his musket over his shoulder, and was shrugged up in his cloak; his heavy, flaxen mustache was stiff and white with frost. He had just been relieved from his post as sentry, and it was no child's play to patrol Deerfield village on a day like that, nor had it been for many previous days. The weather had been so severe that even the French and Indians, lurking like hungry wolves in the neighborhood, had hesitated to descend upon the town, and had stayed in camp.

"What mean you, Silence?" he said.

"What I say," returned Silence, in a strained voice. "I have seen blotches of blood everywhere all day. The enemy will be upon us."

David laughed loudly, and Silence caught his arm. "Don't laugh so loud," she whispered. Then David laughed again. "You be all overwrought, sweetheart," said he. "I have kept guard all the afternoon by the northern palisades, and I have seen not so much as a red fox on the meadow. I tell thee the French and Indians have gone back to Canada. There is no more need of fear."

"I have started all day and all last night at the sound of war-whoops," said Silence.

"Thy head is nigh turned with these troublous times, poor lass. We must cross the road now to Ensign Sheldon's house. Come quickly, or you will perish in this cold."

"Nay, my head is not turned," said Silence, as they hurried on over the crust; "the enemy be hiding in the forests beyond the meadows. David, they be not gone."

"And I tell thee they be gone, sweetheart. Think you not we should have seen their camp smoke had they been there? And we have had trusty scouts out. Come in, and my aunt, Hannah Sheldon, shall talk thee out of this folly."

The front windows of John Sheldon's house were all flickering red from the hearth fire. David flung open the door, and they entered. There was such a goodly blaze from the great logs in the wide fireplace that even the shadows in the remote corners of the large keeping-room were dusky red, and the faces of all the people in the room had a clear red glow upon them.

Goodwife Hannah Sheldon stood before the fire, stirring some porridge in a great pot that hung on the crane; some fair-haired children sat around a basket shelling corn, a slight young girl in a snuff-yellow gown was spinning, and an old woman in a quilted hood crouched in a corner of the fireplace, holding out her lean hands to the heat.

Goodwife Sheldon turned around when the door opened. "Good-day, Mistress Silence Hoit," she called out, and her voice was sweet, but deep like a man's. "Draw near to the fire, for in truth you must be near perishing with the cold."

"There'll be fire enough ere morning, I trow, to warm the whole township," said the old woman in the corner. Her small black eyes gleamed sharply out of the gloom of her great hood; her yellow face was all drawn and puckered towards the center of her shrewdly leering mouth.

"Now you hush your croaking, Goody Crane," cried Hannah Sheldon. "Draw the stool near to the fire for Silence, David. I cannot stop stirring, or the porridge will burn. How fares your aunt this cold weather, Silence?"

"Well, except for her rheumatism," replied Silence. She sat down on the stool that David placed for her, and slipped her blanket back from her head. Her beautiful face, full of a grave and delicate stateliness, drooped towards the fire, her smooth fair hair was folded in clear curves like the leaves of a lily around her ears, and she wore a high, transparent, tortoise-shell comb like a coronet in the knot at the back of her head.

David Walcott had pulled off his cap and cloak, and stood looking down at her. "Silence is all overwrought by this talk of Indians," he remarked, presently, and a blush came over his weather-beaten blond face at the tenderness in his own tone.

"The Indians have gone back to Canada," said Goodwife Sheldon, in a magisterial voice. She stirred the porridge faster; it was steaming fiercely.

"So I tell her," said David.

Silence looked up in Hannah Sheldon's sober, masterly face. "Goodwife, may I have a word in private with you?" she asked, in a half-whisper.

"As soon as I take the porridge off," replied Goodwife Sheldon.

"God grant it be not the last time she takes the porridge off!" said the old woman.

Hannah Sheldon laughed. "Here be Goody Crane in a sorry mind tonight," said she. "Wait till she have a sup of this good porridge, and I trow she'll pack off the Indians to Canada in a half-hour!"

Hannah began dipping out the porridge. When she had placed generous dishes of it on the table and bidden everybody draw up, she motioned to Silence. "Now, Mistress Silence," said she, "come into the bedroom if you would have a word with me."

Silence followed her into the little north room opening out of the keeping-room, where Ensign John Sheldon and his wife Hannah had slept for many years. It was icy cold, and the thick fur of frost on the little window-panes sent out sparkles in the candle-light. The two women stood beside the great chintz draped and canopied bed, Hannah holding the flaring candle. "Now, what is it?" said she.

"Oh, Goodwife Sheldon!" said Silence. Her face remained quite still, but it was as if one could see her soul fluttering beneath it.

"You be all overwrought, as David saith," cried Goodwife Sheldon, and her voice had a motherly harshness in it. Silence had no mother, and her lover, David Walcott, had none. Hannah was his aunt, and loved him like her son, so she felt towards Silence as towards her son's betrothed.

"In truth I know not what it is," said Silence, in a kind of reserved terror, "but there has been all day a great heaviness of spirit upon me, and last night I dreamed. All day I have fancied I saw blood here and there. Sometimes, when I have looked out of the window, the whole snow hath suddenly glared with red. Goodwife Sheldon, think you the Indians and the French have in truth gone back to Canada?"

Goodwife Sheldon hesitated a moment, then she spoke up cheerily. "In truth have they!" cried she. "John said but this noon that naught of them had been seen for some time."

"So David said," returned Silence; "but this heaviness will not be driven away. You know how Parson Williams hath spoken in warning in the pulpit and elsewhere, and besought us to be vigilant. He holdeth that the savages be not gone."

Hannah Sheldon smiled. "Parson Williams is a godly man, but prone ever to look upon the dark side," said she.

"If the Indians should come tonight—" said Silence.

"I tell ye they will not come, child. I shall lay me down in that bed a-trusting in the Lord, and having no fear against the time I shall arise from it."

"If the Indians should come—Goodwife Sheldon, be not angered; hear me. If they should come, I pray you keep David here to defend you in this house, and let him not out to seek me. You know well that our house is musket-proof as well as this, and it has long been agreed that they who live nearest, whose houses have not thick walls, shall come to ours and help us make defense. I pray you let not David out of the house to seek me, should there be a surprise tonight. I pray you give me your promise for this, Goodwife Sheldon."

Hannah Sheldon laughed. "In truth will I give thee the promise, if it makes thee easier, child," said she. "At the very first war-screech will I tie David in the chimney-corner with my apron-string, unless you lend me yours. But there will be no war-screech tonight, nor tomorrow night, nor the night after that. The Lord will preserve His people that trust in Him. Today have I set a web of linen in the loom, and I have candles ready to dip tomorrow, and the day after that I have a quilting. I look not for Indians. If they come I will set them to work. Fear not for David, sweetheart. In truth you should have a bolder heart, an' you look to be a soldier's wife some day."

"I would I had never been aught to him, that he might not be put in jeopardy to defend me!" said Silence, and her words seemed visible in a white cloud at her mouth.

"We must not stay here in the cold," said Goodwife Sheldon. "Out with ye, Silence, and have a sup of hot porridge, and then David shall see ye home."

Silence sipped a cup of the hot porridge obediently, then she pinned her red blanket over her head. Hannah Sheldon assisted her, bringing it warmly over her face. "'Tis bitter cold," she said. "Now have no more fear, Mistress Silence; the Indians will not come tonight; but do you come over tomorrow, and keep me company while I dip the candles."

"There'll be company enough—there'll be a whole house-ful," muttered the old woman in the corner, but nobody heeded her. She was a lonely and wretched old creature whom people sheltered from pity, although she was somewhat feared and held in ill repute. There were rumors that she was well versed in all the dark lore of witchcraft, and held commerce with unlawful beings. The children of Deerfield village looked askance at her, and clung to their mothers if they met her on the street, for they whispered among themselves that old Goody Crane rode through the air on a broom in the night-time.

Silence and David passed out into the keen night. "If you meet my good-man, hasten him home, for the porridge is cooling," Hannah Sheldon called after them.

They met not a soul on Deerfield street, and parted at Silence's door. David would have entered had she bidden him, but she said peremptorily that she had a hard task of spinning that evening, and then she wished him good-night, and without a kiss, for Silence Hoit was chary of caresses. But tonight she called him back ere he was fairly in the street. "David," she called, and he ran back.

"What is it, Silence?" he asked.

She put back her blanket, threw her arms around his neck, and clung to him trembling.

"Why, sweetheart," he whispered, "what has come over thee?"

"You know—this house is made like—a fort," she said, bringing out her words in gasps, "and—there are muskets, and—powder stored in it, and—Captain Moulton, and his sons, and—John Carson will come, and make—a stand in it. I have—no fear should—the Indians come. Remember that I have no fear, and shall be safe here, David."

David laughed, and patted her clinging shoulders. "Yes, I will remember, Silence," he said; "but the Indians will not come."

"Remember that I am safe here, and have no fear," she repeated. Then she kissed him of her own accord, as if she had been his wife, and entered the house, and he went away, wondering.

Silence's aunt, Widow Eunice Bishop, did not look up when the door opened; she was knitting by the fire, sitting erect with her mouth pursed. She had a hostile expression, as if she were listening to some opposite argument. Silence hung her blanket on a peg; she stood irresolute a minute, then she breathed on the frosty window and cleared a space through which she could look out. Her aunt gave a quick, fierce glance at her, then she tossed back her head and knitted. Silence stood staring out of the little peep-hole in the frosty pane. Her aunt glanced at her again, then she spoke.

"I should think if you had been out gossiping and gadding for two hours, you had better get yourself at some work now," she said, "unless your heart be set on idling. A pretty housewife you'll make!"

"Come here quick, quick!" Silence cried out.

Her aunt started, but she would not get up; she knitted, scowling. "I cannot afford to idle if other folk can," said she. "I have no desire to keep running to windows and standing there gaping, as you have done all this day."

"Oh, aunt, I pray you to come," said Silence, and she turned her white face over her shoulder towards her aunt; "there is somewhat wrong surely."

Widow Bishop got up, still scowling, and went over to the window. Silence stood aside and pointed to the little clear circle in the midst of the frost. "Over there to the north," she said, in a quick, low voice.

Her aunt adjusted her horn spectacles and bent her head stiffly. "I see naught," said she.

"A red glare in the north!"

"A red glare in the north! Be ye out of your mind, wench! There be no red glare in the north. Everything be quiet in the town. Get ye away from the window and to your work. I have no more patience with such doings. Here have I left my knitting for nothing, and I just about setting the heel. You'd best keep to your spinning instead of spying out of the window at your own nightmares, and gadding about the town after David Walcott. Pretty doings for a modest maid, I call it, following after young men in this fashion!"

Silence turned on her aunt, and her blue eyes gleamed dark; she held up her head like a queen. "I follow not after young men," she said.

56

"Heard I not David Walcott's voice at the door? Went you not to Goodwife Sheldon's, where he lives? Was it not his voice—hey?"

"Yes, 'twas, an' I had a right to go there an' I chose, an' 'twas naught unmaidenly," said Silence.

"'Twas unmaidenly in my day," retorted her aunt; "perhaps 'tis different now." She had returned to her seat, and was clashing her knitting-needles like two swords in a duel.

Silence pulled a spinning-wheel before the fire and fell to work. The wheel turned so rapidly that the spokes were a revolving shadow; there was a sound as if a bee had entered the room.

"I stayed at home, and your uncle did the courting," Widow Eunice Bishop continued, in a voice that demanded response.

But Silence made none. She went on spinning. Her aunt eyed her maliciously. "I never went after nightfall to his house that he might see me home," said she. "I trow my mother would have locked me up in the garret, and kept me on meal and water for a week, had I done aught so bold."

Silence spun on. Her aunt threw her head back, and knitted, jerking out her elbows. Neither of them spoke again until the clock struck nine. Then Widow Bishop wound her ball of yarn closer, and stuck in the knitting-needles, and rose. "'Tis time to put out the candle," she said, "and *I* have done a good day's work, and feel need of rest. They that have idled cannot make it up by wasting tallow." She threw open the door that led to her bedroom, and a blast of icy confined air rushed in. She untied the black cap that framed her nervous face austerely, and her gray head, with its tight rosette of hair on the crown, appeared. Silence set her spinning-wheel back, and raked the ashes over the hearth fire. Then she took the candle and climbed the stairs to her own chamber. Her aunt was already in bed, her pale, white-frilled face sunk in the icy feather pillow; but she did not bid her good-night: not on account of her anger; there was seldom any such formal courtesy exchanged between the women. Silence's chamber had one side sloping with the slope of the roof, and in it were two dormer-windows looking towards the north. She set her candle on the table, breathed on one of these windows, as she had on the one downstairs, and looked out. She stood there several minutes, then she turned away, shaking her head. The room was very cold. She let down her smooth fair hair, and her fingers began to redden; she took off her kerchief; then she stopped, and looked hesitatingly at her bed, with its blue curtains. She set her mouth hard, and put on her kerchief. Then she sat down on the edge of her bed and waited. After a while she pulled a quilt from the bed and wrapped it around her. Still she did not shiver. She had blown out the candle, and the room was very dark. All her nerves seemed screwed tight like fiddle-strings, and her thoughts beat upon them and made terrific waves of sound in her ears. She saw sparks and flashes like diamond fire in the darkness. She had her hands clinched tight, but she did not feel her hands nor her feet—she did not feel her whole body. She sat so until two o'clock in the morning. When the clock down in the keeping-room struck the hours, the peals shocked her back for a minute to her old sense of herself; then she lost it again. Just after the clock struck two, while the silvery reverberation of the bell tone was still in her ears, and she was breathing a little freer, a great rosy glow suffused the frosty windows. A horrible discord of sound arose without. Above everything else came something like a peal of laughter from wild beasts or fiends.

Silence arose and went downstairs. Her aunt rushed out of her bedroom, shrieking, and caught hold of her. "Oh, Silence, what is it, what is it?" she cried.

"Get away till I light a candle," said Silence. She fairly pushed her aunt off, shoveled the ashes from the coals in the fireplace, and lighted a candle. Then she threw some wood on the smoldering fire. Her aunt was running around the room screaming. There came a great pound on the door.

"It's the Indians! it's the Indians! don't let 'em in!" shrieked her aunt. "Don't let them in! don't let them!" She placed her lean shoulder in her white bed-gown against the door. "Go away! go away!" she yelled. "You can't come in! O Lord Almighty, save us!"

"You stand off," said Silence. She took hold of her aunt's shoulders. "Be quiet," she commanded. Then she called out, in a firm voice, "Who is there?"

At the shout in response she drew the great iron bolts quickly and flung open the heavy nail-studded door. There was a press of frantic, white-faced people into the room; then the door was slammed to and the bolts shot. It was very still in the room, except for the shuffling rush of the men's feet, and now and then a stern, gasping order. The children did not cry; all the noise was without. The house might have stood in the midst of some awful wilderness peopled with fiendish beasts, from the noise without. The cries seemed actually in the room. The children's eyes glared white over their mothers' shoulders.

The men hurriedly strengthened the window-shutters with props of logs, and fitted the muskets into the loop-holes. Suddenly there was a great crash at the door, and a wilder yell outside. The muskets opened fire, and some of the women rushed to the door and pressed fiercely against it with their delicate shoulders, their white, desperate faces turning back dumbly, like a spiritual phalanx of defense. Silence and her aunt were among them.

Suddenly Widow Eunice Bishop, at a fresh onslaught upon the door, and a fiercer yell, lifted up her voice and shrieked back in a rage as mad as theirs. Her speech, too, was almost inarticulate, and the sense of it lost in a savage frenzy; her tongue stuttered over abusive epithets; but for a second she prevailed over the terrible chorus without. It was like the solo of a fury. Then louder yells drowned her out; the muskets cracked faster; the men rammed in the charges; the savages fell back somewhat; the blows on the door ceased.

Silence ran up the stairs to her chamber, and peeped cautiously out of a little dormer-window. Deerfield village was roaring with flames, the sky and snow were red, and leaping through the glare came the painted savages, a savage white face and the waving sword of a French officer in their midst. The awful warwhoops and the death-cries of her friends and neighbors sounded in her ears. She saw, close under her window, the dark sweep of the tomahawk, the quick glance of the scalping-knife, and the red starting of caps of blood. She saw infants dashed through the air, and the backward-straining forms of shrieking women dragged down the street; but she saw not David Walcott anywhere.

She eyed in an agony some dark bodies lying like logs in the snow. A wild impulse seized her to run out, turn their dead faces, and see that none of them was her lover's. Her room was full of red light; everything in it showed distinctly. The roof of the next house crashed in, and the sparks and cinders shot up like a volcano. There was a great outcry of terror from below, and Silence hurried down. The Indians were trying to fire the house from the west side. They had piled a bank of brush against it, and the men had hacked new loop-holes and were beating them back.

John Carson's wife clutched Silence as she entered the keeping-room. "They are trying to set the house on fire," she gasped, "and—the bullets are giving out!" The woman held a little child hugged close to her breast; she strained him closer. "They shall not have him, anyway," she said. Her mouth looked white and stiff.

"Put him down and help, then," said Silence. She began pulling the pewter plates off the dresser.

"What be you doing with my pewter plates?" screamed her aunt at her elbow.

Silence said nothing. She went on piling the plates under her arm.

"Think you I will have the pewter plates I have had ever since I was wed, melted to make bullets for those limbs of Satan?"

Silence carried the plates to the fire; the women piled on wood and made it hotter. John Carson's wife laid her baby on the settle and helped, and Widow Bishop brought out her pewter spoons, and her silver cream-jug when the pewter ran low, and finally her dead husband's knee-buckles from the cedar chest. All the pewter and silver in Widow Eunice Bishop's house were melted down that night. The women worked with desperate zeal to supply the men with bullets, and just before the ammunition failed, the Indians left Deerfield village, with their captives in their train.

The men had stopped firing at last. Everything was quiet outside, except for the flurry of musket-shots down on the meadow, where the skirmish was going on between the Hatfield men and the retreating French and Indians. The dawn was breaking, but not a shutter had been stirred in the Bishop house; the inmates were clustered together, their ears straining for another outburst of slaughter.

Suddenly there was a strange crackling sound overhead; a puff of hot smoke came into the room from the stairway. The roof had caught fire from the shower of sparks, and the staunch house that had withstood all the fury of the savages was going the way of its neighbors.

The men rushed up the stair, and fell back. "We can't save it!" Captain Isaac Moulton said, hoarsely. He was an old man, and his white hair tossed wildly around his powder-blackened face.

Widow Eunice Bishop scuttled into her bedroom, and got her best silk hood and her gilt-framed looking-glass. "Silence, get out the feather-bed!" she shrieked.

The keeping-room was stifling with smoke. Captain Moulton loosened a window-shutter cautiously and peered out. "I see no sign of the savages," he said. They unbolted the door, and opened it inch by inch, but there was no exultant shout in response. The crack of muskets on the meadow sounded louder; that was all.

Widow Eunice Bishop pushed forward before the others; the danger by fire to her household goods had driven her own danger from her mind, which could compass but one terror at a time. "Let me forth!" she cried; and she laid the looking-glass and silk hood on the snow, and pelted back into the smoke for her feather-bed and the best andirons.

Silence carried out the spinning-wheel, and the others caught up various articles which they had wit to see in the panic. They piled them up on the snow outside, and huddled together, staring fearfully down the village street. They saw, amid the smoldering ruins, Ensign John Sheldon's house standing.

"We must make for that," said Captain Isaac Moulton, and they started. The men went before and behind, with their muskets in readiness, and the women and children walked between. Widow Bishop carried the looking-glass; somebody had helped her to bring out her feather-bed, and she had dragged it to a clean place well away from the burning house.

The dawnlight lay pale and cold in the east; it was steadily overcoming the fire-glow from the ruins. Nobody would have known Deerfield village. The night before the sun had gone down upon the snowy slants of humble roofs and the peaceful rise of smoke from pleasant hearth fires. The curtained windows had gleamed out one by one with mild candle-light, and serene faces of white-capped matrons preparing supper had passed them. Now, on both sides of Deerfield street were beds of glowing red coals; grotesque ruins of door-posts and chimneys in the semblances of blackened martyrs stood crumbling in the midst of them, and twisted charred heaps, which the people eyed trembling, lay in the old doorways. The snow showed great red patches in the gathering light, and in them lay still bodies that seemed to move.

Silence Hoit sprang out from the hurrying throng, and turned the head of one dead man whose face she could not see. The horror of his red crown did not move her. She only saw that he was not David Walcott. She stooped and wiped off her hands in some snow.

"That is Israel Bennett," the others groaned.

John Carson's wife had been the dead man's sister. She hugged her baby tighter, and pressed more closely to her husband's back. There was no longer any sound of musketry on the meadows. There was not a sound to be heard except the wind in the dry trees and the panting breaths of the knot of people.

A dead baby lay directly in the path, and a woman caught it up, and tried to warm it at her breast. She wrapped her cloak around it, and wiped its little bloody face with her apron. "'Tis not dead," she declared, frantically; "the child is not dead!" She had not shed a tear nor uttered a wail before, but now she began sobbing aloud over the dead child. It was Goodwife Barnard's, and no kin to her; she was a single woman. The others were looking right and left for lurking savages. She looked only at the little cold face on her bosom. "The child breathes," she said, and hurried on faster that she might get succor for it.

The party halted before Ensign John Sheldon's house. The stout door was fast, but there was a hole in it, as if hacked by a tomahawk. The men tried it and shook it. "Open, open, Goodwife Sheldon!" they hallooed. "Friends! friends! Open the door!" But there was no response.

Silence Hoit left the throng at the door, and began clambering up on a slant of icy snow to a window which was flung wide open. The window-sill was stained with blood, and so was the snow.

One of the men caught Silence and tried to hold her back. "There may be Indians in there," he whispered, hoarsely.

But Silence broke away from him, and was in through the window, and the men followed her, and unbolted the door for the women, who pressed in wildly, and flung it to again. A child who was among them, little Comfort Arms, stationed herself directly with her tiny back against the door, with her mouth set like a soldier's, and her blue eyes gleaming fierce under her flaxen locks. "They shall not get in," said she. Somehow she had gotten hold of a great horse-pistol, which she carried like a doll.

Nobody heeded her, Silence least of all. She stared about the room, with her lips parted. Right before her on the hearth lay a little three-year-old girl, Mercy Sheldon, her pretty head in a pool of blood, but Silence cast only an indifferent glance when the others gathered about her, groaning and sighing.

Suddenly Silence sprang towards a dark heap near the pantry door, but it was only a woman's quilted petticoat.

The spinning-wheel lay broken on the floor, and all the simple furniture was strewn about wildly. Silence went into Goodwife Sheldon's bedroom, and the others followed her, trembling, all except little Comfort Arms, who stood unflinchingly with her back pressed against the door, and the single woman, Grace Mather; she stayed behind, and put wood on the fire, after she had picked up the quilted petticoat, and laid the dead baby tenderly wrapped in it on the settle. Then she pulled the settle forward before the fire, and knelt before it, and fell to chafing the little limbs of the dead baby, weeping as she did so.

Goodwife Sheldon's bedroom was in wild disorder. A candle still burned, although it was very low, on the table, whose linen cover had great red finger-prints on it. Goodwife Sheldon's decent clothes were tossed about on the floor; the curtains of the bed were half torn away. Silence pressed forward unshrinkingly towards the bed; the others, even the men, hung back. There lay Goodwife Sheldon dead in her bed. All the light in the room, the candle-light and the low daylight, seemed to focus upon her white, frozen profile propped stiffly on the pillow, where she had fallen back when the bullet came through that hole in the door.

Silence looked at her. "Where is David, Goodwife Sheldon?" said she.

Eunice Bishop sprang forward. "Be you clean out of your mind, Silence Hoit?" she cried. "Know you not she's dead? She's dead! Oh, she's dead, she's dead! An' here's her best silk hood trampled underfoot on the floor!" Eunice snatched up the hood, and seized Silence by the arm, but she pushed her back.

"Where is David? Where is he gone?" she demanded again of the dead woman.

The other women came crowding around Silence then, and tried to soothe her and reason with her, while their own faces were white with horror and woe. Goodwife Sarah Spear, an old woman whose sons lay dead in the street outside, put an arm around the girl, and tried to draw her head to her broad bosom.

"Mayhap you will find him, sweetheart," she said. "He's not among the dead out there."

But Silence broke away from the motherly arm, and sped wildly through the other rooms, with the people at her heels, and her aunt crying vainly after her. They found no more dead in the house; naught but ruin and disorder, and bloody footprints and handprints of savages.

When they returned to the keeping-room, Silence seated herself on a stool by the fire, and held out her hands towards the blaze to warm them. The daylight was broad outside now, and the great clock that had come from overseas ticked; the Indians had not touched that.

Captain Isaac Moulton lifted little Mercy Sheldon from the hearth and carried her to her dead mother in the bedroom, and two of the older women went in there and shut the door. Little Comfort Arms still stood with her back against the outer door, and Grace Mather tended the dead baby on the settle.

"What do ye with that dead child?" a woman called out roughly to her.

"I tell ye 'tis not dead; it breathes," returned Grace Mather; and she never turned her harsh, plain face from the dead child.

"An' I tell ye 'tis dead."

"An' I tell ye 'tis not dead. I need but some hot posset for it."

Goodwife Carson began to weep. She hugged her own living baby tighter. "Let her alone!" she sobbed. "I wonder our wits be not all gone." She went sobbing over to little Comfort Arms at the door. "Come away, sweetheart, and draw near the fire," she pleaded, brokenly.

The little girl looked obstinately up at her. "They shall not come in," she said. "The wicked savages shall not come in again."

"No more shall they, an' the Lord be willing, sweet. But, I pray you, come away from the door now."

Comfort shook her head, and she looked like her father as he fought on the Deerfield meadows.

"The savages are gone, sweet."

But Comfort answered not a word, and Goodwife Carson sat down and began to nurse her baby. One of the women hung the porridge-kettle over the fire; another put some potatoes in the ashes to bake. Presently the two women came out of Goodwife Sheldon's bedroom with grave, strained faces, and held their stiff blue fingers out to the hearth fire.

Eunice Bishop, who was stirring the porridge, looked at them with sharp curiosity. "How look they?" she whispered.

"As peaceful as if they slept," replied Goodwife Spear, who was one of the women.

"And the child's head?"

"We put on her little white cap with the lace frills."

Eunice stirred the bubbling porridge, scowling in the heat and steam; some of the women laid the table with Hannah Sheldon's linen cloth and pewter dishes, and presently the breakfast was dished up.

Little Comfort Arms had sunk at the foot of the nail-studded door in a deep slumber. She slept at her post like the faithless sentry whose slumbers the night before had brought about the destruction of Deerfield village. Goodwife Spear raised her up, but her curly head drooped helplessly.

"Wake up, Comfort, and have a sup of hot porridge," she called in her ear.

She led her over to the table, Comfort stumbling weakly at arm's-length, and set her on a stool with a dish of porridge before her, which she ate uncertainly in a dazed fashion, with her eyes filming and her head nodding.

They all gathered gravely around the table, except Silence Hoit and Grace Mather. Silence sat still, staring at the fire, and Grace had dipped out a little cup of the hot porridge, and was trying to feed it to the dead baby, with crooning words.

"Silence, why come you not to the table?" her aunt called out.

"I want nothing," answered Silence.

"I see not why you should so set yourself up before the others, as having so much more to bear," said Eunice, sharply. "There is Goodwife Spear, with her sons unburied on the road yonder, and she eats her porridge with good relish."

John Carson's wife set her baby on her husband's knee, and carried a dish of porridge to Silence.

"Try and eat it, sweet," she whispered. She was near Silence's age.

Silence looked up at her. "I want it not," said she.

"But he may not be dead, sweet. He may presently be home. You would not he should find you spent and fainting. Perchance he may have wounds for you to tend."

68

Silence seized the dish and began to eat the porridge in great spoonfuls, gulping it down fast.

The people at the table eyed her sadly and whispered, and they also cast frequent glances at Grace Mather bending over the dead baby. Once Captain Isaac Moulton called out to her in his gruff old voice, which he tried to soften, and she answered back, sharply: "Think ye I will leave this child while it breathes, Captain Isaac Moulton? In faith I am the only one of ye all who has regard to it."

But suddenly, when the meal was half over, Grace Mather arose, and gathered up the little dead baby, carried it into Goodwife Sheldon's bedroom, and was gone some time.

"She has lost her wits," said Eunice Bishop. "Think you not we should follow her? She may do some harm."

"Nay, let her be," said Goodwife Spear.

When at last Grace Mather came out of the bedroom, and they all turned to look at her, her face was stern but quite composed. "I found a little clean linen shift in the chest," she said to Goodwife Spear, who nodded gravely. Then she sat down at the table and ate.

The people, as they ate, cast frequent glances at the barred door and the shuttered windows. The daylight was broad outside, but there was no glimmer of it in the room, and the candles were lighted. They dared not yet remove the barricades, and the muskets were in readiness: the Indians might return.

All at once there was a shrill clamor at the door, and men sprang to their muskets. The women clutched each other, panting.

"Unbar the door!" shrieked a quavering old voice. "I tell ye, unbar the door! I be nigh frozen a-standing here. Unbar the door! The Indians are gone hours ago."

"'Tis Goody Crane," cried Eunice Bishop.

Captain Isaac Moulton shot back the bolts and opened the door a little way, while the men stood close at his back, and Goody Crane slid in like a swift black shadow out of the daylight.

She crouched down close to the fire, trembling and groaning, and the women gave her some hot porridge.

"Where have ye been?" demanded Eunice Bishop.

"Where they found me not," replied the old woman, and there was a sudden leer like a light in the gloom of her great hood. She motioned towards the bedroom door.

"Goody Sheldon sleeps late this morning, and so doth Mercy," said she. "I trow she will not dip her candles today."

The people looked at each other; a subtler horror than that of the night before shook their spirits.

Captain Isaac Moulton towered over the old woman on the hearth. "How knew you Goodwife Sheldon and Mercy were dead?" he asked, sternly.

The old woman leered up at him undauntedly; her head bobbed. There was a curious grotesqueness about her blanketed and hooded figure when in motion. There was so little of the old woman herself visible that motion surprised, as it would have done in a puppet. "Told I not Goody Sheldon last night she would never stir porridge again?" said she. "Who stirred the porridge this morning? I trow Goody Sheldon's hands be too stiff and too cold, though they have stirred well in their day. Hath she dipped her candles yet? Hath she begun on her weaving? I trow 'twill be a long day ere Mary Sheldon's linen-chest be filled, if she herself go a-gadding to Canada and her mother sleep so late."

"Eat this hot porridge and stop your croaking," said Goodwife Spear, stooping over her.

The old woman extended her two shaking hands for the dish. "That was what she said last night," she returned. "The living echo the dead, and that is enough wisdom for a witch."

"You'll be burned for a witch yet, Goody Crane, an' you be not careful," cried Eunice Bishop.

"There is fire enough outside to burn all the witches in the land," muttered the old woman, sipping her porridge. Suddenly she eyed Silence sitting motionless opposite. "Where be your sweetheart this fine morning, Silence Hoit?" she inquired.

Silence looked at her. There was a strange likeness between the glitter in her blue eyes and that in Goody Crane's black ones.

The old woman's great hood nodded over the porridge-dish. "I can tell ye, Mistress Silence," she said, thickly, as she ate. "He is gone to Canada on a moose-hunt, and unless I be far wrong, he hath taken thy wits with him."

"How know you David Walcott is gone to Canada?" cried Eunice Bishop; and Silence stared at her with her hard blue eyes.

Silence's soft fair hair hung all matted like uncombed flax over her pale cheeks. There was a rigid, dead look about her girlish forehead and her sweet mouth.

"I know," returned Goody Crane, nodding her head.

The women washed the pewter dishes, set them back on the dresser, and swept the floor. Little Comfort Arms had been carried upstairs and laid in the bed whence poor Mary Sheldon had been dragged and haled to Canada. The men stood talking near their stacked muskets. One of the shutters had been opened and the candles put out. The winter sun shone in the window as it had shone before, but the poor folk in Ensign Sheldon's keeping-room saw it with a certain shock, as if it were a stranger. That morning their own hearts had in them such strangeness that they transferred it like motion to all familiar objects. The very iron dogs in the Sheldon fireplace seemed on the leap with tragedy, and the porridge-kettle swung darkly out of some former age.

Now and then one of the men opened the door cautiously and peered out and listened. The reek of the smoldering village came in at the door, but there was not a sound except the whistling howl of the savage north wind, which still swept over the valley. There was not a shot to be heard from the meadows. The men discussed the wisdom of leaving the women for a short space and going forth to explore, but Widow Eunice Bishop interposed, thrusting her sharp face in among them.

"Here we be," scolded she, "a passel of women and children, and Hannah Sheldon and Mercy a-lying dead, and me with my house burnt down, and nothing saved except my silk hood and my looking-glass and my feather-bed, and it's a mercy if that's not all smooched, and you talk of going off and leaving us!"

The men looked doubtfully at one another; then there was the hissing creak of footsteps on the snow outside, and Widow Bishop screamed. "Oh, the Indians have come back!" she proclaimed.

Silence looked up.

The door was tried from without.

"Who's there?" cried out Captain Moulton.

"John Sheldon," responded a hoarse voice. "Who's inside?"

Captain Moulton threw open the door, and John Sheldon stood there. His severe and sober face was painted like an Indian's with blood and powder grime; he stood staring in at the company.

"Come in, quick, and let us bar the door!" screamed Eunice Bishop.

John Sheldon came in hesitatingly, and stood looking around the room.

"Have you but just come from the meadows?" inquired Captain Moulton. But John Sheldon did not seem to hear him. He stared at the company, who all stood still staring back at him; then he looked hard and long at the doors, as if expecting some one to enter. The eyes of the others followed his, but no one spoke.

"Where's Hannah?" asked John Sheldon.

Then the women began to weep.

"She's in there," sobbed John Carson's wife, pointing to the bedroom door—"in there with little Mercy, Goodman Sheldon."

"Is—the child hurt, and—Hannah a-tending her?"

The women wept, and pushed each other forward to tell him, but Captain Isaac Moulton spoke out, and drove the knife home like an honest soldier, who will kill if he must, but not mangle.

"Goodwife Sheldon lies yonder, shot dead in her bed, and we found the child dead on the hearth-stone," said Isaac Moulton.

John Sheldon turned his gaze on him.

"The judgments of the Lord are just and righteous altogether," said Isaac Moulton, confronting him with stern defiance.

"Amen," returned John Sheldon. He took off his cloak, and hung it up on the peg as he was used.

"Where is David Walcott?" asked Silence, standing before him.

"David, he is gone with the Indians to Canada, and the boys, Ebenezer and Remembrance."

"Where is David?"

"I tell ye, lass, he is gone with the French and Indians to Canada; and you need be thankful he was but your sweetheart, and ye not wed, with a half-score of babes to be taken too. The curse that was upon the women of Jerusalem is upon the women of Deerfield." John Sheldon looked sternly into Silence's white wild face; then his voice softened. "Take heart, lass," said he.

"Erelong I shall go to Governor Dudley and get help, and then after them to Canada, and fetch them back. Take heart; I will fetch thee thy sweetheart presently."

Silence returned to her seat in the fireplace. Goody Crane looked across at her. "He will come back over the north meadow," she whispered. "Keep watch over the north meadow; but 'twill be a long day ere ye see him."

Silence paid seemingly little heed. She paid little heed to Ensign John Sheldon relating how the French and Indians, with Hertel de Rouville at their head, were on the road to Canada with their captives; of the fight on the meadow between the retreating foe and the brave band of Deerfield and Hatfield men, who had made a stand there to intercept them; how they had been obliged to cease firing because the captives were threatened; and the pitiful tale of Parson John Williams, two of whose children were killed, dragged through the wilderness with the others, and his sick wife.

"Had folk listened to him, we had all been safe in our good houses with our belongings," cried Eunice Bishop.

"They will not drag Goodwife Williams far," said Goody Crane, "nor the babe at her breast. I trow well it hath stopped wailing ere now."

"How know you that?" questioned Eunice Bishop, turning sharply on her.

But the old woman only nodded her head, and Silence paid no heed, for she was not there. Her slender girlish shape sat by the hearth fire in John Sheldon's house in Deerfield, her fair head showed like a delicate flower, but Silence Hoit was following her lover to Canada. Every step that he took painfully through pathless forests, on treacherous ice, and desolate snow fields, she took more painfully still; every knife gleaming over his head she saw. She bore his every qualm of hunger and pain and cold, and it was all the harder because they struck on her bare heart with no flesh between, for she sat in the flesh in Deerfield, and her heart went with her lover to Canada.

The sun stood higher, but it was still bitter cold; the blue frost on the windows did not melt, and the icicles on the eaves, which nearly touched the sharp snow-drifts underneath, did not drip. The desolate survivors of the terrible night began work among the black ruins of their homes. They cared as well as they might for the dead in Deerfield street, and the dead on the meadow where the fight had been. Their muscles were all tense with the cold, their faces seamed and blue with it, but their hearts were strained with a fiercer cold than that. Not one man of them but had one or more slain, with dead face upturned, seeking his in the morning light, or on that awful road to Canada. Ever as the men worked they turned their eyes northward, and met grimly the icy blast of the north wind, and sometimes to their excited fancies it seemed to bring to their ears the cries of their friends who were facing it also, and they stood still and listened.

Silence Hoit crept out of the house and down the road a little way, and then stood looking over the meadow towards the north. Her fair hair tossed in the wind, her pale cheeks turned pink, the wind struck full upon her delicate figure. She had come out without her blanket.

"David!" she called. "David! David! David!" The north wind bore down upon her, shrieking with a wild fury like a savage of the air; the dry branches of a small tree near her struck her in the face. "David!" she called again. "David! David!" She swelled out her white throat like a bird, and her voice was shrill and sweet and far-reaching. The men moving about on the meadow below, and stooping over the dead, looked up at her, but she did not heed them. She had come through a break in the palisades; on each side of her the frozen snow-drifts slanted sharply to their tops, and they glittered with blue lights like glaciers in the morning sun over those drifts the enemy had passed the night before.

The men on the meadow saw Silence's hair blowing like a yellow banner between the drifts of snow.

"The poor lass has come out bareheaded," said Ensign Sheldon. "She is near out of her mind for David Walcott."

"A man should have no sweetheart in these times, unless he would her heart be broke," said a young man beside him. He was hardly more than a boy, and his face was as rosy as a girl's in the wind. He kept close to Ensign Sheldon, and his mind was full of young Mary Sheldon traveling to Canada on her weary little feet. He had often, on a Sabbath day, looked across the meeting-house at her, and thought that there was no maiden like her in Deerfield.

Ensign John Sheldon thought of his sweetheart lying with her heart still in her freezing bedroom, and stooped over a dead Hatfield man whose face was frozen into the snow.

The young man, whose name was Freedom Wells, bent over to help him. Then he started. "What's that?" he cried.

"'Tis only Silence Hoit calling David Walcott again," replied Ensign Sheldon.

The voice had sounded like Mary Sheldon's to Freedom. The tears rolled over his boyish cheeks as he put his hands into the snow and tried to dig it away from the dead man's face.

"David! David! David!" called Silence.

Suddenly her aunt threw a wiry arm around her. "Be you gone clean daft," she shrieked against the wind, "standing here calling David Walcott? Know you not he is a half-day's journey towards Canada, an' the savages have not scalped him and left him by the way? Standing here with your hair blowing and no blanket! Into the house with ye!"

Silence followed her aunt unresistingly. The women in Ensign Sheldon's house were hard at work. They were baking in the great brick oven, spinning, and even dipping poor Goodwife Sheldon's candles.

"Bind up your hair, like an honest maid, and go to spinning," said Eunice, and she pointed to the spinning-wheel which had been saved from her own house. "We that be spared have to work, and not sit down and trot our own hearts on our knees. There is scarce a yard of linen left in Deerfield, to say naught of woolen cloth. Bind up your hair!"

And Silence bound up her hair, and sat down by her wheel meekly, and yet with a certain dignity. Indeed, through all the disorder of her mind, that delicate maiden dignity never forsook her, and there was never aught but respect shown her.

As time went on, it became quite evident that although the fair semblance of Silence Hoit still walked the Deerfield street, sat in the meeting-house, and toiled at the spinning-wheel and the loom, yet she was as surely not there as though she had been haled to Canada with the other captives on that terrible February night. It became the general opinion that Silence Hoit would never be quite her old self again and walk in the goodly company of all her fair wits unless David Walcott should be redeemed from captivity and restored to her. Then, it was accounted possible, the mending of the calamity which had brought her disorder upon her might remove it.

"Ye wait," Widow Eunice Bishop would say, hetchelling flax the while as though it were the scalp-locks of the enemy—"ye wait. If once David Walcott show his face, ye'll see Silence Hoit be not so lacking. She hath a tenderer heart than some I could mention, who go about smiling when their nearest of kin lay in torment in Indian lodges. She cares naught for picking up a new sweetheart. She hath a steady heart that be not so easy turned as some. Silence was never a light hussy, a-dancing hither and thither off the bridle-path for a new flower on the bushes. An', for all ye call her lacking now, there be not a maid in Deerfield does such a day's task as she."

And that last statement was quite true. All the Deerfield women, the matrons and maidens, toiled unceasingly, with a kind of stern patience like that which served their husbands and lovers in the frontier corn-fields, and which served all the dauntless border settlers, who were forced continually to rebuild after destruction, like wayside ants whose nests are always being trampled underfoot. There was need of unflinching toil at wheel and loom, for there was great scarcity of household linen in Deerfield, and Silence Hoit's shapely white maiden hands flinched less than any.

Nevertheless, many a day, in the morning when the snowy meadows were full of blue lights, at sunset when all the snow levels were rosy, but more particularly in wintry moonlight when the country was like a waste of silver, would Silence Hoit leave suddenly her household task, and hasten to the terrace overlooking the north meadow, and shriek out: "David! David! David Walcott!"

The village children never jeered at her, as they would some-times jeer at Goody Crane if not restrained by their elders. They eyed with a mixture of wonder and admiration Silence's beautiful bewildered face, with the curves of gold hair around the pink cheeks, and the fret-work of tortoise-shell surmounting it. David Walcott had given Silence her shell comb, and she was never seen without it.

Many a time when Silence called to David from the terrace of the north meadow, some of the little village maids in their homespun pinafores would join her and call with her. They had no fear of her, as they had of Goody Crane.

Indeed, Goody Crane, after the massacre, was in worse repute than ever in Deerfield. There were dark rumors concerning her whereabouts upon that awful night. Some among the devout and godly were fain to believe that the old woman had been in league with the powers of darkness and their allies the savages, and had so escaped harm. Some even whispered that in the thickest of the slaughter, when Deerfield was in the midst of that storm of fire, old Goody Crane's laugh had been heard, and one, looking up, had spied her high overhead riding her broomstick, her face red with the glare of the flames. The old woman was sheltered under protest, and had Deerfield not been a frontier town, and graver matters continually in mind, she might have come to harm in consequence of the gloomy suspicions concerning her.

Many a night after the massacre would the windows fly up and anxious faces peer out. It was as if the ears of the people were tuned up to the pitch of the Indian warwhoops, and their very thoughts made the nights ring with them.

The palisades were well looked to; there was never a slope of frozen snow again to form foothold for the enemy, and the sentry never slept at his post. But the anxious women listened all winter for the warwhoops, and many a time it seemed they heard them. In the midst of their nervous terror it was often a sore temptation to consult old Goody Crane, since she was held to have occult knowledge.

"I'll warrant old Goody Crane could tell us in a twinkling whether or no the Indians would come before morning," Eunice Bishop said one fierce windy night that called to mind the one of the massacre.

"Knowledge got in unlawful ways would avail us naught," returned Goodwife Spear. "I trow the Lord be yet able to protect His people."

"I doubt not that," said Eunice Bishop, "but I would like well to know if I had best bury my hood and my spinning-wheel and looking-glass in a snow-drift tonight. I have no mind the Indians shall get them. I warrant she knows well."

But Eunice Bishop did not consult Goody Crane, although she watched her narrowly and had a sharp ear to her mutterings as she sat in the chimney-corner. Eunice and Silence were living in John Sheldon's house, as did many of the survivors for some time after the massacre. It was the largest house in the village, and most of its original inhabitants were dead or gone into captivity. The people all huddled together fearfully in the few houses that were left, and the women's spinning-wheels and looms jostled each other.

As soon as the weather moderated, the work of building new dwellings commenced, and went on bravely with the advance of the spring. The air was full of the calls of spring birds and the strokes of axes and hammers. A little house was built on the site of their old one for Widow Bishop and Silence Hoit. Widow

Sarah Spear also lived with them, and Goody Crane took frequent shelter at their fireside. So they were a household of women, with loaded muskets at hand, and spinning-wheels and looms at full hum. They had but a scanty household store, although Widow Bishop tried in every way to increase it. Several times during the summer she took perilous journeys to Hatfield and Squakheak, for the purpose of bartering skeins of yarn or rolls of wool for household articles. In December, when Ensign Sheldon with young Freedom Wells went down to Boston to consult with Governor Dudley concerning an expedition to Canada to redeem the captives, Widow Eunice Bishop, having saved a few shillings, burdened him with a commission to purchase for her a new cap and a pair of bellows. She was much angered when he returned without them, having quite forgotten them in his press of business.

On the day when John Sheldon and Freedom Wells started upon their terrible journey of three hundred miles to redeem the captives, Eunice Bishop scolded well as she spun by her hearth fire.

"I trow they will bring back nobody," said she, her nose high in air, and her voice shrilling over the drone of the wheel; "an' they could not do the bidding of a poor lone widow-woman, and fetch her the cap and bellows from Boston, they'll fetch nobody home from Canada. I would I had ear of Governor Dudley. I trow men with minds upon their task would be sent." Eunice kept jerking her head as she scolded, and spun like a bee angry with its own humming.

Silence sat knitting, and paid no heed. She had paid no heed to any of the talk about Ensign Sheldon's and Freedom Wells's journey to Canada. She had not seemed to listen when Widow Spear had tried to explain the matter to her. "It may be, sweetheart, if it be the will of the Lord, that they will bring David back to thee," she had said over and over, and Silence had knitted and made no response.

She was the only one in Deerfield who was not torn with excitement and suspense as the months went by, and the only one unmoved by joy or disappointment when in May John Sheldon and Freedom Wells returned with five of the captives. But David Walcott was not among them.

"Said I not 'twould be so?" scolded Eunice Bishop. "Knew I not 'twould be so when they forgot to get the cap and the bellows in Boston? The one of all the captives that could have saved a poor maid's wits they leave behind. There's Mary Sheldon come home, and she a-coloring red before Freedom Wells, and everybody in the room a-seeing it. I trow they might have done somewhat for poor Silence," and Eunice broke down and wailed and wept, but Silence shed not a tear. Before long she stole out to the terrace and called "David! David! David!" over the north meadow, and strained her blue eyes towards Canada, and held out her fair arms, but it was with no new disappointment and desolation.

There was never a day nor a night that Silence called not over the north meadow like a spring bird from the bush to her absent mate, and people heard her and sighed and shuddered. One afternoon in the last of the month of June, as Silence was thrusting her face between the leaves of a wild cherry-tree and calling "David! David! David!" David himself broke through the thicket and stood before her. He and three other young men had escaped from their captivity and come home, and the four, crawling half dead across the meadow, had heard Silence's voice from the terrace above, and David, leaving the others, had made his way to her.

"Silence!" he said, and held out his poor arms, panting.

But Silence looked past him. "David! David! David Walcott!" she called.

David could scarcely stand for trembling, and he grasped a branch of the cherry-tree to steady himself, and swayed with it.

"Know—you not—who I am, Silence?" he said.

But she made as though she did not hear, and called again, always looking past him. And David Walcott, being near spent with fatigue and starvation, wound himself feebly around the trunk of the tree, and the tears dropped over his cheeks as he looked at her; and she called past him, until some women came and led him away and tried to comfort him, telling him how it was with her, and that she would soon know him when he looked more like himself.

But the summer wore away and she did not know him, although he constantly followed her beseechingly. His elders even reproved him for paying so little heed to his work in the colony. "It is not meet for a young man to be so weaned from usefulness by grief for a maid," said they. But David Walcott would at any time leave his reaping-hook in the corn and his axe in the tree, leave aught but his post as sentry, when he heard Silence calling him over the north meadow. He would stand at her elbow and say, in his voice that broke like a woman's: "Here I am, sweetheart, at thy side. I pray thee turn thy head." But she would not let her eyes rest upon him for more than a second's space, turning them ever past him towards Canada, and called in his very ears with a sad longing that tore his heart: "David! David! David!" It was as if her mind, reaching out always and speeding fast in search of him, had gotten such impetus that she passed the very object of her search and knew it not.

Now and then would David Walcott grow desperate, fling his arms around her, and kiss her upon her cold delicate lips and cheeks as if he would make her recognize him by force; but she would free herself from him with a passionless resentment that left him helpless.

One day in autumn, when the borders of the Deerfield meadows were a smoky purple with wild asters, and golden-rods flashed out like golden flames in the midst of them, David Walcott had been pleading vainly with Silence as she stood calling on the north terrace. Suddenly he turned and rushed away, and his face was all convulsed like a weeping child's. As he came out of the thicket he met the old woman Goody Crane, and would fain have hidden his face from her, but she stopped him.

"Prithee stop a moment's space, Master David Walcott," said she.

"What would you?" David cried out in a surly tone, and he dashed the back of his hand across his eyes.

"'Tis full moon tonight," said the old woman, in a whisper. "Come out here tonight when the moon shall be an hour high, and I promise ye she shall know ye."

The young man stared at her.

"I tell ye Mistress Silence Hoit shall know ye tonight," repeated the old woman. Her voice sounded hollow in the depths of her great hood, which she donned early in the fall. Her eyes in the gloom of it gleamed with a small dark brightness.

"I'll have no witch-work tried on her," said David, roughly.

"I'll try no witch-work but mine own wits," said Goody Crane. "If they would hang me for a witch for that, then they may. None but I can cure her. I tell ye, come out here tonight when the moon is an hour high; and mind ye wear a white sheep's fleece over your shoulders. I'll harm her not so much with my witch-work as ye'll do with your love, for all your prating."

The old woman pushed past him to where Silence stood calling, and waited there, standing in the shadow cast by the wild cherry-tree until she ceased and turned away. Then she caught hold of the skirt of her gown, and David stood, hidden by the thicket, listening.

"I prithee, Mistress Silence Hoit, listen but a moment," said Goody Crane.

Silence paused, and smiled at her gently and wearily.

"Give me your hand," demanded the old woman.

And Silence held out her hand, flashing white in the green gloom, as if she cared not.

The old woman turned the palm, bending her hooded head low over it. "He draweth near!" she cried out suddenly; "he draweth near, with a white sheep's fleece over his shoulders! He cometh through the woods from Canada. He will cross the meadow when the moon is an hour high tonight. He will wear a white sheep's fleece over his shoulders, and ye'll know him by that."

Silence's wandering eyes fastened upon her face.

The old woman caught hold of her shoulders and shook her to and fro. "David! David! David Walcott!" she screamed. "David Walcott with a white sheep's fleece on his back! On the meadow! Tonight when the moon's an hour high! Be ye out here tonight, Silence Hoit, if ye'd see him a-coming down from the north!"

Silence gasped faintly when the old woman released her and went muttering away. Presently she crept home, and sat down with her knitting-work in the chimney-place.

When Eunice Bishop hung on the porridge-kettle, Goody Crane lifted the latch-string and came in. It was growing dusky, but the moon would not rise for an hour yet. Goody Crane sat opposite Silence, with her eyes fixed upon her, and Silence, in spite of herself, kept looking at her. A gold brooch at the old woman's throat glittered in the firelight, and that seemed to catch Silence's eyes. She finally knitted with them fixed upon it.

She scarcely took her eyes away when she ate her supper; then she sat down to her knitting and knitted, and gazed, in spite of herself, at the gold spot on the old woman's throat.

The moon arose; the tree branches before the windows tossed half in silver light; the air was shrill with crickets. Silence stirred uneasily, and dropped stitches in her knitting-work. "He draweth near," muttered Goody Crane, and Silence quivered.

The moon was a half-hour high. Widow Bishop was spinning, Widow Spear was winding quills, and Silence knitted. "He draweth near," muttered Goody Crane.

"I'll have no witchcraft!" Silence cried out, suddenly and sharply. Her aunt stopped spinning, and Widow Spear started.

"What's that?" said her aunt. But Silence was knitting again.

"What meant you by that?" asked her aunt, sharply.

"I have dropped a stitch," said Silence.

Her aunt spun again, with occasional wary glances. The moon was three-quarters of an hour high. Silence gazed steadily at the gold brooch at Goody Crane's throat.

"The moon is near an hour high; you had best be going," said the old woman, in a low monotone.

Silence arose directly.

"Where go you at this time of night?" grumbled her aunt. But Silence glided past her.

"You'll lose your good name as well as your wits," cried Eunice. But she did not try to stop Silence, for she knew it was useless.

"A white sheep's fleece over his shoulders," muttered Goody Crane as Silence went out of the door; and the other women marveled what she meant.

Silence Hoit went swiftly and softly down Deerfield street to her old haunt on the north meadow terrace. She pushed in among the wild cherry-trees, which waved, white with the moonlight, like ghostly arms in her face. Then she called, setting her face towards Canada and the north: "David! David! David!" But her voice had a different tone in it, and it broke with her heart-beats.

David Walcott came slowly across the meadow below; a white fleece of a sheep thrown over his back caught the moonlight. He came on, and on, and on; then he went up the terrace to Silence. Her face, white like a white flower in the moonlight, shone out suddenly close before him. He waited a second, then he spoke. "Silence!" he said.

Then Silence gave a great cry, and threw her arms around his neck, and pressed softly and wildly against him with her wet cheek to his.

"Know you who 'tis, sweetheart?"

"Oh, David, David!"

The trees arched like arbors with the weight of the wild grapes, which made the air sweet; the night insects called from the bushes; Deerfield village and the whole valley lay in the moonlight like a landscape of silver. The lovers stood in each other's arms, motionless, and seemingly fixed as the New England flora around them, as if they too might reappear hundreds of spring-times hence, with their loves as fairly in blossom.

THE SCHOOL-TEACHER'S STORY

have taught school forty-four years. Now I have delivered the keys of my schoolhouse to the committee, I have packed away on the top shelf of my closet a row of primers and readers, geographies, spelling-books, and arithmetics, and I have stopped work for the rest of my life. Through all these forty-four years, I have squeezed resolutely all the sweets out of existence, and stored them up to make a kind of tasteless, but life-sustaining honey for old age. I have never spent one penny unless for the barest necessities. I have added term by term to the sum on my bank-book, until I have been able to build this house, and have a sufficient sum at interest to live upon. I need little, very little, to eat, and I wear my clothes carefully and long.

I was never extravagant in clothes, but once. That was twenty-five years ago, when I was thirty-five, and expected to be married in the spring. I had a green-silk dress then, a bright green. But I had it dyed black, and, after all, got considerable wear out of it, although it was flimsy. Colored silk is apt to be. I had a blue woolen, too, a color I should never have bought, if I had not expected to be married, and that faded. I also had a black-velvet cloak, something that was very costly, and I should not have bought it under any circumstances, but I was foolish. However, that has made my winter bonnets ever since; it was a good piece, and not cut up much.

Looking backward forty-four years, I cannot remember any other extravagance than this outlay in clothes when I expected to be married at thirty-five. I never have bought any candy except a few cough-drops when I had a cold. I have never bought a ribbon even, or a breast-pin. I have always worn my mother's old hair pin, although it was so old-fashioned, and the other girls had pretty gold and coral, or cameo ones.

My mother died when I was fourteen; my father, when I was sixteen; then I began to teach. My father left me nothing. Mother was sick all her life nearly, and he could not lay up a cent. However, there was enough to pay his funeral expenses, and I was thankful for that. I sometimes wonder what my father would say if he could see me now, and know how I am situated. I wonder if he would think I had done pretty well. I don't know how it can make any difference to him now; he is past all such earthly vanities, even if he knows about them, but I do sometimes feel glad I have done so well, on his account. Anybody has to have some account beside their own, even if it is somebody's that's dead.

I have built this house, with six rooms in it, and a woodshed. I have a little land, too. I keep hens, and I am going to have a vegetable-garden back of the house, and a flower-garden, front. I have good woolen carpets all over the house except the kitchen. I have stuffed parlor furniture, and a marble-topped table, and a marble shelf with a worked plush scarf on it. I have a handsome dining-set, and two nice chamber-sets, and two beautiful silk quilts I pieced from bits my scholars gave me. I shouldn't be ashamed to have anybody go over my house. And I keep it nice, too; you could not find a speck of dust anywhere. Of course, I have nobody to put it out of order, and that makes a difference.

It has always been my habit to look at all the advantage there is in life, and I have found there is an advantage-side to almost everything. I can keep my house a great deal nicer than I could if I were not all alone in the world. I sometimes wonder what I should do, if I had a man coming in with muddy boots, or children tracking in dirt, and stubbing out my carpets, or kicking the paint off my new doors.

To tell the truth, I have never cared much about children, though I have been teaching them forty-four years. I never dared to say so before, but it is true. Once in a while I saw a child that I thought a good deal of, but taking them all together, I have often wondered how their own mothers could stand them. I would have worked my fingers to the bone for the few I did take a notion to. I fairly grudged them to their folks, but the others!—and I had to hide it, too; it wouldn't have done for the children to think I was partial. They had all the meanness of grown-up folks, about apple-cores, and teasing away one another's candy, and the big ones plaguing the little ones; throwing paper-balls, and marking up the walls, and everything else. I know, for one, that there's something in the doctrine of original sin. I guess most women that have taught a district school forty-four years do.

I have never been sure, either, that they learned anything so's to remember it, and have it do them any good. I have always been afraid that, no matter how hard I tried to do my duty by them, it was never quite done, and that I was teaching myself more than anybody else, just as I always seemed to hit my own hands harder than a scholar's when I had to ferule one.

I could travel all over the earth, on the map, and never once lose my way, but I wonder if my scholars could. I can spell through the spelling-book without missing a word, but I know that not one of my scholars could. I can do every sum in the arithmetic, measure the depths of all the wells, calculate the speed of all the dogs and foxes, and say the multiplication-tables by heart, but I am quite sure that no boy or girl ever left my school who could. It seems to me sometimes that I have gone to school to my scholars, instead of my scholars going to school to me, and that I have never been of any benefit to any one of them.

Still, I have sometimes thought that I was, once, and in a strange way, to the strangest scholar I ever had. Before thinking even of this scholar, and this story, I have to review my face, and my whole character, in my mental vision, as before a glass, to establish, as it were, my own reliability to myself. Is it likely that anybody, who looks like that, should tell herself that she saw what she did not see, or heard what she did not hear? Is it likely that anybody, who is like that, should?

But, after all, I was never given to saying things that weren't plain common sense. Still, it has always kind of seemed to me, when I thought of that time in Marshbrook, that it didn't ring like any known metal. But there may be some metals that really are on earth, though they are not known, I suppose, and anybody might hear them ring, and be honest enough about it.

It was just twenty-five years ago today, that I went to Marshbrook to teach the Number One district-school. It was right in the middle of the spring-time. I had given up my old school, because I was expecting to be married that May. But when I found out he'd changed his mind toward me, I felt as if I ought to go to work again. I'd laid out a good deal of money on my clothes, and I knew I'd have to make it up someway, as long as I was always going to have nobody but myself to depend on, the way I always had.

Maria Rogers had my old school. She had come from the east village to teach it, when I gave it up, and it wasn't more'n three weeks before he began to go with her. She was good-looking, always smiling, though it always seemed to me it was a kind of silly smile. I was always sober and set-looking, and I couldn't smile easy even if I felt like it. Her hair curled, too. I tried to curl mine, but it wouldn't look like hers. I wouldn't believe it at first, when folks came and told me he was going with her, and they thought I ought to know; but after a while I saw enough to satisfy me, myself. I wrote him a letter, and told him I'd found out he had changed his mind, and he had my best wishes for his welfare and prosperity; and then I began to look out for another school. He didn't marry Maria Rogers till the spring term was through. She wanted the money for her wedding-clothes. She was a poor girl, or I could have had my old school. As it was, she had him, and my school, too.

I don't know as I should have got any till fall, if the teacher of the Number One district in Marshbrook hadn't left suddenly. One of the committee came for me the next day, and said I'd got to go there, whether or no. I asked why the other teacher had left, and he said she wasn't very well—"kind of hystericky," he called it. He was an old man, and a doctor. I looked him straight in the face when he spoke, and I knew there was something behind what he said, and he knew I did.

"I'll give you fifty cents a week more, seeing as you come to oblige," says he.

"Very well," says I. I knew what it all meant. I had heard about district Number One in Marshbrook, ever since I could remember. They could never keep a teacher there through the spring term. There wasn't any trouble fall, and winter, but the teacher would leave in the spring term. They always tried to hush it up, and nobody ever knew exactly what they left for. I rather guess they bound the teachers over not to tell, maybe paid them a little extra. Anyway, nobody ever knew exactly what it was, but it got whispered round there was something wrong about the Number One schoolhouse.

Nobody but a stranger or somebody that was along in years and pretty courageous could be hired to go there and teach the spring term. The chances were that old Doctor Emmons couldn't get another soul beside me for love nor money, and if I wouldn't go, the school would have to be shut up till fall. But I didn't care anything about the stories. I never was one of the kind that listen, and hark, and screech, and I had had enough real things to think and worry about. Then I had a kind of feeling then, I suppose it was wicked, that it didn't matter much what happened anyway, after what had happened.

So I just packed up my trunk, while Doctor Emmons waited, and then he put it in behind his wagon, and carried me over to Marshbrook. It was about six miles away.

Marshbrook was named after the brook there, that runs through marshy land, and gets soaked up in it some seasons of the year. That spring it was quite high, and the land all around it was yellow as gold with cowslips. We rode beside it quite a way, and the doctor said his wife had boiled cowslip-greens twice. He talked considerable about such things being better for folks to eat than meat, too. He didn't say a word about the school, till he set me down at the house where I was going to board. Then he said I looked as if I wasn't fidgety, and he hadn't any notion but what I should get along well, and like the school. Then he said, kind of as if he hated to, but thought he'd better, that he guessed

I might just as well make up my mind not to stay after school at night much, and not to keep the scholars. The schoolhouse was in rather a lonesome place, and some stragglers might come along; then, too, it was rather damp there, being near the brook, after the dew fell, and he didn't think it was very healthy. I said, "Very well," and then Mr. Orrin Simonds, the man where I was going to board, came out, and they carried my trunk between them, into the house.

I began school the next morning, and got along well enough. The school was quite a large one, about forty in it, and none of them very old. They behaved well as usual, and I taught them the best I knew how. I ought to have done better by them than I had ever done for other scholars, for I hadn't any outlook for myself to take my mind off. I suppose I always had had a little, though I had hardly known it myself, and I ought to have been ashamed of it.

I did not stay after school for some weeks, not because I was afraid of anything, for I wasn't, but I hadn't any call to. I didn't mind what Doctor Emmons had said at all, as far as I was concerned, but I thought I wouldn't keep the scholars anyway, so if anything did come up, I wouldn't be blamed on their account. There wasn't anybody to blame me on mine, if I didn't give up the school—and I wasn't going to do that, anyway.

I went to meeting the Sunday after I went to Marshbrook. I suppose some folks thought I would get somebody to carry me home to meeting, seeing it was only six miles, and I belonged to the church there, but I felt as if I had just as soon see some new faces.

Maria Rogers used to sit right in front of me at home.

I noticed that folks in the meeting-house at Marshbrook eyed me some. I don't know whether it was because I had come to teach the Number One school, or because I wore my green silk. I suppose it did look 'most too fine, but I had it, and it was a pleasant Sunday, and I thought I might just as well wear it, though somehow, every time I looked down at my lap as I sat in meeting, there was something about the color seemed to strike over me, and make me sick. I never liked green very well, but he did, and that was why I got it. I liked it better after it was colored, though it seemed a shame to have all the stiffening taken out of it. It was a beautiful piece.

I had a good boarding-place, just Mr. Simonds and his wife, and she was as neat as wax, and a good cook. She was a kind of woodeny, and didn't talk much, but I didn't feel much like talking, and I liked it full as well. She used to have supper early, about as soon as I got home from school, and then I used to go upstairs to my chamber, and sit by myself. Mrs. Simonds didn't neighbor much, she said, but I guess after I came, folks run in more. I'd hear them talking downstairs. I guess they wanted to find out how I was getting along at the Number One school.

Once Mrs. Simonds said, if she was in my place, she'd make her plans not to stay after school. She didn't seem any more fidgety herself than a wooden post, but I guess she'd heard so much from the neighbors, she thought she ought to say something.

I said I hadn't had any occasion to stay after school, and I hadn't. I didn't really have any occasion the night I did stay, but I felt kind of down at the heel, and I didn't want any supper, and I just sat there on the platform behind my desk, after the scholars marched out of the room.

I don't know how long I sat there—quite a while, I suppose, for it began to grow dusky. The frogs peeped as if they were in the room, and there was a damp wind blew in the window, and I could smell wintergreen, and swamp-pinks. It was all I could do to keep the children from chewing wintergreen-leaves in school-time. They were real thick all around the schoolhouse.

All of a sudden, as I sat there, I had a queer feeling as if there was somebody in the room, and I looked up. I saw, down in the middle of the room, a little white arm raised in the dusk. It was the way the children did, when they wanted to ask something, and I thought for a second that one had stayed or come back, unbeknown to me, and was raising an arm. Of course, that was queer, but it was the only reason I could think of, and it flashed through my head.

"What is it?" says I, and then I heard a little girl's voice pipe up:

"'Please, teacher, find my doll for me, and hear my next lesson in the primer.'"

"What?" says I, for it didn't seem to me I could have heard right. And then the voice said it over again, and that little white arm crooked out of the gloom.

I got up, and went down the aisle between the desks, and when I came close enough, I saw a little girl, in a queer, straight white dress, almost like a nightgown, sitting there. Her little face was so white in the gloom, it made me creep, and her features looked set; even her mouth didn't move when she spoke. It was open a little, and the words just seemed to flow out between her lips.

"'Please, teacher, find my doll for me, and hear my next lesson in the primer,'" says she, over again, dreadful pitiful.

I put my hand on her shoulder, and then I jumped and took it away, for I never felt anything so cold as her little shoulder was. It seemed as if the cold struck to my heart from it, and I had to catch my breath.

"What is your name?" says I, as soon as I could.

96

"'Mary Williams, aged six years, three months, and five days,'" says she.

Then my blood ran cold, but I tried to reason it out to myself again, that she was some child I hadn't seen, that had run in there, and maybe she wasn't quite right in her mind.

"Well," says I, "you had better run home now. If you want to come to school, you can come at nine o'clock tomorrow morning, if your mother is willing. Then I will hear your lesson, and maybe you will find your doll, but you mustn't bring it to school. I can't have any dolls brought to school."

With that she rose up, and dropped a queer little courtesy that made a puff of icy-cold wind in my face, and was out of the room, very fast, as if she slid or floated, without taking any steps at all.

I put on my bonnet and locked up the schoolhouse, and went home then. Looking back, I can't say as I felt scared or nervous at all. I know I didn't walk a mite faster when I went past the old graveyard. There was an old graveyard near the schoolhouse, and the children used to play there at recess.

When I got home, Mrs. Simonds asked why I hadn't been home, and if I didn't want any supper, but she didn't act surprised nor curious. She never seemed surprised or curious at anything.

I went upstairs to my chamber, and sat down and thought it over. It seemed to me there must be some aboveboard reason for it. As I thought it over, I remembered that there had been a strange, faint, choking smell about the child, and then I put my own dress-skirt up to my face, and I smelled it then. I hung my dress out of the window to air, when I took it off.

The next morning, when the scholars filed in to school, I tried to think that strange little girl might be among them, but she wasn't, and she didn't come in the afternoon.

That night I stayed after school again. I had made up my mind I would. I waited, and after a while, that little white arm showed out of the dusk, but I had not seen the child come into the room.

I asked her again what she wanted, and she piped up, just as she did before:

"'Please, teacher, find my doll for me, and hear me say the next lesson in the primer.'"

I got up and went to her just as I had before, and there she was just the same, and the faint smell came into my face.

"Where did you lose your doll?" says I.

But she wouldn't say.

"'Please, teacher, find my doll for me, and hear me say my lesson in the primer,'" says she, with a kind of a wail. I never heard anything so pitiful as it was. It seemed to me, somehow, as if all the wants I had ever had myself, sounded in that child's voice, and as if she was begging for something I had lost myself.

But I spoke decidedly. It was always my way with children. I found it worked better.

"Now you run right home," says I, "and you come tomorrow, and I'll give you your doll and hear your lesson in the primer."

And then she rose up and courtesied, just as she had before, and was gone.

I did not try to follow her.

That evening, I went around to old Doctor Emmons' and asked Mrs. Emmons if I could see the doctor a few minutes.

I guess she suspected what had happened, for she looked at me real sharp, and said she hoped I wasn't getting nervous and overwrought with school-teaching. I said I wasn't. I just wanted to see the doctor about a new scholar; and she left me in the sitting-room, and called him in.

I asked him, pointblank, if anything had ever happened there in Marshbrook, and he wouldn't tell me at first.

"I suppose you want to give the school up. I thought you were old enough to behave yourself," says he. He was pretty short sometimes, but he meant well.

"I've done the best I could by the school," says I.

"Why couldn't you come home when school was done, as you were told to, instead of staying there in that lonesome place, and getting hystericky?" says he. "I don't know as I can get another teacher this term. The schoolhouse will have to be shut up. It's a pity all the female school-teachers in creation couldn't be ducked a few times, and get the fidgets out of them. I'll get a man for the place next time. I've had enough of women."

"I don't want to give up the school," says I.

"What are you talking about, then?" says he.

"I want to know if anything has ever happened here in Marshbrook," says I. "I don't want to give up the school if anything has happened."

He finally told me how a little girl had been murdered, some fifty or sixty years ago, on her way to school, on the brook-road. They found her laying dead beside a clump of swamp-pinks, with a great bruise on the back of her neck, as if she'd been hit by a stone, and her doll and her primer were laying in the road, where she'd dropped them when she run from whoever killed her. They never found him.

"Was her name Mary Williams?" says I.

"How did you know it?" says the doctor.

"She told me," says I.

The old doctor turned as white as a sheet.

"You ain't hystericky?" says he.

When he found out I wasn't scared, and didn't want to give up the school, he wanted to know what I'd seen, and asked a good many questions. I told him as short as I could, and then I went home.

The next morning before school, I got some linen rags from Mrs. Simonds, and a piece of bright-blue thibet, and I made a real pretty little rag-baby. I'd never made one before, but I couldn't see why I didn't make it as well as anybody. I raveled out a little of an old black stocking I had, for its hair, and I colored its cheeks and mouth with cranberry juice, and made its eyes with blue ink. I found, too, an old primer, that Mrs. Simonds said her mother had studied, for I thought that might have been like the one the child was carrying to school, when she was killed.

That night I stayed after school again, and waited until I saw the little white arm raised out of the dusk. She did not wait for me to speak that time. She piped up, quick:

"'Please, teacher, find my doll for me, and hear me say my lesson in the primer.'"

"Put your arm down, and be quiet," says I, "and I will hear your lesson." I put the rag-doll in my pocket, and took the old primer I had found, and went to her.

"Find the place, and go on with your lesson," says I, and I gave her the book. She turned over the leaves, as if she were quite accustomed to it, and I saw at once that I had the right book. It was a queer little primer, that had been written by an old minister in Marshbrook, and used in the schools there for some time. She found the place soon, and began to read, piping up quite loud. You could have heard her out-of-doors; the windows were open. The piece was called "The Character of a Good Child." She read it very well. I only had her spell out a few of the words.

"You have got your lesson very well," said I. Then I took the doll out of my pocket, and gave it to her. She fairly snatched for it with her little, white, gleaming hands and they touched mine, and I felt the cold strike to my heart again.

She hugged the doll tight, and kissed it with her stiff, parted lips. Then she held it off, and looked at it.

"Please, teacher, find my doll for me," says she, with a great wail and I saw she knew it wasn't her own old doll.

"Hush," says I, "I can't find a doll that's been lost fifty years. This doll is just exactly as good. Now, you'd better take it, and run home."

But she just gave that pitiful cry again: "Please, teacher, find my doll for me."

"You are not behaving pretty at all," says I. "That doll is just as good." Then, I don't know what possessed me to say it, but I says: "She hasn't got any mother, either."

She just hugged the doll tight, and kissed it again then, and didn't say another word against it.

"Now, you'd better run home," says I.

She rose up, and courtesied, and I was all ready to spring. I followed her. I didn't know as I could keep her in sight, but I did, and she went into the old graveyard. I saw a gleam of white in there a minute; then it was gone.

That evening, I went to Doctor Emmons, and told him what had happened.

"Now," says I, "I want to know where that child was buried."

"She was buried in the old Williams tomb," says he.

Then I asked him to take a lantern, and go to the graveyard with me, and look in that tomb. I didn't know as I could make him for quite a while. He said the Williams family had all died out, and gone away. There wasn't one of them left in town. He didn't exactly know who had the key of the tomb, and he kept looking at me real sharp. I suppose he was afraid I was getting hystericky. I guess he got pretty sure at last that I wasn't, for I taught that Marshbrook Number One school seven years after that, though any young thing could have done it, and stayed after school every night in the spring terms, for that little girl never came to scare anybody again. He kept looking at me that night, and then he felt my pulse and counted it by his watch.

"You don't want to give the school up?" says he.

"No, I don't," says I.

He went out after a while, and presently he came back with a lighted lantern and a key. I don't know where he got it. Then we went down the road to the graveyard. It was a dark night, and it was misting a little. He went along in front with the lantern, and I followed on behind. He didn't speak a word the whole way. I guess he felt kind of grouty at having to come out. I didn't care if he was. I was bound to find out.

When we came to the old graveyard, he opened the gate, and we went in. His lantern lit up all the old headstones, and trees, and scraggy bushes, as we went across to the Williams tomb. It wasn't very far from the gate. A lot of little bushes were growing out of the humped-up roof, and I read "Williams" in the stonework over the iron door. The doctor fitted the key in the lock, while I held the lantern. I felt the way I used to when I was a child, when I waked up in the dark, in the night, but I held the lantern as steady as if my hand had been an iron hook.

It was hard to turn the key in the rusty padlock, and the doctor worked quite a long time, but finally it snapped back, and he pulled off the padlock, and slipped the hasp. But even then he could not open the door until he had cleared away some stones and pulled up some little plants, that had grown over the threshold, by the roots.

After he had done that, he opened the door, and a puff of that same strange odor which I had noticed about the child, came in my face. He took the lantern and stepped down and into the tomb, and I after him. All of a sudden he stopped short, and caught hold of my arm. There, on the floor of the tomb, in the lantern-light, right before us, lay the doll, and the primer.

THE WIND IN THE ROSE-BUSH

ord Village has no railroad station, being on the other side of the river from Porter's Falls, and accessible only by the ford which gives it its name, and a ferry line.

The ferry-boat was waiting when Rebecca Flint got off the train with her bag and lunch basket. When she and her small trunk were safely embarked she sat stiff and straight and calm in the ferry-boat as it shot swiftly and smoothly across stream. There was a horse attached to a light country wagon on board, and he pawed the deck uneasily. His owner stood near, with a wary eye upon him, although he was chewing, with as dully reflective an expression as a cow. Beside Rebecca sat a woman of about her own age, who kept looking at her with furtive curiosity; her husband, short and stout and saturnine, stood near her. Rebecca paid no attention to either of them. She was tall and spare and pale, the type of a spinster, yet with rudimentary lines and expressions of matronhood. She all unconsciously held her shawl, rolled up in a canvas bag, on her left hip, as if it had been a child. She wore a settled frown of dissent at life, but it was the frown of a mother who regarded life as a froward child, rather than as an overwhelming fate.

The other woman continued staring at her; she was mildly stupid, except for an over-developed curiosity which made her at times sharp beyond belief. Her eyes glittered, red spots came on her flaccid cheeks; she kept opening her mouth to speak, making little abortive motions. Finally she could endure it no longer; she nudged Rebecca boldly.

"A pleasant day," said she.

Rebecca looked at her and nodded coldly.

"Yes, very," she assented.

"Have you come far?"

"I have come from Michigan."

"Oh!" said the woman, with awe. "It's a long way," she remarked presently.

"Yes, it is," replied Rebecca, conclusively.

Still the other woman was not daunted; there was something which she determined to know, possibly roused thereto by a vague sense of incongruity in the other's appearance. "It's a long ways to come and leave a family," she remarked with painful slyness.

"I ain't got any family to leave," returned Rebecca shortly.

"Then you ain't—"

"No, I ain't."

"Oh!" said the woman.

Rebecca looked straight ahead at the race of the river.

It was a long ferry. Finally Rebecca herself waxed unexpectedly loquacious. She turned to the other woman and inquired if she knew John Dent's widow who lived in Ford Village. "Her husband died about three years ago," said she, by way of detail.

The woman started violently. She turned pale, then she flushed; she cast a strange glance at her husband, who was regarding both women with a sort of stolid keenness.

"Yes, I guess I do," faltered the woman finally.

"Well, his first wife was my sister," said Rebecca with the air of one imparting important intelligence.

"Was she?" responded the other woman feebly. She glanced at her husband with an expression of doubt and terror, and he shook his head forbiddingly.

"I'm going to see her, and take my niece Agnes home with me," said Rebecca.

Then the woman gave such a violent start that she noticed it.

"What is the matter?" she asked.

"Nothin', I guess," replied the woman, with eyes on her husband, who was slowly shaking his head, like a Chinese toy.

"Is my niece sick?" asked Rebecca with quick suspicion.

"No, she ain't sick," replied the woman with alacrity, then she caught her breath with a gasp.

"When did you see her?"

"Let me see; I ain't seen her for some little time," replied the woman. Then she caught her breath again.

"She ought to have grown up real pretty, if she takes after my sister. She was a real pretty woman," Rebecca said wistfully.

"Yes, I guess she did grow up pretty," replied the woman in a trembling voice.

"What kind of a woman is the second wife?"

The woman glanced at her husband's warning face. She continued to gaze at him while she replied in a choking voice to Rebecca:

"I—guess she's a nice woman," she replied. "I—don't know, I—guess so. I—don't see much of her."

"I felt kind of hurt that John married again so quick," said Rebecca; "but I suppose he wanted his house kept, and Agnes wanted care. I wasn't so situated that I could take her when her mother died. I had my own mother to care for, and I was school-teaching. Now mother has gone, and my uncle died six months ago and left me quite a little property, and I've given up my school, and I've come for Agnes. I guess she'll be glad to go with me, though I suppose her stepmother is a good woman, and has always done for her."

The man's warning shake at his wife was fairly portentous.

"I guess so," said she.

"John always wrote that she was a beautiful woman," said Rebecca.

Then the ferry-boat grated on the shore.

John Dent's widow had sent a horse and wagon to meet her sister-in-law. When the woman and her husband went down the road, on which Rebecca in the wagon with her trunk soon passed them, she said reproachfully:

"Seems as if I'd ought to have told her, Thomas."

"Let her find it out herself," replied the man. "Don't you go to burnin' your fingers in other folks' puddin', Maria."

"Do you s'pose she'll see anything?" asked the woman with a spasmodic shudder and a terrified roll of her eyes.

"See!" returned her husband with stolid scorn. "Better be sure there's anything to see."

"Oh, Thomas, they say—"

"Lord, ain't you found out that what they say is mostly lies?"

"But if it should be true, and she's a nervous woman, she might be scared enough to lose her wits," said his wife, staring uneasily after Rebecca's erect figure in the wagon disappearing over the crest of the hilly road.

"Wits that's so easy upset ain't worth much," declared the man. "You keep out of it, Maria."

Rebecca in the meantime rode on in the wagon, beside a flaxen-headed boy, who looked, to her understanding, not very bright. She asked him a question, and he paid no attention. She repeated it, and he responded with a bewildered and incoherent grunt. Then she let him alone, after making sure that he knew how to drive straight.

They had traveled about half a mile, passed the village square, and gone a short distance beyond, when the boy drew up with a sudden Whoa! before a very prosperous-looking house. It had been one of the aboriginal cottages of the vicinity, small and white, with a roof extending on one side over a piazza, and a tiny "L" jutting out in the rear, on the right hand. Now the cottage was transformed by dormer windows, a bay window on the piazza-less side, a carved railing down the front steps, and a modern hard-wood door.

"Is this John Dent's house?" asked Rebecca.

The boy was as sparing of speech as a philosopher. His only response was in flinging the reins over the horse's back, stretching out one foot to the shaft, and leaping out of the wagon, then going around to the rear for the trunk. Rebecca got out and went toward the house. Its white paint had a new gloss; its blinds were an immaculate apple green; the lawn was trimmed as smooth as velvet, and it was dotted with scrupulous groups of hydrangeas and cannas.

"I always understood that John Dent was well-to-do," Rebecca reflected comfortably. "I guess Agnes will have considerable. I've got enough, but it will come in handy for her schooling. She can have advantages."

The boy dragged the trunk up the fine gravel-walk, but before he reached the steps leading up to the piazza, for the house stood on a terrace, the front door opened and a fair, frizzled head of a very large and handsome woman appeared. She held up her black silk skirt, disclosing voluminous ruffles of starched embroidery, and waited for Rebecca. She smiled placidly, her pink, double-chinned face widened and dimpled, but her blue eyes were wary and calculating. She extended her hand as Rebecca climbed the steps.

"This is Miss Flint, I suppose," said she.

"Yes, ma'am," replied Rebecca, noticing with bewilderment a curious expression compounded of fear and defiance on the other's face.

"Your letter only arrived this morning," said Mrs. Dent, in a steady voice. Her great face was a uniform pink, and her china-blue eyes were at once aggressive and veiled with secrecy.

"Yes, I hardly thought you'd get my letter," replied Rebecca. "I felt as if I could not wait to hear from you before I came. I supposed you would be so situated that you could have me a little while without putting you out too much, from what John used to write me about his circumstances, and when I had that money so unexpected I felt as if I must come for Agnes. I suppose you will be willing to give her up. You know she's my own blood, and of course she's no relation to you, though you must have got attached to her. I know from her picture what a sweet girl she must be, and John always said she looked like her own mother, and Grace was a beautiful woman, if she was my sister."

Rebecca stopped and stared at the other woman in amazement and alarm. The great handsome blonde creature stood speechless, livid, gasping, with her hand to her heart, her lips parted in a horrible caricature of a smile.

"Are you sick!" cried Rebecca, drawing near. "Don't you want me to get you some water!"

Then Mrs. Dent recovered herself with a great effort. "It is nothing," she said. "I am subject to—spells. I am over it now. Won't you come in, Miss Flint?"

As she spoke, the beautiful deep-rose color suffused her face, her blue eyes met her visitor's with the opaqueness of turquoise—with a revelation of blue, but a concealment of all behind.

Rebecca followed her hostess in, and the boy, who had waited quiescently, climbed the steps with the trunk. But before they entered the door a strange thing happened. On the upper terrace, close to the piazza-post, grew a great rose-bush, and on it, late in the season though it was, one small red, perfect rose.

Rebecca looked at it, and the other woman extended her hand with a quick gesture. "Don't you pick that rose!" she brusquely cried.

Rebecca drew herself up with stiff dignity.

"I ain't in the habit of picking other folks' roses without leave," said she.

As Rebecca spoke she started violently, and lost sight of her resentment, for something singular happened. Suddenly the rose-bush was agitated violently as if by a gust of wind, yet it was a remarkably still day. Not a leaf of the hydrangea standing on the terrace close to the rose trembled.

"What on earth—" began Rebecca, then she stopped with a gasp at the sight of the other woman's face. Although a face, it gave somehow the impression of a desperately clutched hand of secrecy.

"Come in!" said she in a harsh voice, which seemed to come forth from her chest with no intervention of the organs of speech. "Come into the house. I'm getting cold out here."

"What makes that rose-bush blow so when there isn't any wind?" asked Rebecca, trembling with vague horror, yet resolute.

"I don't see as it is blowing," returned the woman calmly. And as she spoke, indeed, the bush was quiet.

"It was blowing," declared Rebecca.

"It isn't now," said Mrs. Dent. "I can't try to account for everything that blows out-of-doors. I have too much to do."

She spoke scornfully and confidently, with defiant, unflinching eyes, first on the bush, then on Rebecca, and led the way into the house.

"It looked queer," persisted Rebecca, but she followed, and also the boy with the trunk.

Rebecca entered an interior, prosperous, even elegant, according to her simple ideas. There were Brussels carpets, lace curtains, and plenty of brilliant upholstery and polished wood.

"You're real nicely situated," remarked Rebecca, after she had become a little accustomed to her new surroundings and the two women were seated at the tea-table.

Mrs. Dent stared with a hard complacency from behind her silver-plated service. "Yes, I be," said she.

"You got all the things new?" said Rebecca hesitatingly, with a jealous memory of her dead sister's bridal furnishings.

"Yes," said Mrs. Dent; "I was never one to want dead folks' things, and I had money enough of my own, so I wasn't beholden to John. I had the old duds put up at auction. They didn't bring much."

"I suppose you saved some for Agnes. She'll want some of her poor mother's things when she is grown up," said Rebecca with some indignation.

The defiant stare of Mrs. Dent's blue eyes waxed more intense. "There's a few things up garret," said she.

"She'll be likely to value them," remarked Rebecca. As she

spoke she glanced at the window. "Isn't it most time for her to be coming home?" she asked.

"'Most time," answered Mrs. Dent carelessly; "but when she gets over to Addie Slocum's she never knows when to come home."

"Is Addie Slocum her intimate friend?"

"Intimate as any."

"Maybe we can have her come out to see Agnes when she's living with me," said Rebecca wistfully. "I suppose she'll be likely to be homesick at first."

"Most likely," answered Mrs. Dent.

"Does she call you mother?" Rebecca asked.

"No, she calls me Aunt Emeline," replied the other woman shortly. "When did you say you were going home?"

"In about a week, I thought, if she can be ready to go so soon," answered Rebecca with a surprised look.

She reflected that she would not remain a day longer than she could help after such an inhospitable look and question.

"Oh, as far as that goes," said Mrs. Dent, "it wouldn't make any difference about her being ready. You could go home whenever you felt that you must, and she could come afterward."

"Alone?"

"Why not? She's a big girl now, and you don't have to change cars."

"My niece will go home when I do, and not travel alone; and if I can't wait here for her, in the house that used to be her mother's and my sister's home, I'll go and board somewhere," returned Rebecca with warmth.

"Oh, you can stay here as long as you want to. You're welcome," said Mrs. Dent.

Then Rebecca started. "There she is!" she declared in a trembling, exultant voice. Nobody knew how she longed to see the girl.

"She isn't as late as I thought she'd be," said Mrs. Dent, and again that curious, subtle change passed over her face, and again it settled into that stony impassiveness.

Rebecca stared at the door, waiting for it to open. "Where is she?" she asked presently.

"I guess she's stopped to take off her hat in the entry," suggested Mrs. Dent.

Rebecca waited. "Why don't she come? It can't take her all this time to take off her hat."

For answer Mrs. Dent rose with a stiff jerk and threw open the door.

"Agnes!" she called. "Agnes!" Then she turned and eyed Rebecca. "She ain't there."

"I saw her pass the window," said Rebecca in bewilderment.

"You must have been mistaken."

"I know I did," persisted Rebecca.

"You couldn't have."

"I did. I saw first a shadow go over the ceiling, then I saw her in the glass there"—she pointed to a mirror over the sideboard opposite—"and then the shadow passed the window."

"How did she look in the glass?"

"Little and light-haired, with the light hair kind of tossing over her forehead."

"You couldn't have seen her."

"Was that like Agnes?"

"Like enough; but of course you didn't see her. You've been thinking so much about her that you thought you did."

"You thought *you* did."

"I thought I saw a shadow pass the window, but I must have been mistaken. She didn't come in, or we would have seen her before now. I knew it was too early for her to get home from Addie Slocum's, anyhow."

When Rebecca went to bed Agnes had not returned. Rebecca had resolved that she would not retire until the girl came, but she was very tired, and she reasoned with herself that she was foolish. Besides, Mrs. Dent suggested that Agnes might go to the church social with Addie Slocum. When Rebecca suggested that she be sent for and told that her aunt had come, Mrs. Dent laughed meaningly.

"I guess you'll find out that a young girl ain't so ready to leave a sociable, where there's boys, to see her aunt," said she.

"She's too young," said Rebecca incredulously and indignantly.

"She's sixteen," replied Mrs. Dent; "and she's always been great for the boys."

"She's going to school four years after I get her before she thinks of boys," declared Rebecca.

"We'll see," laughed the other woman.

After Rebecca went to bed, she lay awake a long time listening for the sound of girlish laughter and a boy's voice under her window; then she fell asleep.

The next morning she was down early. Mrs. Dent, who kept no servants, was busily preparing breakfast.

"Don't Agnes help you about breakfast?" asked Rebecca.

"No, I let her lay," replied Mrs. Dent shortly.

"What time did she get home last night?"

"She didn't get home."

"What?"

"She didn't get home. She stayed with Addie. She often does."

"Without sending you word?"

"Oh, she knew I wouldn't worry."

"When will she be home?"

"Oh, I guess she'll be along pretty soon."

Rebecca was uneasy, but she tried to conceal it, for she knew of no good reason for uneasiness. What was there to occasion alarm in the fact of one young girl staying overnight with another? She could not eat much breakfast. Afterward she went out on the little piazza, although her hostess strove furtively to stop her.

"Why don't you go out back of the house? It's real pretty—a view over the river," she said.

"I guess I'll go out here," replied Rebecca. She had a purpose: to watch for the absent girl.

Presently Rebecca came hustling into the house through the sitting-room, into the kitchen where Mrs. Dent was cooking.

"That rose-bush!" she gasped.

Mrs. Dent turned and faced her.

"What of it?"

"It's a-blowing."

"What of it?"

"There isn't a mite of wind this morning."

Mrs. Dent turned with an inimitable toss of her fair head. "If you think I can spend my time puzzling over such nonsense as—" she began, but Rebecca interrupted her with a cry and a rush to the door.

"There she is now!" she cried.

She flung the door wide open, and curiously enough a breeze came in and her own gray hair tossed, and a paper blew off the table to the floor with a loud rustle, but there was nobody in sight.

"There's nobody here," Rebecca said.

She looked blankly at the other woman, who brought her rolling-pin down on a slab of pie-crust with a thud.

"I didn't hear anybody," she said calmly.

"*I saw somebody pass that window!*"

"You were mistaken again."

"I *know* I saw somebody."

"You couldn't have. Please shut that door."

Rebecca shut the door. She sat down beside the window and looked out on the autumnal yard, with its little curve of foot-path to the kitchen door.

"What smells so strong of roses in this room?" she said presently. She sniffed hard.

"I don't smell anything but these nutmegs."

"It is not nutmeg."

"I don't smell anything else."

"Where do you suppose Agnes is?"

"Oh, perhaps she has gone over the ferry to Porter's Falls with Addie. She often does. Addie's got an aunt over there, and Addie's got a cousin, a real pretty boy."

"You suppose she's gone over there?"

"Mebbe. I shouldn't wonder."

"When should she be home?"

"Oh, not before afternoon."

Rebecca waited with all the patience she could muster. She kept reassuring herself, telling herself that it was all natural, that the other woman could not help it, but she made up her mind that if Agnes did not return that afternoon she should be sent for.

When it was four o'clock she started up with resolution. She had been furtively watching the onyx clock on the sitting-room mantel; she had timed herself. She had said that if Agnes was not home by that time she should demand that she be sent for. She rose and stood before Mrs. Dent, who looked up coolly from her embroidery.

"I've waited just as long as I'm going to," she said. "I've come 'way from Michigan to see my own sister's daughter and take her home with me. I've been here ever since yesterday—twenty-four hours—and I haven't seen her. Now I'm going to. I want her sent for."

Mrs. Dent folded her embroidery and rose.

"Well, I don't blame you," she said. "It is high time she came home. I'll go right over and get her myself."

Rebecca heaved a sigh of relief. She hardly knew what she had suspected or feared, but she knew that her position had been one of antagonism if not accusation, and she was sensible of relief.

"I wish you would," she said gratefully, and went back to her chair, while Mrs. Dent got her shawl and her little white head-tie. "I wouldn't trouble you, but I do feel as if I couldn't wait any longer to see her," she remarked apologetically.

"Oh, it ain't any trouble at all," said Mrs. Dent as she went out. "I don't blame you; you have waited long enough."

Rebecca sat at the window watching breathlessly until Mrs. Dent came stepping through the yard alone. She ran to the door and saw, hardly noticing it this time, that the rose-bush was again violently agitated, yet with no wind evident elsewhere.

"Where is she?" she cried.

Mrs. Dent laughed with stiff lips as she came up the steps over the terrace. "Girls will be girls," said she. "She's gone with Addie to Lincoln. Addie's got an uncle who's conductor on the train, and lives there, and he got 'em passes, and they're goin' to stay to Addie's Aunt Margaret's a few days. Mrs. Slocum said Agnes didn't have time to come over and ask me before the train went, but she took it on herself to say it would be all right, and—"

"Why hadn't she been over to tell you?" Rebecca was angry, though not suspicious. She even saw no reason for her anger.

"Oh, she was putting up grapes. She was coming over just as soon as she got the black off her hands. She heard I had company, and her hands were a sight. She was holding them over sulfur matches."

"You say she's going to stay a few days?" repeated Rebecca dazedly.

"Yes; till Thursday, Mrs. Slocum said."

"How far is Lincoln from here?"

"About fifty miles. It'll be a real treat to her. Mrs. Slocum's sister is a real nice woman."

"It is goin' to make it pretty late about my goin' home."

"If you don't feel as if you could wait, I'll get her ready and send her on just as soon as I can," Mrs. Dent said sweetly.

"I'm going to wait," said Rebecca grimly.

The two women sat down again, and Mrs. Dent took up her embroidery.

"Is there any sewing I can do for her?" Rebecca asked finally in a desperate way. "If I can get her sewing along some—"

Mrs. Dent arose with alacrity and fetched a mass of white from the closet. "Here," she said, "if you want to sew the lace on this nightgown. I was going to put her to it, but she'll be glad enough to get rid of it. She ought to have this and one more before she goes. I don't like to send her away without some good underclothing."

Rebecca snatched at the little white garment and sewed feverishly.

That night she wakened from a deep sleep a little after midnight and lay a minute trying to collect her faculties and explain to herself what she was listening to. At last she discovered that it was the then popular strains of "The Maiden's Prayer" floating up through the floor from the piano in the sitting-room below. She jumped up, threw a shawl over her nightgown, and hurried downstairs trembling. There was nobody in the sitting-room; the piano was silent. She ran to Mrs. Dent's bedroom and called hysterically:

"Emeline! Emeline!"

"What is it?" asked Mrs. Dent's voice from the bed. The voice was stern, but had a note of consciousness in it.

"Who—who was that playing 'The Maiden's Prayer' in the sitting-room, on the piano?"

"I didn't hear anybody."

"There was some one."

"I didn't hear anything."

"I tell you there was some one. But—*there ain't anybody there.*"

"I didn't hear anything."

"I did—somebody playing 'The Maiden's Prayer' on the piano. Has Agnes got home? I *want to know.*"

"Of course Agnes hasn't got home," answered Mrs. Dent with rising inflection. "Be you gone crazy over that girl? The last boat from Porter's Falls was in before we went to bed. Of course she ain't come."

"I heard—"

"You were dreaming."

"I wasn't; I was broad awake."

Rebecca went back to her chamber and kept her lamp burning all night.

The next morning her eyes upon Mrs. Dent were wary and blazing with suppressed excitement. She kept opening her mouth as if to speak, then frowning, and setting her lips hard. After breakfast she went upstairs, and came down presently with her coat and bonnet.

"Now, Emeline," she said, "I want to know where the Slocums live."

Mrs. Dent gave a strange, long, half-lidded glance at her. She was finishing her coffee.

"Why?" she asked.

"I'm going over there and find out if they have heard anything from her daughter and Agnes since they went away. I don't like what I heard last night."

"You must have been dreaming."

"It don't make any odds whether I was or not. Does she play 'The Maiden's Prayer' on the piano? I want to know."

"What if she does? She plays it a little, I believe. I don't know. She don't half play it, anyhow; she ain't got an ear."

"That wasn't half played last night. I don't like such things happening. I ain't superstitious, but I don't like it. I'm going. Where do the Slocums live?"

"You go down the road over the bridge past the old grist mill, then you turn to the left; it's the only house for half a mile. You can't miss it. It has a barn with a ship in full sail on the cupola."

"Well, I'm going. I don't feel easy."

About two hours later Rebecca returned. There were red spots on her cheeks. She looked wild. "I've been there," she said, "and there isn't a soul at home. Something *has* happened."

"What has happened?"

"I don't know. Something. I had a warning last night. There wasn't a soul there. They've been sent for to Lincoln."

"Did you see anybody to ask?" asked Mrs. Dent with thinly concealed anxiety.

"I asked the woman that lives on the turn of the road. She's stone deaf. I suppose you know. She listened while I screamed at her to know where the Slocums were, and then she said, 'Mrs. Smith don't live here.' I didn't see anybody on the road, and that's the only house. What do you suppose it means?"

"I don't suppose it means much of anything," replied Mrs. Dent coolly. "Mr. Slocum is conductor on the railroad, and he'd be away anyway, and Mrs. Slocum often goes early when he does, to spend the day with her sister in Porter's Falls. She'd be more likely to go away than Addie."

"And you don't think anything has happened?" Rebecca asked with diminishing distrust before the reasonableness of it.

"Land, no!"

Rebecca went upstairs to lay aside her coat and bonnet. But she came hurrying back with them still on.

"Who's been in my room?" she gasped. Her face was pale as ashes.

Mrs. Dent also paled as she regarded her.

"What do you mean?" she asked slowly.

"I found when I went upstairs that—little nightgown of—Agnes's on—the bed, laid out. It was—*laid out*. The sleeves were folded across the bosom, and there was that little red rose between them. Emeline, what is it? Emeline, what's the matter? Oh!"

Mrs. Dent was struggling for breath in great, choking gasps. She clung to the back of a chair. Rebecca, trembling herself so she could scarcely keep on her feet, got her some water.

As soon as she recovered herself Mrs. Dent regarded her with eyes full of the strangest mixture of fear and horror and hostility.

"What do you mean talking so?" she said in a hard voice.

"It *is there*."

"Nonsense. You threw it down and it fell that way."

"It was folded in my bureau drawer."

"It couldn't have been."

"Who picked that red rose?"

"Look on the bush," Mrs. Dent replied shortly.

Rebecca looked at her; her mouth gaped. She hurried out of the room. When she came back her eyes seemed to protrude. (She had in the meantime hastened upstairs, and come down with tottering steps, clinging to the banisters.)

"Now I want to know what all this means?" she demanded.

"What what means?"

"The rose is on the bush, and it's gone from the bed in my room! Is this house haunted, or what?"

"I don't know anything about a house being haunted. I don't believe in such things. Be you crazy?" Mrs. Dent spoke with gathering force. The color flashed back to her cheeks.

"No," said Rebecca shortly. "I ain't crazy yet, but I shall be if this keeps on much longer. I'm going to find out where that girl is before night."

Mrs. Dent eyed her.

"What be you going to do?"

"I'm going to Lincoln."

A faint triumphant smile overspread Mrs. Dent's large face.

"You can't," said she; "there ain't any train."

"No train?"

"No; there ain't any afternoon train from the Falls to Lincoln."

"Then I'm going over to the Slocums' again tonight."

However, Rebecca did not go; such a rain came up as deterred even her resolution, and she had only her best dresses with her. Then in the evening came the letter from the Michigan village which she had left nearly a week ago. It was from her cousin, a single woman, who had come to keep her house while she was away. It was a pleasant unexciting letter enough, all the first of it, and related mostly how she missed Rebecca; how she hoped she was having pleasant weather and kept her health; and how her friend, Mrs. Greenaway, had come to stay with her since she had felt lonesome the first night in the house; how she hoped Rebecca would have no objections to this, although nothing had been said about it, since she had not realized that she might be nervous alone. The cousin was painfully conscientious, hence the letter. Rebecca smiled in spite of her disturbed mind as she read it, then her eye caught the postscript. That was in a different hand, purporting to be written by the friend, Mrs. Hannah Greenaway, informing her that the cousin had fallen down the cellar stairs and broken her hip, and was in a dangerous condition, and begging Rebecca to return at once, as she herself was rheumatic and unable to nurse her properly, and no one else could be obtained.

Rebecca looked at Mrs. Dent, who had come to her room with the letter quite late; it was half-past nine, and she had gone upstairs for the night.

"Where did this come from?" she asked.

"Mr. Amblecrom brought it," she replied.

"Who's he?"

"The postmaster. He often brings the letters that come on the late mail. He knows I ain't anybody to send. He brought yours about your coming. He said he and his wife came over on the ferry-boat with you."

"I remember him," Rebecca replied shortly. "There's bad news in this letter."

Mrs. Dent's face took on an expression of serious inquiry.

"Yes, my Cousin Harriet has fallen down the cellar stairs—they were always dangerous—and she's broken her hip, and I've got to take the first train home tomorrow."

"You don't say so. I'm dreadfully sorry."

"No, you ain't sorry!" said Rebecca, with a look as if she leaped. "You're glad. I don't know why, but you're glad. You've wanted to get rid of me for some reason ever since I came. I don't know why. You're a strange woman. Now you've got your way, and I hope you're satisfied."

"How you talk."

Mrs. Dent spoke in a faintly injured voice, but there was a light in her eyes.

"I talk the way it is. Well, I'm going tomorrow morning, and I want you, just as soon as Agnes Dent comes home, to send her out to me. Don't you wait for anything. You pack what clothes she's got, and don't wait even to mend them, and you buy her ticket. I'll leave the money, and you send her along. She don't have to change cars. You start her off, when she gets home, on the next train!"

"Very well," replied the other woman. She had an expression of covert amusement.

"Mind you do it."

"Very well, Rebecca."

Rebecca started on her journey the next morning. When she arrived, two days later, she found her cousin in perfect health. She found, moreover, that the friend had not written the postscript in the cousin's letter. Rebecca would have returned to Ford Village the next morning, but the fatigue and nervous strain had been too much for her. She was not able to move from her bed. She had a species of low fever induced by anxiety and fatigue. But she could write, and she did, to the Slocums, and she received no answer. She also wrote to Mrs. Dent; she even sent numerous telegrams, with no response. Finally she wrote to the postmaster, and an answer arrived by the first possible mail. The letter was short, curt, and to the purpose. Mr. Amblecrom, the postmaster, was a man of few words, and especially wary as to his expressions in a letter.

"Dear madam," he wrote, "your favor rec'ed. No Slocums in Ford's Village. All dead. Addie ten years ago, her mother two years later, her father five. House vacant. Mrs. John Dent said to have neglected stepdaughter. Girl was sick. Medicine not given. Talk of taking action. Not enough evidence. House said to be haunted. Strange sights and sounds. Your niece, Agnes Dent, died a year ago, about this time.

"Yours truly,

"THOMAS AMBLECROM."

THE VACANT LOT

hen it became generally known in Townsend Center that the Townsends were going to move to the city, there was great excitement and dismay. For the Townsends to move was about equivalent to the town's moving. The Townsend ancestors had founded the village a hundred years ago. The first Townsend had kept a wayside hostelry for man and beast, known as the "Sign of the Leopard." The sign-board, on which the leopard was painted a bright blue, was still extant, and prominently so, being nailed over the present Townsend's front door. This Townsend, by name David, kept the village store. There had been no tavern since the railroad was built through Townsend Center in his father's day. Therefore the family, being ousted by the march of progress from their chosen employment, took up with a general country store as being the next thing to a country tavern, the principal difference consisting in the fact that all the guests were transients, never requiring bedchambers, securing their rest on the tops of sugar and flour barrels and codfish boxes, and their refreshment from stray nibblings at the stock in trade, to the profitless deplenishment of raisins and loaf sugar and crackers and cheese.

The flitting of the Townsends from the home of their ancestors was due to a sudden access of wealth from the death of a relative and the desire of Mrs. Townsend to secure better advantages for her son George, sixteen years old, in the way of education, and for her daughter Adrianna, ten years older, better matrimonial opportunities. However, this last inducement for leaving Townsend Center was not openly stated, only ingeniously surmised by the neighbors.

"Sarah Townsend don't think there's anybody in Townsend Center fit for her Adrianna to marry, and so she's goin' to take her to Boston to see if she can't pick up somebody there," they said. Then they wondered what Abel Lyons would do. He had been a humble suitor for Adrianna for years, but her mother had not approved, and Adrianna, who was dutiful, had repulsed him delicately and rather sadly. He was the only lover whom she had ever had, and she felt sorry and grateful; she was a plain, awkward girl, and had a patient recognition of the fact.

But her mother was ambitious, more so than her father, who was rather pugnaciously satisfied with what he had, and not easily disposed to change. However, he yielded to his wife and consented to sell out his business and purchase a house in Boston and move there.

David Townsend was curiously unlike the line of ancestors from whom he had come. He had either retrograded or advanced, as one might look at it. His moral character was certainly better, but he had not the fiery spirit and eager grasp at advantage which had distinguished them. Indeed, the old Townsends, though prominent and respected as men of property and influence, had reputations not above suspicions. There was more than one dark whisper regarding them handed down from mother to son in the village, and especially was this true of the first Townsend, he who built the tavern bearing the Sign of the Blue Leopard. His portrait, a hideous effort of contemporary art, hung in the garret of David Townsend's home. There was many a tale of wild roistering, if no worse, in that old roadhouse, and high stakes, and quarreling in cups, and blows, and money gotten in evil fashion, and the matter hushed up with a high hand for inquirers by the imperious Townsends who terrorized everybody. David Townsend terrorized nobody. He had gotten his little competence from his store by honest methods—the exchanging of sterling goods and true weights for country produce and country shillings. He was sober and reliable, with intense self-respect and a decided talent for the management of money. It was principally for this reason that he took great delight in his sudden wealth by legacy. He had thereby greater opportunities for the exercise of his native shrewdness in a bargain. This he evinced in his purchase of a house in Boston.

One day in spring the old Townsend house was shut up, the Blue Leopard was taken carefully down from his lair over the front door, the family chattels were loaded on the train, and the Townsends departed. It was a sad and eventful day for Townsend Center. A man from Barre had rented the store—David had decided at the last not to sell—and the old familiars congregated in melancholy fashion and talked over the situation. An enormous pride over their departed townsman became evident. They paraded him, flaunting him like a banner in the eyes of the new man. "David is awful smart," they said; "there won't nobody get the better of him in the city if he has lived in Townsend Center all his life. He's got his eyes open. Know what he paid for his house in Boston? Well, sir, that house cost twenty-five thousand dollars, and David he bought it for five. Yes, sir, he did."

"Must have been some out about it," remarked the new man, scowling over his counter. He was beginning to feel his disparaging situation.

"Not an out, sir. David he made sure on't. Catch him gettin' bit. Everythin' was in apple-pie order, hot an' cold water and all, and in one of the best locations of the city—real high-up street. David he said the rent in that street was never under a thousand. Yes, sir, David he got a bargain—five thousand dollars for a twenty-five-thousand-dollar house."

"Some out about it!" growled the new man over the counter.

However, as his fellow townsmen and allies stated, there seemed to be no doubt about the desirableness of the city house which David Townsend had purchased and the fact that he had secured it for an absurdly low price. The whole family were at first suspicious. It was ascertained that the house had cost a round sum only a few years ago; it was in perfect repair; nothing whatever was amiss with plumbing, furnace, anything. There was not even a soap factory within smelling distance, as Mrs. Townsend had vaguely surmised. She was sure that she had heard of houses being undesirable for such reasons, but there was no soap factory. They all sniffed and peeked; when the first rainfall came they looked at the ceiling, confidently expecting to see dark spots where the leaks had commenced, but there were none. They were forced to confess that their suspicions were allayed, that the house was perfect, even overshadowed with the mystery of a lower price than it was worth. That, however, was an additional perfection in the opinion of the Townsends, who had their share of New England thrift. They had lived just one month in their new house, and were happy, although at times somewhat lonely from missing the society of Townsend Center, when the trouble began. The Townsends, although they lived in a fine house in a genteel, almost fashionable, part of the city, were true to their antecedents and kept, as they had been accustomed, only one maid. She was

129

the daughter of a farmer on the outskirts of their native village, was middle-aged, and had lived with them for the last ten years. One pleasant Monday morning she rose early and did the family washing before breakfast, which had been prepared by Mrs. Townsend and Adrianna, as was their habit on washing-days. The family were seated at the breakfast table in their basement dining-room, and this maid, whose name was Cordelia, was hanging out the clothes in the vacant lot. This vacant lot seemed a valuable one, being on a corner. It was rather singular that it had not been built upon. The Townsends had wondered at it and agreed that they would have preferred their own house to be there. They had, however, utilized it as far as possible with their innocent, rural disregard of property rights in unoccupied land.

"We might just as well hang out our washing in that vacant lot," Mrs. Townsend had told Cordelia the first Monday of their stay in the house. "Our little yard ain't half big enough for all our clothes, and it is sunnier there, too."

So Cordelia had hung out the wash there for four Mondays, and this was the fifth. The breakfast was about half finished—they had reached the buckwheat cakes—when this maid came rushing into the dining-room and stood regarding them, speechless, with a countenance indicative of the utmost horror. She was deadly pale. Her hands, sodden with soapsuds, hung twitching at her sides in the folds of her calico gown; her very hair, which was light and sparse, seemed to bristle with fear. All the Townsends turned and looked at her. David and George rose with a half-defined idea of burglars.

"Cordelia Battles, what is the matter?" cried Mrs. Townsend. Adrianna gasped for breath and turned as white as the maid. "What is the matter?" repeated Mrs. Townsend, but the maid was unable to speak. Mrs. Townsend, who could be peremptory, sprang up, ran to the frightened woman and shook her violently. "Cordelia Battles, you speak," said she, "and not stand there staring that way, as if you were struck dumb! What is the matter with you?"

Then Cordelia spoke in a fainting voice.

"There's—somebody else—hanging out clothes—in the vacant lot," she gasped, and clutched at a chair for support.

"Who?" cried Mrs. Townsend, rousing to indignation, for already she had assumed a proprietorship in the vacant lot. "Is it the folks in the next house? I'd like to know what right they have! We are next to that vacant lot."

"I—dunno—who it is," gasped Cordelia.

"Why, we've seen that girl next door go to mass every morning," said Mrs. Townsend. "She's got a fiery red head. Seems as if you might know her by this time, Cordelia."

"It ain't that girl," gasped Cordelia. Then she added in a horror-stricken voice, "I couldn't see who 'twas."

They all stared.

"Why couldn't you see?" demanded her mistress. "Are you struck blind?"

"No, ma'am."

"Then why couldn't you see?"

"All I could see was—" Cordelia hesitated, with an expression of the utmost horror.

"Go on," said Mrs. Townsend, impatiently.

"All I could see was the shadow of somebody, very slim, hanging out the clothes, and—"

"What?"

"I could see the shadows of the things flappin' on their line."

"You couldn't see the clothes?"

"Only the shadow on the ground."

"What kind of clothes were they?"

"Queer," replied Cordelia, with a shudder.

"If I didn't know you so well, I should think you had been drinking," said Mrs. Townsend. "Now, Cordelia Battles, I'm going out in that vacant lot and see myself what you're talking about."

"I can't go," gasped the woman.

With that Mrs. Townsend and all the others, except Adrianna, who remained to tremble with the maid, sallied forth into the vacant lot. They had to go out the area gate into the street to reach it. It was nothing unusual in the way of vacant lots. One large poplar tree, the relic of the old forest which had once flourished there, twinkled in one corner; for the rest, it was overgrown with coarse weeds and a few dusty flowers. The Townsends stood just inside the rude board fence which divided the lot from the street and stared with wonder and horror, for Cordelia had told the truth. They all saw what she had described—the shadow of an exceedingly slim woman moving along the ground with up-stretched arms, the shadows of strange, nondescript garments flapping from a shadowy line, but when they looked up for the substance of the shadows nothing was to be seen except the clear, blue October air.

"My goodness!" gasped Mrs. Townsend. Her face assumed a strange gathering of wrath in the midst of her terror. Suddenly she made a determined move forward, although her husband strove to hold her back.

"You let me be," said she. She moved forward. Then she recoiled and gave a loud shriek. "The wet sheet flapped in my

132

face," she cried. "Take me away, take me away!" Then she fainted. Between them they got her back to the house. "It was awful," she moaned when she came to herself, with the family all around her where she lay on the dining-room floor. "Oh, David, what do you suppose it is?"

"Nothing at all," replied David Townsend stoutly. He was remarkable for courage and staunch belief in actualities. He was now denying to himself that he had seen anything unusual.

"Oh, there was," moaned his wife.

"I saw something," said George, in a sullen, boyish bass.

The maid sobbed convulsively and so did Adrianna for sympathy.

"We won't talk any about it," said David. "Here, Jane, you drink this hot tea—it will do you good; and Cordelia, you hang out the clothes in our own yard. George, you go and put up the line for her."

"The line is out there," said George, with a jerk of his shoulder.

"Are you afraid?"

"No, I ain't," replied the boy resentfully, and went out with a pale face.

After that Cordelia hung the Townsend wash in the yard of their own house, standing always with her back to the vacant lot. As for David Townsend, he spent a good deal of his time in the lot watching the shadows, but he came to no explanation, although he strove to satisfy himself with many.

"I guess the shadows come from the smoke from our chimneys, or else the poplar tree," he said.

"Why do the shadows come on Monday mornings, and no other?" demanded his wife.

David was silent.

Very soon new mysteries arose. One day Cordelia rang the dinner-bell at their usual dinner hour, the same as in Townsend Center, high noon, and the family assembled. With amazement Adrianna looked at the dishes on the table.

"Why, that's queer!" she said.

"What's queer?" asked her mother.

Cordelia stopped short as she was about setting a tumbler of water beside a plate, and the water slopped over.

"Why," said Adrianna, her face paling, "I—thought there was boiled dinner. I—smelt cabbage cooking."

"I knew there would something else come up," gasped Cordelia, leaning hard on the back of Adrianna's chair.

"What do you mean?" asked Mrs. Townsend sharply, but her own face began to assume the shocked pallor which it was so easy nowadays for all their faces to assume at the merest suggestion of anything out of the common.

"I smelt cabbage cooking all the morning up in my room," Adrianna said faintly, "and here's codfish and potatoes for dinner."

The Townsends all looked at one another. David rose with an exclamation and rushed out of the room. The others waited tremblingly. When he came back his face was lowering.

"What did you—" Mrs. Townsend asked hesitatingly.

"There's some smell of cabbage out there," he admitted reluctantly. Then he looked at her with a challenge. "It comes from the next house," he said. "Blows over our house."

"Our house is higher."

"I don't care; you can never account for such things."

"Cordelia," said Mrs. Townsend, "you go over to the next house and you ask if they've got cabbage for dinner."

Cordelia switched out of the room, her mouth set hard. She came back promptly.

"Says they never have cabbage," she announced with gloomy triumph and a conclusive glance at Mr. Townsend. "Their girl was real sassy."

"Oh, father, let's move away; let's sell the house," cried Adrianna in a panic-stricken tone.

"If you think I'm going to sell a house that I got as cheap as this one because we smell cabbage in a vacant lot, you're mistaken," replied David firmly.

"It isn't the cabbage alone," said Mrs. Townsend.

"And a few shadows," added David. "I am tired of such nonsense. I thought you had more sense, Jane."

"One of the boys at school asked me if we lived in the house next to the vacant lot on Wells Street and whistled when I said 'Yes,'" remarked George.

"Let him whistle," said Mr. Townsend.

After a few hours the family, stimulated by Mr. Townsend's calm, common sense, agreed that it was exceedingly foolish to be disturbed by a mysterious odor of cabbage. They even laughed at themselves.

"I suppose we have got so nervous over those shadows hanging out clothes that we notice every little thing," conceded Mrs. Townsend.

"You will find out some day that that is no more to be regarded than the cabbage," said her husband.

"You can't account for that wet sheet hitting my face," said Mrs. Townsend, doubtfully.

"You imagined it."

"I *felt* it."

That afternoon things went on as usual in the household until nearly four o'clock. Adrianna went downtown to do some shopping. Mrs. Townsend sat sewing beside the bay window in her room, which was a front one in the third story. George had not got home. Mr. Townsend was writing a letter in the library. Cordelia was busy in the basement; the twilight, which was coming earlier and earlier every night, was beginning to gather, when suddenly there was a loud crash which shook the house from its foundations. Even the dishes on the sideboard rattled, and the glasses rang like bells. The pictures on the walls of Mrs. Townsend's room swung out from the walls. But that was not all: every looking-glass in the house cracked simultaneously—as nearly as they could judge—from top to bottom, then shivered into fragments over the floors. Mrs. Townsend was too frightened to scream. She sat huddled in her chair, gasping for breath, her eyes, rolling from side to side in incredulous terror, turned toward the street. She saw a great black group of people crossing it just in front of the vacant lot. There was something inexpressibly strange and gloomy about this moving group; there was an effect of sweeping, wavings and foldings of sable draperies and gleams of deadly white faces; then they passed. She twisted her head to see, and they disappeared in the vacant lot. Mr. Townsend came hurrying into the room; he was pale, and looked at once angry and alarmed.

"Did you fall?" he asked inconsequently, as if his wife, who was small, could have produced such a manifestation by a fall.

"Oh, David, what is it?" whispered Mrs. Townsend.

"Darned if I know!" said David.

"Don't swear. It's too awful. Oh, see the looking-glass, David!"

"I see it. The one over the library mantel is broken, too."

"Oh, it is a sign of death!"

Cordelia's feet were heard as she staggered on the stairs. She almost fell into the room. She reeled over to Mr. Townsend and clutched his arm. He cast a sidewise glance, half furious, half commiserating at her.

"Well, what is it all about?" he asked.

"I don't know. What is it? Oh, what is it? The looking-glass in the kitchen is broken. All over the floor. Oh, oh! What is it?"

"I don't know any more than you do. I didn't do it."

"Lookin'-glasses broken is a sign of death in the house," said Cordelia. "If it's me, I hope I'm ready; but I'd rather die than be so scared as I've been lately."

Mr. Townsend shook himself loose and eyed the two trembling women with gathering resolution.

"Now, look here, both of you," he said. "This is nonsense. You'll die sure enough of fright if you keep on this way. I was a fool myself to be startled. Everything it is is an earthquake."

"Oh, David!" gasped his wife, not much reassured.

"It is nothing but an earthquake," persisted Mr. Townsend. "It acted just like that. Things always are broken on the walls, and the middle of the room isn't affected. I've read about it."

Suddenly Mrs. Townsend gave a loud shriek and pointed.

"How do you account for that," she cried, "if it's an earthquake? Oh, oh, oh!"

She was on the verge of hysterics. Her husband held her firmly by the arm as his eyes followed the direction of her rigid pointing finger. Cordelia looked also, her eyes seeming converged to a bright point of fear. On the floor in front of the broken looking-glass lay a mass of black stuff in a grewsome long ridge.

"It's something you dropped there," almost shouted Mr. Townsend.

"It ain't. Oh!"

Mr. Townsend dropped his wife's arm and took one stride toward the object. It was a very long crape veil. He lifted it, and it floated out from his arm as if imbued with electricity.

"It's yours," he said to his wife.

"Oh, David, I never had one. You know, oh, you know I—shouldn't—unless you died. How came it there?"

"I'm darned if I know," said David, regarding it. He was deadly pale, but still resentful rather than afraid.

"Don't hold it; don't!"

"I'd like to know what in thunder all this means?" said David. He gave the thing an angry toss and it fell on the floor in exactly the same long heap as before.

Cordelia began to weep with racking sobs. Mrs. Townsend reached out and caught her husband's hand, clutching it hard with ice-cold fingers.

"What's got into this house, anyhow?" he growled.

"You'll have to sell it. Oh, David, we can't live here."

"As for my selling a house I paid only five thousand for when it's worth twenty-five, for any such nonsense as this, I won't!"

David gave one stride toward the black veil, but it rose from the floor and moved away before him across the room at exactly the same height as if suspended from a woman's head. He pursued it, clutching vainly, all around the room, then he swung himself on his heel with an exclamation and the thing fell to the floor again in the long heap. Then were heard hurrying feet on the stairs and Adrianna burst into the room. She ran straight to her father and clutched his arm; she tried to speak, but she chattered unintelligibly; her face was blue. Her father shook her violently.

"Adrianna, do have more sense!" he cried.

"Oh, David, how can you talk so?" sobbed her mother.

"I can't help it. I'm mad!" said he with emphasis. "What has got into this house and you all, anyhow?"

"What is it, Adrianna, poor child," asked her mother. "Only look what has happened here."

"It's an earthquake," said her father staunchly; "nothing to be afraid of."

"How do you account for *that?*" said Mrs. Townsend in an awful voice, pointing to the veil.

Adrianna did not look—she was too engrossed with her own terrors. She began to speak in a breathless voice.

"I—was—coming—by the vacant lot," she panted, "and—I—I—had my new hat in a paper bag and—a parcel of blue ribbon, and—I saw a crowd, an awful—oh! a whole crowd of people with white faces, as if—they were dressed all in black."

"Where are they now?"

"I don't know. Oh!" Adrianna sank gasping feebly into a chair.

"Get her some water, David," sobbed her mother.

David rushed with an impatient exclamation out of the room and returned with a glass of water which he held to his daughter's lips.

"Here, drink this!" he said roughly.

"Oh, David, how can you speak so?" sobbed his wife.

"I can't help it. I'm mad clean through," said David.

Then there was a hard bound upstairs, and George entered. He was very white, but he grinned at them with an appearance of unconcern.

"Hullo!" he said in a shaking voice, which he tried to control. "What on earth's to pay in that vacant lot now?"

"Well, what is it?" demanded his father.

"Oh, nothing, only—well, there are lights over it exactly as if there was a house there, just about where the windows would be. It looked as if you could walk right in, but when you look close there are those old dried-up weeds rattling away on the ground the same as ever. I looked at it and couldn't believe my eyes. A woman saw it, too. She came along just as I did. She gave one look, then she screeched and ran. I waited for some one else, but nobody came."

Mr. Townsend rushed out of the room.

"I daresay it'll be gone when he gets there," began George, then he stared round the room. "What's to pay here?" he cried.

"Oh, George, the whole house shook all at once, and all the looking-glasses broke," wailed his mother, and Adrianna and Cordelia joined.

George whistled with pale lips. Then Mr. Townsend entered.

"Well," asked George, "see anything?"

"I don't want to talk," said his father. "I've stood just about enough."

"We've got to sell out and go back to Townsend Center," cried his wife in a wild voice. "Oh, David, say you'll go back."

"I won't go back for any such nonsense as this, and sell a twenty-five thousand dollar house for five thousand," said he firmly.

But that very night his resolution was shaken. The whole family watched together in the dining-room. They were all afraid to go to bed—that is, all except possibly Mr. Townsend. Mrs. Townsend declared firmly that she for one would leave that awful house and go back to Townsend Center whether he came or not, unless they all stayed together and watched, and Mr. Townsend yielded. They chose the dining-room for the reason that it was nearer the

street should they wish to make their egress hurriedly, and they took up their station around the dining-table on which Cordelia had placed a luncheon.

"It looks exactly as if we were watching with a corpse," she said in a horror-stricken whisper.

"Hold your tongue if you can't talk sense," said Mr. Townsend.

The dining-room was very large, finished in oak, with a dark blue paper above the wainscotting. The old sign of the tavern, the Blue Leopard, hung over the mantel-shelf. Mr. Townsend had insisted on hanging it there. He had a curious pride in it. The family sat together until after midnight and nothing unusual happened. Mrs. Townsend began to nod; Mr. Townsend read the paper ostentatiously. Adrianna and Cordelia stared with roving eyes about the room, then at each other as if comparing notes on terror. George had a book which he studied furtively. All at once Adrianna gave a startled exclamation and Cordelia echoed her. George whistled faintly. Mrs. Townsend awoke with a start and Mr. Townsend's paper rattled to the floor.

"Look!" gasped Adrianna.

The sign of the Blue Leopard over the shelf glowed as if a lantern hung over it. The radiance was thrown from above. It grew brighter and brighter as they watched. The Blue Leopard seemed to crouch and spring with life. Then the door into the front hall opened—the outer door, which had been carefully locked. It squeaked and they all recognized it. They sat staring. Mr. Townsend was as transfixed as the rest. They heard the outer door shut, then the door into the room swung open and slowly that awful black group of people which they had seen in the afternoon entered. The Townsends with one accord rose and huddled together in a far corner; they all held to each other and stared.

The people, their faces gleaming with a whiteness of death, their black robes waving and folding, crossed the room. They were a trifle above mortal height, or seemed so to the terrified eyes which saw them. They reached the mantel-shelf where the sign-board hung, then a black-draped long arm was seen to rise and make a motion, as if plying a knocker. Then the whole company passed out of sight, as if through the wall, and the room was as before. Mrs. Townsend was shaking in a nervous chill, Adrianna was almost fainting, Cordelia was in hysterics. David Townsend stood glaring in a curious way at the sign of the Blue Leopard. George stared at him with a look of horror. There was something in his father's face which made him forget everything else. At last he touched his arm timidly.

"Father," he whispered.

David turned and regarded him with a look of rage and fury, then his face cleared; he passed his hand over his forehead.

"Good Lord! What *did* come to me?" he muttered.

"You looked like that awful picture of old Tom Townsend in the garret in Townsend Center, father," whimpered the boy, shuddering.

"Should think I might look like 'most any old cuss after such darned work as this," growled David, but his face was white. "Go and pour out some hot tea for your mother," he ordered the boy sharply. He himself shook Cordelia violently. "Stop such actions!" he shouted in her ears, and shook her again. "Ain't you a church member?" he demanded; "what be you afraid of? You ain't done nothin' wrong, have ye?"

Then Cordelia quoted Scripture in a burst of sobs and laughter.

"Behold, I was shapen in iniquity; and in sin did my mother conceive me," she cried out. "If I ain't done wrong, mebbe them

142

that's come before me did, and when the Evil One and the Powers of Darkness is abroad I'm liable, I'm liable!" Then she laughed loud and long and shrill.

"If you don't hush up," said David, but still with that white terror and horror on his own face, "I'll bundle you out in that vacant lot whether or no. I mean it."

Then Cordelia was quiet, after one wild roll of her eyes at him. The color was returning to Adrianna's cheeks; her mother was drinking hot tea in spasmodic gulps.

"It's after midnight," she gasped, "and I don't believe they'll come again tonight. Do you, David?"

"No, I don't," said David conclusively.

"Oh, David, we mustn't stay another night in this awful house."

"We won't. Tomorrow we'll pack off bag and baggage to Townsend Center, if it takes all the fire department to move us," said David.

Adrianna smiled in the midst of her terror. She thought of Abel Lyons.

The next day Mr. Townsend went to the real estate agent who had sold him the house.

"It's no use," he said, "I can't stand it. Sell the house for what you can get. I'll give it away rather than keep it."

Then he added a few strong words as to his opinion of parties who sold him such an establishment. But the agent pleaded innocent for the most part.

"I'll own I suspected something wrong when the owner, who pledged me to secrecy as to his name, told me to sell that place for what I could get, and did not limit me. I had never heard anything, but I began to suspect something was wrong. Then I made a few inquiries and found out that there was a rumor in the neighborhood that there was something out of the usual about that vacant lot. I had wondered myself why it wasn't built upon. There was a story about it's being undertaken once, and the contract made, and the contractor dying; then another man took it and one of the workmen was killed on his way to dig the cellar, and the others struck. I didn't pay much attention to it. I never believed much in that sort of thing anyhow, and then, too, I couldn't find out that there had ever been anything wrong about the house itself, except as the people who had lived there were said to have seen and heard queer things in the vacant lot, so I thought you might be able to get along, especially as you didn't look like a man who was timid, and the house was such a bargain as I never handled before. But this you tell me is beyond belief."

"Do you know the names of the people who formerly owned the vacant lot?" asked Mr. Townsend.

"I don't know for certain," replied the agent, "for the original owners flourished long before your or my day, but I do know that the lot goes by the name of the old Gaston lot. What's the matter? Are you ill?"

"No; it is nothing," replied Mr. Townsend. "Get what you can for the house; perhaps another family might not be as troubled as we have been."

"I hope you are not going to leave the city?" said the agent, urbanely.

"I am going back to Townsend Center as fast as steam can carry me after we get packed up and out of that cursed house," replied Mr. David Townsend.

He did not tell the agent nor any of his family what had caused him to start when told the name of the former owners of the lot.

He remembered all at once the story of a ghastly murder which had taken place in the Blue Leopard. The victim's name was Gaston and the murderer had never been discovered.

LUELLA MILLER

lose to the village street stood the one-story house in which Luella Miller, who had an evil name in the village, had dwelt. She had been dead for years, yet there were those in the village who, in spite of the clearer light which comes on a vantage-point from a long-past danger, half believed in the tale which they had heard from their childhood. In their hearts, although they scarcely would have owned it, was a survival of the wild horror and frenzied fear of their ancestors who had dwelt in the same age with Luella Miller. Young people even would stare with a shudder at the old house as they passed, and children never played around it as was their wont around an untenanted building. Not a window in the old Miller house was broken: the panes reflected the morning sunlight in patches of emerald and blue, and the latch of the sagging front door was never lifted, although no bolt secured it. Since Luella Miller had been carried out of it, the house had had no tenant except one friendless old soul who had no choice between that and the far-off shelter of the open sky. This old woman, who had survived her kindred and friends, lived in the house one week, then one morning no smoke came out of the chimney, and a body of neighbors, a score strong, entered and found her dead in her bed. There were dark whispers as to the cause of her death, and there were those who testified to an expression of fear so exalted that it showed forth the state of the departing soul upon the dead face. The old woman had been hale and hearty when she entered the house, and in seven days she was dead; it seemed that she had fallen a victim to some uncanny power. The minister talked in the pulpit with covert severity against the sin of superstition; still the belief prevailed. Not a soul in the village but would have chosen the almshouse rather than that dwelling. No vagrant, if he heard the tale, would seek shelter beneath that old roof, unhallowed by nearly half a century of superstitious fear.

There was only one person in the village who had actually known Luella Miller. That person was a woman well over eighty, but a marvel of vitality and unextinct youth. Straight as an arrow, with the spring of one recently let loose from the bow of life, she moved about the streets, and she always went to church, rain or shine. She had never married, and had lived alone for years in a house across the road from Luella Miller's.

This woman had none of the garrulousness of age, but never in all her life had she ever held her tongue for any will save her own, and she never spared the truth when she essayed to present it. She it was who bore testimony to the life, evil, though possibly wittingly or designedly so, of Luella Miller, and to her personal appearance. When this old woman spoke—and she had the gift of description, although her thoughts were clothed in the rude vernacular of her native village—one could seem to see Luella Miller as she had really looked. According to this woman, Lydia Anderson by name, Luella Miller had been a beauty of a type rather unusual in New England. She had been a slight, pliant sort of creature, as ready with a strong yielding to fate and as unbreakable as a willow. She had glimmering lengths of straight, fair hair, which she wore softly looped round a long, lovely face. She had blue eyes full of soft pleading, little slender, clinging hands, and a wonderful grace of motion and attitude.

"Luella Miller used to sit in a way nobody else could if they sat up and studied a week of Sundays," said Lydia Anderson, "and it was a sight to see her walk. If one of them willows over there on the edge of the brook could start up and get its roots free of the ground, and move off, it would go just the way Luella Miller used to. She had a green shot silk she used to wear, too, and a hat with green ribbon streamers, and a lace veil blowing across her face and out sideways, and a green ribbon flyin' from her waist. That was what she came out bride in when she married Erastus Miller. Her name before she was married was Hill. There was always a sight of 'l's' in her name, married or single. Erastus Miller was good lookin', too, better lookin' than Luella. Sometimes I used to think that Luella wa'n't so handsome after all. Erastus just about worshiped her. I used to know him pretty well. He lived next door to me, and we went to school together. Folks used to say he was waitin' on me, but he wa'n't. I never thought he was except once or twice when he said things that some girls might have suspected meant somethin'. That was before Luella came here to teach the district school. It was funny how she came to get it, for folks said she hadn't any education, and that one of the big girls, Lottie Henderson, used to do all the teachin' for her, while she sat back and did embroidery work on a cambric pocket-handkerchief. Lottie Henderson was a real smart girl, a splendid scholar, and she just set her eyes by Luella, as all the girls did. Lottie would have made a real smart woman, but she died when Luella had been here about a year—just faded away and died: nobody knew what aided her. She dragged herself to that schoolhouse and helped Luella teach till the very last minute. The committee all knew how Luella didn't do much of the work herself, but they winked at it. It wa'n't long after Lottie died that Erastus married her. I always thought he hurried it up because she wa'n't fit to teach. One of the big boys used to help her after Lottie died, but he hadn't much government, and the school didn't do very well, and Luella might have had to give it up, for the committee couldn't have shut their eyes to things much longer. The boy that helped her was a real honest, inno- cent sort of fellow, and he was a good scholar, too. Folks said he overstudied, and that was the reason he was took crazy the year after Luella married, but I don't know. And I don't know what made Erastus Miller go into consumption of the blood the year after he was married: consumption wa'n't in his family. He just grew weaker and weaker, and went almost bent double when he tried to wait on Luella, and he spoke feeble, like an old man. He worked terrible hard till the last trying to save up a little to leave Luella. I've seen him out in the worst storms on a wood-sled—he used to cut and sell wood—and he was hunched up on top lookin' more dead than alive. Once I couldn't stand it: I went over and helped him pitch some wood on the cart—I was always strong in my arms. I wouldn't stop for all he told me to, and I guess he was glad enough for the help. That was only a week before he died. He fell on the kitchen floor while he was gettin' breakfast. He always got the breakfast and let Luella lay abed. He did all the sweepin' and the washin' and the ironin' and most of the cookin'. He couldn't bear to have Luella lift her finger, and she let him do for her. She lived like a queen for all the work she did. She didn't even do her sewin'. She said it made her shoulder ache to sew, and poor Erastus's sister Lily used to do all her sewin'. She wa'n't able to, either; she was never strong in her back, but she did it beautifully. She had to, to suit Luella, she was so dreadful particular. I never saw anythin' like the fagottin' and hemstitchin' that Lily Miller did for Luella. She made all Luella's weddin' outfit, and that green silk dress, after Maria Babbit cut it. Maria she cut it for nothin', and she did a lot more cuttin' and fittin' for nothin' for Luella, too. Lily Miller went to live with Luella after Erastus died. She gave up her home, though she was real attached to it and wa'n't a mite afraid to stay alone. She rented it and she went to live with Luella right away after the funeral."

Then this old woman, Lydia Anderson, who remembered Luella Miller, would go on to relate the story of Lily Miller. It seemed that on the removal of Lily Miller to the house of her dead brother, to live with his widow, the village people first began to talk. This Lily Miller had been hardly past her first youth, and a most robust and blooming woman, rosy-cheeked, with curls of strong, black hair overshadowing round, candid temples and bright dark eyes. It was not six months after she had taken up her residence with her sister-in-law that her rosy color faded and her pretty curves became wan hollows. White shadows began to show in the black rings of her hair, and the light died out of her eyes, her features sharpened, and there were pathetic lines at her mouth, which yet wore always an expression of utter sweetness and even happiness. She was devoted to her sister; there was no doubt that she loved her with her whole heart, and was perfectly content in her service. It was her sole anxiety lest she should die and leave her alone.

"The way Lily Miller used to talk about Luella was enough to make you mad and enough to make you cry," said Lydia Anderson. "I've been in there sometimes toward the last when she was too feeble to cook and carried her some blanc-mange or custard—somethin' I thought she might relish, and she'd thank me, and when I asked her how she was, say she felt better than she did yesterday, and asked me if I didn't think she looked better, dreadful pitiful, and say poor Luella had an awful time takin' care of her and doin' the work—she wa'n't strong enough to do anythin'—when all the time Luella wa'n't liftin' her finger and poor Lily didn't get any care except what the neighbors gave her, and Luella eat up everythin' that was carried in for Lily. I had it real straight that she did. Luella used to just sit and cry and do nothin'. She did act real fond of Lily, and she pined away considerable, too. There was those that thought she'd go into a decline herself. But after Lily died, her Aunt Abby Mixter came, and then Luella picked up and grew as fat and rosy as ever. But poor Aunt Abby begun to droop just the way Lily had, and I guess somebody wrote to her married daughter, Mrs. Sam Abbot, who lived in Barre, for she wrote her mother that she must leave right away and come and make her a visit, but Aunt Abby wouldn't go. I can see her now. She was a real good-lookin' woman, tall and large, with a big, square face and a high forehead that looked of itself kind of benevolent and good. She just tended out on Luella as if she had been a baby, and when her married daughter sent for her she wouldn't stir one inch. She'd always thought a lot of her daughter, too, but she said Luella needed her and her married daughter didn't. Her daughter kept writin' and writin', but it didn't do any good. Finally she came, and when she saw how bad her mother looked, she broke down and cried and all but went on her knees to have her come away. She spoke her mind out to Luella, too. She told her that she'd killed her husband and everybody that had anythin' to do with her, and she'd thank her to leave her mother alone. Luella went into hysterics, and Aunt

Abby was so frightened that she called me after her daughter went. Mrs. Sam Abbot she went away fairly cryin' out loud in the buggy, the neighbors heard her, and well she might, for she never saw her mother again alive. I went in that night when Aunt Abby called for me, standin' in the door with her little green-checked shawl over her head. I can see her now. 'Do come over here, Miss Anderson,' she sung out, kind of gasping for breath. I didn't stop for anythin'. I put over as fast as I could, and when I got there, there was Luella laughin' and cryin' all together, and Aunt Abby trying to hush her, and all the time she herself was white as a sheet and shakin' so she could hardly stand. 'For the land sakes, Mrs. Mixter,' says I, 'you look worse than she does. You ain't fit to be up out of your bed.'

"'Oh, there ain't anythin' the matter with me,' says she. Then she went on talkin' to Luella. 'There, there, don't, don't, poor little lamb,' says she. 'Aunt Abby is here. She ain't goin' away and leave you. Don't, poor little lamb.'

"'Do leave her with me, Mrs. Mixter, and you get back to bed,' says I, for Aunt Abby had been layin' down considerable lately, though somehow she contrived to do the work.

"'I'm well enough,' says she. 'Don't you think she had better have the doctor, Miss Anderson?'

"'The doctor,' says I, 'I think *you* had better have the doctor. I think you need him much worse than some folks I could mention.' And I looked right straight at Luella Miller laughin' and cryin' and goin' on as if she was the center of all creation. All the time she was actin' so—seemed as if she was too sick to sense anythin'—she was keepin' a sharp lookout as to how we took it out of the corner of one eye. I see her. You could never cheat me about Luella Miller. Finally I got real mad and I run home and I got a bottle of valerian I had, and I poured some boilin' hot water on a handful of catnip, and I mixed up that catnip tea with most half a wineglass of valerian, and I went with it over to Luella's. I marched right up to Luella, a-holdin' out of that cup, all smokin'. 'Now,' says I, 'Luella Miller, *you swaller this!*'

"'What is—what is it, oh, what is it?' she sort of screeches out. Then she goes off a-laughin' enough to kill.

"'Poor lamb, poor little lamb,' says Aunt Abby, standin' over her, all kind of tottery, and tryin' to bathe her head with camphor.

"'*You swaller this right down,*' says I. And I didn't waste any ceremony. I just took hold of Luella Miller's chin and I tipped her head back, and I caught her mouth open with laughin', and I clapped that cup to her lips, and I fairly hollered at her: 'Swaller, swaller, swaller!' and she gulped it right down. She had to, and I guess it did her good. Anyhow, she stopped cryin' and laughin' and let me put her to bed, and she went to sleep like a baby inside of half an hour. That was more than poor Aunt Abby did. She lay awake all that night and I stayed with her, though she tried not to have me; said she wa'n't sick enough for watchers. But I stayed, and I made some good cornmeal gruel and I fed her a teaspoon every little while all night long. It seemed to me as if she was jest dyin' from bein' all wore out. In the mornin' as soon as it was light I run over to the Bisbees and sent Johnny Bisbee for the doctor. I told him to tell the doctor to hurry, and he come pretty quick. Poor Aunt Abby didn't seem to know much of anythin' when he got there. You couldn't hardly tell she breathed, she was so used up. When the doctor had gone, Luella came into the room lookin' like a baby in her ruffled nightgown. I can see her now. Her eyes were as blue and her face all pink and white like a blossom, and she looked at Aunt Abby in the bed sort of innocent and surprised. 'Why,' says she, 'Aunt Abby ain't got up yet?'

"'No, she ain't,' says I, pretty short.

"'I thought I didn't smell the coffee,' says Luella.

"'Coffee,' says I. 'I guess if you have coffee this mornin' you'll make it yourself.'

"'I never made the coffee in all my life,' says she, dreadful astonished. 'Erastus always made the coffee as long as he lived, and then Lily she made it, and then Aunt Abby made it. I don't believe I *can* make the coffee, Miss Anderson.'

"'You can make it or go without, jest as you please,' says I.

"'Ain't Aunt Abby goin' to get up?' says she.

"'I guess she won't get up,' says I, 'sick as she is.' I was gettin' madder and madder. There was somethin' about that little pink-and-white thing standin' there and talkin' about coffee, when she had killed so many better folks than she was, and had jest killed another, that made me feel 'most as if I wished somebody would up and kill her before she had a chance to do any more harm.

"'Is Aunt Abby sick?' says Luella, as if she was sort of aggrieved and injured.

"'Yes,' says I, 'she's sick, and she's goin' to die, and then you'll be left alone, and you'll have to do for yourself and wait on yourself, or do without things.' I don't know but I was sort of hard, but it was the truth, and if I was any harder than Luella Miller had been I'll give up. I ain't never been sorry that I said it. Well, Luella, she up and had hysterics again at that, and I jest let her have 'em. All I did was to bundle her into the room on the other side of the entry where Aunt Abby couldn't hear her, if she wa'n't past it—I don't know but she was—and set her down hard in a chair and told her not to come back into the other room, and she minded. She had her hysterics in there till she got tired. When she found out that nobody was comin' to coddle her and do for her she stopped. At least I suppose she did. I had all I could do with poor Aunt Abby tryin' to keep the breath of life in her. The doctor had told me that she was dreadful low, and give me some very strong medicine to give to her in drops real often, and told me real particular about the nourishment. Well, I did as he told me real faithful till she wa'n't able to swaller any longer. Then I had her daughter sent for. I had begun to realize that she wouldn't last any time at all. I hadn't realized it before, though I spoke to Luella the way I did. The doctor he came, and Mrs. Sam Abbot, but when she got there it was too late; her mother was dead. Aunt Abby's daughter just give one look at her mother layin' there, then she turned sort of sharp and sudden and looked at me.

"'Where is she?' says she, and I knew she meant Luella.

"'She's out in the kitchen,' says I. 'She's too nervous to see folks die. She's afraid it will make her sick.'

"The Doctor he speaks up then. He was a young man. Old Doctor Park had died the year before, and this was a young fellow just out of college. 'Mrs. Miller is not strong,' says he, kind of severe, 'and she is quite right in not agitating herself.'

"'You are another, young man; she's got her pretty claw on you,' thinks I, but I didn't say anythin' to him. I just said over to Mrs. Sam Abbot that Luella was in the kitchen, and Mrs. Sam Abbot she went out there, and I went, too, and I never heard anythin' like the way she talked to Luella Miller. I felt pretty hard to Luella myself, but this was more than I ever would have dared to say. Luella she was too scared to go into hysterics. She jest flopped. She seemed to jest shrink away to nothin' in that kitchen chair, with Mrs. Sam Abbot standin' over her and talkin' and tellin' her the truth. I guess the truth was most too much for her and no mistake, because Luella presently actually did faint away, and there wa'n't any sham about it, the way I always suspected there was about them hysterics. She fainted dead away and we had to lay her flat on the floor, and the Doctor he came runnin' out and he said somethin' about a weak heart dreadful fierce to Mrs. Sam Abbot, but she wa'n't a mite scared. She faced him jest as white as even Luella was layin' there lookin' like death and the Doctor feelin' of her pulse.

"'Weak heart,' says she, 'weak heart; weak fiddlesticks! There ain't nothin' weak about that woman. She's got strength enough to hang onto other folks till she kills 'em. Weak? It was my poor mother that was weak: this woman killed her as sure as if she had taken a knife to her.'

"But the Doctor he didn't pay much attention. He was bendin' over Luella layin' there with her yellow hair all streamin' and her pretty pink-and-white face all pale, and her blue eyes like stars gone out, and he was holdin' onto her hand and smoothin' her forehead, and tellin' me to get the brandy in Aunt Abby's room, and I was sure as I wanted to be that Luella had got somebody else to hang onto, now Aunt Abby was gone, and I thought of poor Erastus Miller, and I sort of pitied the poor young Doctor, led away by a pretty face, and I made up my mind I'd see what I could do.

"I waited till Aunt Abby had been dead and buried about a month, and the Doctor was goin' to see Luella steady and folks were beginnin' to talk; then one evenin', when I knew the Doctor had been called out of town and wouldn't be round, I went over to Luella's. I found her all dressed up in a blue muslin with white polka dots on it, and her hair curled jest as pretty, and there wa'n't a young girl in the place could compare with her.

There was somethin' about Luella Miller seemed to draw the heart right out of you, but she didn't draw it out of *me*. She was settin' rocking in the chair by her sittin'-room window, and Maria Brown had gone home. Maria Brown had been in to help her, or rather to do the work, for Luella wa'n't helped when she didn't do anythin'. Maria Brown was real capable and she didn't have any ties; she wa'n't married, and lived alone, so she'd offered. I couldn't see why she should do the work any more than Luella; she wa'n't any too strong; but she seemed to think she could and Luella seemed to think so, too, so she went over and did all the work—washed, and ironed, and baked, while Luella sat and rocked. Maria didn't live long afterward. She began to fade away just the same fashion the others had. Well, she was warned, but she acted real mad when folks said anythin': said Luella was a poor, abused woman, too delicate to help herself, and they'd ought to be ashamed, and if she died helpin' them that couldn't help themselves she would—and she did.

"'I s'pose Maria has gone home,' says I to Luella, when I had gone in and sat down opposite her.

"'Yes, Maria went half an hour ago, after she had got supper and washed the dishes,' says Luella, in her pretty way.

"'I suppose she has got a lot of work to do in her own house tonight,' says I, kind of bitter, but that was all thrown away on Luella Miller. It seemed to her right that other folks that wa'n't any better able than she was herself should wait on her, and she couldn't get it through her head that anybody should think it *wa'n't* right.

"'Yes,' says Luella, real sweet and pretty, 'yes, she said she had to do her washin' tonight. She has let it go for a fortnight along of comin' over here.'

"'Why don't she stay home and do her washin' instead of comin' over here and doin' *your* work, when you are just as well able, and enough sight more so, than she is to do it?' says I.

"Then Luella she looked at me like a baby who has a rattle shook at it. She sort of laughed as innocent as you please. 'Oh, I can't do the work myself, Miss Anderson,' says she. 'I never did. Maria *has* to do it.'

"Then I spoke out: 'Has to do it!' says I. 'Has to do it! She don't have to do it, either. Maria Brown has her own home and enough to live on. She ain't beholden to you to come over here and slave for you and kill herself.'

"Luella she jest set and stared at me for all the world like a doll-baby that was so abused that it was comin' to life.

"'Yes,' says I, 'she's killin' herself. She's goin' to die just the way Erastus did, and Lily, and your Aunt Abby. You're killin' her jest as you did them. I don't know what there is about you, but you seem to bring a curse,' says I. 'You kill everybody that is fool enough to care anythin' about you and do for you.'

"She stared at me and she was pretty pale.

"'And Maria ain't the only one you're goin' to kill,' says I. 'You're goin' to kill Doctor Malcom before you're done with him.'

"Then a red color came flamin' all over her face. 'I ain't goin' to kill him, either,' says she, and she begun to cry.

"'Yes, you *be!*' says I. Then I spoke as I had never spoke before. You see, I felt it on account of Erastus. I told her that she hadn't any business to think of another man after she'd been married to one that had died for her: that she was a dreadful woman; and she was, that's true enough, but sometimes I have wondered lately if she knew it—if she wa'n't like a baby with scissors in its hand cuttin' everybody without knowin' what it was doin'.

158

"Luella she kept gettin' paler and paler, and she never took her eyes off my face. There was somethin' awful about the way she looked at me and never spoke one word. After awhile I quit talkin' and I went home. I watched that night, but her lamp went out before nine o'clock, and when Doctor Malcom came drivin' past and sort of slowed up he see there wa'n't any light and he drove along. I saw her sort of shy out of meetin' the next Sunday, too, so he shouldn't go home with her, and I begun to think mebbe she did have some conscience after all. It was only a week after that that Maria Brown died—sort of sudden at the last, though everybody had seen it was comin'. Well, then there was a good deal of feelin' and pretty dark whispers. Folks said the days of witchcraft had come again, and they were pretty shy of Luella. She acted sort of offish to the Doctor and he didn't go there, and there wa'n't anybody to do anythin' for her. I don't know how she *did* get along. I wouldn't go in there and offer to help her—not because I was afraid of dyin' like the rest, but I thought she was just as well able to do her own work as I was to do it for her, and I thought it was about time that she did it and stopped killin' other folks. But it wa'n't very long before folks began to say that Luella herself was goin' into a decline jest the way her husband, and Lily, and Aunt Abby and the others had, and I saw myself that she looked pretty bad. I used to see her goin' past from the store with a bundle as if she could hardly crawl, but I remembered how Erastus used to wait and 'tend when he couldn't hardly put one foot before the other, and I didn't go out to help her.

"But at last one afternoon I saw the Doctor come drivin' up like mad with his medicine chest, and Mrs. Babbit came in after supper and said that Luella was real sick.

"'I'd offer to go in and nurse her,' says she, 'but I've got my children to consider, and mebbe it ain't true what they say, but it's queer how many folks that have done for her have died.'

"I didn't say anythin', but I considered how she had been Erastus's wife and how he had set his eyes by her, and I made up my mind to go in the next mornin', unless she was better, and see what I could do; but the next mornin' I see her at the window, and pretty soon she came steppin' out as spry as you please, and a little while afterward Mrs. Babbit came in and told me that the Doctor had got a girl from out of town, a Sarah Jones, to come there, and she said she was pretty sure that the Doctor was goin' to marry Luella.

"I saw him kiss her in the door that night myself, and I knew it was true. The woman came that afternoon, and the way she flew around was a caution. I don't believe Luella had swept since Maria died. She swept and dusted, and washed and ironed; wet clothes and dusters and carpets were flyin' over there all day, and every time Luella set her foot out when the Doctor wa'n't there there was that Sarah Jones helpin' of her up and down the steps, as if she hadn't learned to walk.

"Well, everybody knew that Luella and the Doctor were goin' to be married, but it wa'n't long before they began to talk about his lookin' so poorly, jest as they had about the others; and they talked about Sarah Jones, too.

"Well, the Doctor did die, and he wanted to be married first, so as to leave what little he had to Luella, but he died before the minister could get there, and Sarah Jones died a week afterward.

"Well, that wound up everything for Luella Miller. Not another soul in the whole town would lift a finger for her. There got to be a sort of panic. Then she began to droop in good earnest. She used to have to go to the store herself, for Mrs. Babbit was afraid to let Tommy go for her, and I've seen her goin' past and stoppin' every two or three steps to rest. Well, I stood it as long as I could, but one day I see her comin' with her arms full and stoppin' to lean against the Babbit fence, and I run out and took her bundles and carried them to her house. Then I went home and never spoke one word to her though she called after me dreadful kind of pitiful. Well, that night I was taken sick with a chill, and I was sick as I wanted to be for two weeks. Mrs. Babbit had seen me run out to help Luella and she came in and told me I was goin' to die on account of it. I didn't know whether I was or not, but I considered I had done right by Erastus's wife.

"That last two weeks Luella she had a dreadful hard time, I guess. She was pretty sick, and as near as I could make out nobody dared go near her. I don't know as she was really needin' anythin' very much, for there was enough to eat in her house and it was warm weather, and she made out to cook a little flour gruel every day, I know, but I guess she had a hard time, she that had been so petted and done for all her life.

"When I got so I could go out, I went over there one morning. Mrs. Babbit had just come in to say she hadn't seen any smoke and she didn't know but it was somebody's duty to go in, but she couldn't help thinkin' of her children, and I got right up, though I hadn't been out of the house for two weeks, and I went in there, and Luella she was layin' on the bed, and she was dyin'.

"She lasted all that day and into the night. But I sat there after the new doctor had gone away. Nobody else dared to go there. It was about midnight that I left her for a minute to run home and get some medicine I had been takin', for I begun to feel rather bad.

"It was a full moon that night, and just as I started out of my door to cross the street back to Luella's, I stopped short, for I saw something."

Lydia Anderson at this juncture always said with a certain defiance that she did not expect to be believed, and then proceeded in a hushed voice:

"I saw what I saw, and I know I saw it, and I will swear on my death bed that I saw it. I saw Luella Miller and Erastus Miller, and Lily, and Aunt Abby, and Maria, and the Doctor, and Sarah, all goin' out of her door, and all but Luella shone white in the moonlight, and they were all helpin' her along till she seemed to fairly fly in the midst of them. Then it all disappeared. I stood a minute with my heart poundin', then I went over there. I thought of goin' for Mrs. Babbit, but I thought she'd be afraid. So I went alone, though I knew what had happened. Luella was layin' real peaceful, dead on her bed."

This was the story that the old woman, Lydia Anderson, told, but the sequel was told by the people who survived her, and this is the tale which has become folklore in the village.

Lydia Anderson died when she was eighty-seven. She had continued wonderfully hale and hearty for one of her years until about two weeks before her death.

One bright moonlight evening she was sitting beside a window in her parlor when she made a sudden exclamation, and was out of the house and across the street before the neighbor who was taking care of her could stop her. She followed as fast as possible and found Lydia Anderson stretched on the ground before the door of Luella Miller's deserted house, and she was quite dead.

The next night there was a red gleam of fire athwart the moonlight and the old house of Luella Miller was burned to the ground. Nothing is now left of it except a few old cellar stones and a lilac bush, and in summer a helpless trail of morning glories among the weeds, which might be considered emblematic of Luella herself.

THE SHADOWS ON THE WALL

"Henry had words with Edward in the study the night before Edward died," said Caroline Glynn.

She was elderly, tall, and harshly thin, with a hard colorlessness of face. She spoke not with acrimony, but with grave severity. Rebecca Ann Glynn, younger, stouter and rosy of face between her crinkling puffs of gray hair, gasped, by way of assent. She sat in a wide flounce of black silk in the corner of the sofa, and rolled terrified eyes from her sister Caroline to her sister Mrs. Stephen Brigham, who had been Emma Glynn, the one beauty of the family. She was beautiful still, with a large, splendid, full-blown beauty; she filled a great rocking-chair with her superb bulk of femininity, and swayed gently back and forth, her black silks whispering and her black frills fluttering. Even the shock of death (for her brother Edward lay dead in the house,) could not disturb her outward serenity of demeanor. She was grieved over the loss of her brother: he had been the youngest, and she had been fond of him, but never had Emma Brigham lost sight of her own importance amidst the waters of tribulation. She was always awake to the consciousness of her own stability in the midst of vicissitudes and the splendor of her permanent bearing.

But even her expression of masterly placidity changed before her sister Caroline's announcement and her sister Rebecca Ann's gasp of terror and distress in response.

"I think Henry might have controlled his temper, when poor Edward was so near his end," said she with an asperity which disturbed slightly the roseate curves of her beautiful mouth.

"Of course he did not *know*," murmured Rebecca Ann in a faint tone strangely out of keeping with her appearance.

One involuntarily looked again to be sure that such a feeble pipe came from that full-swelling chest.

"Of course he did not know it," said Caroline quickly. She turned on her sister with a strange sharp look of suspicion. "How could he have known it?" said she. Then she shrank as if from the other's possible answer. "Of course you and I both know he could not," said she conclusively, but her pale face was paler than it had been before.

Rebecca gasped again. The married sister, Mrs. Emma Brigham, was now sitting up straight in her chair; she had ceased rocking, and was eyeing them both intently with a sudden accentuation of family likeness in her face. Given one common intensity of emotion and similar lines showed forth, and the three sisters of one race were evident.

"What do you mean?" said she impartially to them both. Then she, too, seemed to shrink before a possible answer. She even laughed an evasive sort of laugh. "I guess you don't mean anything," said she, but her face wore still the expression of shrinking horror.

"Nobody means anything," said Caroline firmly. She rose and crossed the room toward the door with grim decisiveness.

"Where are you going?" asked Mrs. Brigham.

"I have something to see to," replied Caroline, and the others at once knew by her tone that she had some solemn and sad duty to perform in the chamber of death.

"Oh," said Mrs. Brigham.

After the door had closed behind Caroline, she turned to Rebecca.

"Did Henry have many words with him?" she asked.

"They were talking very loud," replied Rebecca evasively, yet with an answering gleam of ready response to the other's curiosity in the quick lift of her soft blue eyes.

Mrs. Brigham looked at her. She had not resumed rocking. She still sat up straight with a slight knitting of intensity on her fair forehead, between the pretty rippling curves of her auburn hair.

"Did you—hear anything?" she asked in a low voice with a glance toward the door.

"I was just across the hall in the south parlor, and that door was open and this door ajar," replied Rebecca with a slight flush.

"Then you must have—"

"I couldn't help it."

"Everything?"

"Most of it."

"What was it?"

"The old story."

"I suppose Henry was mad, as he always was, because Edward was living on here for nothing, when he had wasted all the money father left him."

Rebecca nodded with a fearful glance at the door.

When Emma spoke again her voice was still more hushed. "I know how he felt," said she. "He had always been so prudent himself, and worked hard at his profession, and there Edward had never done anything but spend, and it must have looked to him as if Edward was living at his expense, but he wasn't."

"No, he wasn't."

"It was the way father left the property—that all the children should have a home here—and he left money enough to buy the food and all if we had all come home."

"Yes."

"And Edward had a right here according to the terms of father's will, and Henry ought to have remembered it."

"Yes, he ought."

"Did he say hard things?"

"Pretty hard from what I heard."

"What?"

"I heard him tell Edward that he had no business here at all, and he thought he had better go away."

"What did Edward say?"

"That he would stay here as long as he lived and afterward, too, if he was a mind to, and he would like to see Henry get him out; and then—"

"What?"

"Then he laughed."

"What did Henry say."

"I didn't hear him say anything, but—"

"But what?"

"I saw him when he came out of this room."

"He looked mad?"

"You've seen him when he looked so."

Emma nodded; the expression of horror on her face had deepened.

"Do you remember that time he killed the cat because she had scratched him?"

"Yes. Don't!"

Then Caroline re-entered the room. She went up to the stove in which a wood fire was burning—it was a cold, gloomy day of fall—and she warmed her hands, which were reddened from recent washing in cold water.

Mrs. Brigham looked at her and hesitated. She glanced at the door, which was still ajar, as it did not easily shut, being still swollen with the damp weather of the summer. She rose and pushed it together with a sharp thud which jarred the house. Rebecca started painfully with a half exclamation. Caroline looked at her disapprovingly.

"It is time you controlled your nerves, Rebecca," said she.

"I can't help it," replied Rebecca with almost a wail. "I am nervous. There's enough to make me so, the Lord knows."

"What do you mean by that?" asked Caroline with her old air of sharp suspicion, and something between challenge and dread of its being met.

Rebecca shrank.

"Nothing," said she.

"Then I wouldn't keep speaking in such a fashion."

Emma, returning from the closed door, said imperiously that it ought to be fixed, it shut so hard.

"It will shrink enough after we have had the fire a few days," replied Caroline. "If anything is done to it it will be too small; there will be a crack at the sill."

"I think Henry ought to be ashamed of himself for talking as he did to Edward," said Mrs. Brigham abruptly, but in an almost inaudible voice.

"Hush!" said Caroline, with a glance of actual fear at the closed door.

"Nobody can hear with the door shut."

"He must have heard it shut, and—"

"Well, I can say what I want to before he comes down, and I am not afraid of him."

"I don't know who is afraid of him! What reason is there for anybody to be afraid of Henry?" demanded Caroline.

Mrs. Brigham trembled before her sister's look. Rebecca gasped again. "There isn't any reason, of course. Why should there be?"

"I wouldn't speak so, then. Somebody might overhear you and think it was queer. Miranda Joy is in the south parlor sewing, you know."

"I thought she went upstairs to stitch on the machine."

"She did, but she has come down again."

"Well, she can't hear."

"I say again I think Henry ought to be ashamed of himself. I shouldn't think he'd ever get over it, having words with poor Edward the very night before he died. Edward was enough sight better disposition than Henry, with all his faults. I always thought a great deal of poor Edward, myself."

Mrs. Brigham passed a large fluff of handkerchief across her eyes; Rebecca sobbed outright.

"Rebecca," said Caroline admonishingly, keeping her mouth stiff and swallowing determinately.

"I never heard him speak a cross word, unless he spoke cross to Henry that last night. I don't know, but he did from what Rebecca overheard," said Emma.

"Not so much cross as sort of soft, and sweet, and aggravating," sniffled Rebecca.

"He never raised his voice," said Caroline; "but he had his way."

"He had a right to in this case."

"Yes, he did."

"He had as much of a right here as Henry," sobbed Rebecca, "and now he's gone, and he will never be in this home that poor father left him and the rest of us again."

"What do you really think ailed Edward?" asked Emma in hardly more than a whisper. She did not look at her sister.

Caroline sat down in a nearby armchair, and clutched the arms convulsively until her thin knuckles whitened.

"I told you," said she.

Rebecca held her handkerchief over her mouth, and looked at them above it with terrified, streaming eyes.

"I know you said that he had terrible pains in his stomach, and had spasms, but what do you think made him have them?"

"Henry called it gastric trouble. You know Edward has always had dyspepsia."

Mrs. Brigham hesitated a moment. "Was there any talk of an—examination?" said she.

Then Caroline turned on her fiercely.

"No," said she in a terrible voice. "No."

The three sisters' souls seemed to meet on one common ground of terrified understanding through their eyes. The old-fashioned latch of the door was heard to rattle, and a push from without made the door shake ineffectually. "It's Henry," Rebecca sighed rather than whispered. Mrs. Brigham settled herself after a noiseless rush across the floor into her rocking-chair again, and was swaying back and forth with her head comfortably leaning back, when the door at last yielded and Henry Glynn entered. He cast a covertly sharp, comprehensive glance at Mrs. Brigham with her elaborate calm; at Rebecca quietly huddled in the corner of the sofa with her handkerchief to her face and only one small reddened ear as attentive as a dog's uncovered and revealing her alertness for his presence; at Caroline sitting with a strained composure in her armchair by the stove. She met his eyes quite firmly with a look of inscrutable fear, and defiance of the fear and of him.

Henry Glynn looked more like this sister than the others. Both had the same hard delicacy of form and feature, both were tall and almost emaciated, both had a sparse growth of gray blond hair far back from high intellectual foreheads, both had an almost noble aquilinity of feature. They confronted each other with the pitiless immovability of two statues in whose marble lineaments emotions were fixed for all eternity.

Then Henry Glynn smiled and the smile transformed his face. He looked suddenly years younger, and an almost boyish recklessness and irresolution appeared in his face. He flung himself into a chair with a gesture which was bewildering from its incongruity with his general appearance. He leaned his head back, flung one leg over the other, and looked laughingly at Mrs. Brigham.

"I declare, Emma, you grow younger every year," he said.

She flushed a little, and her placid mouth widened at the corners. She was susceptible to praise.

"Our thoughts today ought to belong to the one of us who will *never* grow older," said Caroline in a hard voice.

Henry looked at her, still smiling. "Of course, we none of us forget that," said he, in a deep, gentle voice, "but we have to speak to the living, Caroline, and I have not seen Emma for a long time, and the living are as dear as the dead."

"Not to me," said Caroline.

She rose, and went abruptly out of the room again. Rebecca also rose and hurried after her, sobbing loudly.

Henry looked slowly after them.

"Caroline is completely unstrung," said he.

Mrs. Brigham rocked. A confidence in him inspired by his manner was stealing over her. Out of that confidence she spoke quite easily and naturally.

"His death was very sudden," said she.

Henry's eyelids quivered slightly but his gaze was unswerving.

"Yes," said he; "it was very sudden. He was sick only a few hours."

"What did you call it?"

"Gastric."

"You did not think of an examination?"

"There was no need. I am perfectly certain as to the cause of his death."

Suddenly Mrs. Brigham felt a creep as of some live horror over her very soul. Her flesh prickled with cold, before an inflection of his voice. She rose, tottering on weak knees.

"Where are you going?" asked Henry in a strange, breathless voice.

Mrs. Brigham said something incoherent about some sewing which she had to do, some black for the funeral, and was out of the room. She went up to the front chamber which she occupied. Caroline was there. She went close to her and took her hands, and the two sisters looked at each other.

"Don't speak, don't, I won't have it!" said Caroline finally in an awful whisper.

"I won't," replied Emma.

That afternoon the three sisters were in the study, the large

172

front room on the ground floor across the hall from the south parlor, when the dusk deepened.

Mrs. Brigham was hemming some black material. She sat close to the west window for the waning light. At last she laid her work on her lap.

"It's no use, I cannot see to sew another stitch until we have a light," said she.

Caroline, who was writing some letters at the table, turned to Rebecca, in her usual place on the sofa.

"Rebecca, you had better get a lamp," she said.

Rebecca started up; even in the dusk her face showed her agitation.

"It doesn't seem to me that we need a lamp quite yet," she said in a piteous, pleading voice like a child's.

"Yes, we do," returned Mrs. Brigham peremptorily. "We must have a light. I must finish this tonight or I can't go to the funeral, and I can't see to sew another stitch."

"Caroline can see to write letters, and she is farther from the window than you are," said Rebecca.

"Are you trying to save kerosene or are you lazy, Rebecca Glynn?" cried Mrs. Brigham. "I can go and get the light myself, but I have this work all in my lap."

Caroline's pen stopped scratching.

"Rebecca, we must have the light," said she.

"Had we better have it in here?" asked Rebecca weakly.

"Of course! Why not?" cried Caroline sternly.

"I am sure I don't want to take my sewing into the other room, when it is all cleaned up for tomorrow," said Mrs. Brigham.

"Why, I never heard such a to-do about lighting a lamp."

Rebecca rose and left the room. Presently she entered with a lamp—a large one with a white porcelain shade. She set it on a table, an old-fashioned card-table which was placed against the opposite wall from the window. That wall was clear of bookcases and books, which were only on three sides of the room. That opposite wall was taken up with three doors, the one small space being occupied by the table. Above the table on the old-fashioned paper, of a white satin gloss, traversed by an indeterminate green scroll, hung quite high a small gilt and black-framed ivory miniature taken in her girlhood of the mother of the family. When the lamp was set on the table beneath it, the tiny pretty face painted on the ivory seemed to gleam out with a look of intelligence.

"What have you put that lamp over there for?" asked Mrs. Brigham, with more of impatience than her voice usually revealed. "Why didn't you set it in the hall and have done with it. Neither Caroline nor I can see if it is on that table."

"I thought perhaps you would move," replied Rebecca hoarsely.

"If I do move, we can't both sit at that table. Caroline has her paper all spread around. Why don't you set the lamp on the study table in the middle of the room, then we can both see?"

Rebecca hesitated. Her face was very pale. She looked with an appeal that was fairly agonizing at her sister Caroline.

"Why don't you put the lamp on this table, as she says?" asked Caroline, almost fiercely. "Why do you act so, Rebecca?"

"I should think you *would* ask her that," said Mrs. Brigham. "She doesn't act like herself at all."

Rebecca took the lamp and set it on the table in the middle of the room without another word. Then she turned her back upon it quickly and seated herself on the sofa, and placed a hand over her eyes as if to shade them, and remained so.

"Does the light hurt your eyes, and is that the reason why you didn't want the lamp?" asked Mrs. Brigham kindly.

"I always like to sit in the dark," replied Rebecca chokingly. Then she snatched her handkerchief hastily from her pocket and began to weep. Caroline continued to write, Mrs. Brigham to sew.

Suddenly Mrs. Brigham as she sewed glanced at the opposite wall. The glance became a steady stare. She looked intently, her work suspended in her hands. Then she looked away again and took a few more stitches, then she looked again, and again turned to her task. At last she laid her work in her lap and stared concentratedly. She looked from the wall around the room, taking note of the various objects; she looked at the wall long and intently. Then she turned to her sisters.

"What *is* that?" said she.

"What?" asked Caroline harshly; her pen scratched loudly across the paper.

Rebecca gave one of her convulsive gasps.

"That strange shadow on the wall," replied Mrs. Brigham.

Rebecca sat with her face hidden: Caroline dipped her pen in the inkstand.

"Why don't you turn around and look?" asked Mrs. Brigham in a wondering and somewhat aggrieved way.

"I am in a hurry to finish this letter, if Mrs. Wilson Ebbit is going to get word in time to come to the funeral," replied Caroline shortly.

Mrs. Brigham rose, her work slipping to the floor, and she began walking around the room, moving various articles of furniture, with her eyes on the shadow.

Then suddenly she shrieked out:

"Look at this awful shadow! What is it? Caroline, look, look! Rebecca, look! *What is it?*"

All Mrs. Brigham's triumphant placidity was gone. Her handsome face was livid with horror. She stood stiffly pointing at the shadow.

"Look!" said she, pointing her finger at it. "Look! What is it?"

Then Rebecca burst out in a wild wail after a shuddering glance at the wall:

"Oh, Caroline, there it is again! There it is again!"

"Caroline Glynn, you look!" said Mrs. Brigham. "Look! What is that dreadful shadow?"

Caroline rose, turned, and stood confronting the wall.

"How should I know?" she said.

"It has been there every night since he died," cried Rebecca.

"Every night?"

"Yes. He died Thursday and this is Saturday; that makes three nights," said Caroline rigidly. She stood as if holding herself calm with a vise of concentrated will.

"It—it looks like—like—" stammered Mrs. Brigham in a tone of intense horror.

"I know what it looks like well enough," said Caroline. "I've got eyes in my head."

"It looks like Edward," burst out Rebecca in a sort of frenzy of fear. "Only—"

"Yes, it does," assented Mrs. Brigham, whose horror-stricken tone matched her sister's, "only— Oh, it is awful! What is it, Caroline?"

"I ask you again, how should I know?" replied Caroline. "I see it there like you. How should I know any more than you?"

"It *must* be something in the room," said Mrs. Brigham, staring wildly around.

"We moved everything in the room the first night it came," said Rebecca; "it is not anything in the room."

Caroline turned upon her with a sort of fury. "Of course it is something in the room," said she. "How you act! What do you mean by talking so? Of course it is something in the room."

"Of course, it is," agreed Mrs. Brigham, looking at Caroline suspiciously. "Of course it must be. It is only a coincidence. It just happens so. Perhaps it is that fold of the window curtain that makes it. It must be something in the room."

"It is not anything in the room," repeated Rebecca with obstinate horror.

The door opened suddenly and Henry Glynn entered. He began to speak, then his eyes followed the direction of the others'. He stood stock still staring at the shadow on the wall. It was life size and stretched across the white parallelogram of a door, half across the wall space on which the picture hung.

"What is that?" he demanded in a strange voice.

"It must be due to something in the room," Mrs. Brigham said faintly.

"It is not due to anything in the room," said Rebecca again with the shrill insistency of terror.

"How you act, Rebecca Glynn," said Caroline.

Henry Glynn stood and stared a moment longer. His face showed a gamut of emotions—horror, conviction, then furious incredulity. Suddenly he began hastening hither and thither about the room. He moved the furniture with fierce jerks, turning ever to see the effect upon the shadow on the wall. Not a line of its terrible outlines wavered.

"It must be something in the room!" he declared in a voice which seemed to snap like a lash.

His face changed. The inmost secrecy of his nature seemed evident until one almost lost sight of his lineaments. Rebecca stood close to her sofa, regarding him with woeful, fascinated eyes. Mrs. Brigham clutched Caroline's hand. They both stood in a corner out of his way. For a few moments he raged about the room like a caged wild animal. He moved every piece of furniture; when the moving of a piece did not affect the shadow, he flung it to the floor, the sisters watching.

Then suddenly he desisted. He laughed and began straightening the furniture which he had flung down.

"What an absurdity," he said easily. "Such a to-do about a shadow."

"That's so," assented Mrs. Brigham, in a scared voice which she tried to make natural. As she spoke she lifted a chair near her.

"I think you have broken the chair that Edward was so fond of," said Caroline.

Terror and wrath were struggling for expression on her face. Her mouth was set, her eyes shrinking. Henry lifted the chair with a show of anxiety.

"Just as good as ever," he said pleasantly. He laughed again, looking at his sisters. "Did I scare you?" he said. "I should think you might be used to me by this time. You know my way of wanting to leap to the bottom of a mystery, and that shadow does look—queer, like—and I thought if there was any way of accounting for it I would like to without any delay."

"You don't seem to have succeeded," remarked Caroline dryly, with a slight glance at the wall.

Henry's eyes followed hers and he quivered perceptibly.

"Oh, there is no accounting for shadows," he said, and he laughed again. "A man is a fool to try to account for shadows."

Then the supper bell rang, and they all left the room, but Henry kept his back to the wall, as did, indeed, the others.

Mrs. Brigham pressed close to Caroline as she crossed the hall. "He looked like a demon!" she breathed in her ear.

Henry led the way with an alert motion like a boy; Rebecca brought up the rear; she could scarcely walk, her knees trembled so.

"I can't sit in that room again this evening," she whispered to Caroline after supper.

"Very well, we will sit in the south room," replied Caroline. "I think we will sit in the south parlor," she said aloud; "it isn't as damp as the study, and I have a cold."

So they all sat in the south room with their sewing. Henry read the newspaper, his chair drawn close to the lamp on the table. About nine o'clock he rose abruptly and crossed the hall to the study. The three sisters looked at one another. Mrs. Brigham rose, folded her rustling skirts compactly around her, and began tiptoeing toward the door.

"What are you going to do?" inquired Rebecca agitatedly.

"I am going to see what he is about," replied Mrs. Brigham cautiously.

She pointed as she spoke to the study door across the hall; it was ajar. Henry had striven to pull it together behind him, but it had somehow swollen beyond the limit with curious speed. It was still ajar and a streak of light showed from top to bottom. The hall lamp was not lit.

"You had better stay where you are," said Caroline with guarded sharpness.

"I am going to see," repeated Mrs. Brigham firmly.

Then she folded her skirts so tightly that her bulk with its swelling curves was revealed in a black silk sheath, and she went with a slow toddle across the hall to the study door. She stood there, her eye at the crack.

In the south room Rebecca stopped sewing and sat watching with dilated eyes. Caroline sewed steadily. What Mrs. Brigham, standing at the crack in the study door, saw was this:

Henry Glynn, evidently reasoning that the source of the strange shadow must be between the table on which the lamp stood and the wall, was making systematic passes and thrusts all over and through the intervening space with an old sword which had belonged to his father. Not an inch was left unpierced. He seemed to have divided the space into mathematical sections. He brandished the sword with a sort of cold fury and calculation; the blade gave out flashes of light, the shadow remained unmoved. Mrs. Brigham, watching, felt herself cold with horror.

Finally Henry ceased and stood with the sword in hand and raised as if to strike, surveying the shadow on the wall threateningly. Mrs. Brigham toddled back across the hall and shut the south room door behind her before she related what she had seen.

"He looked like a demon!" she said again. "Have you got any of that old wine in the house, Caroline? I don't feel as if I could stand much more."

Indeed, she looked overcome. Her handsome placid face was worn and strained and pale.

"Yes, there's plenty," said Caroline; "you can have some when you go to bed."

"I think we had all better take some," said Mrs. Brigham. "Oh, my God, Caroline, what—"

"Don't ask and don't speak," said Caroline.

"No, I am not going to," replied Mrs. Brigham; "but—"

Rebecca moaned aloud.

"What are you doing that for?" asked Caroline harshly.

"Poor Edward," returned Rebecca.

"That is all you have to groan for," said Caroline. "There is nothing else."

"I am going to bed," said Mrs. Brigham. "I sha'n't be able to be at the funeral if I don't."

Soon the three sisters went to their chambers and the south parlor was deserted. Caroline called to Henry in the study to put out the light before he came upstairs. They had been gone about an hour when he came into the room bringing the lamp which had stood in the study. He set it on the table and waited a few minutes, pacing up and down. His face was terrible, his fair complexion showed livid; his blue eyes seemed dark blanks of awful reflections.

Then he took the lamp up and returned to the library. He set the lamp on the center table, and the shadow sprang out on the wall. Again he studied the furniture and moved it about, but deliberately, with none of his former frenzy. Nothing affected the shadow. Then he returned to the south room with the lamp and again waited. Again he returned to the study and placed the lamp on the table, and the shadow sprang out upon the wall. It was midnight before he went upstairs. Mrs. Brigham and the other sisters, who could not sleep, heard him.

The next day was the funeral. That evening the family sat in the south room. Some relatives were with them. Nobody entered the study until Henry carried a lamp in there after the others had retired for the night. He saw again the shadow on the wall leap to an awful life before the light.

The next morning at breakfast Henry Glynn announced that he had to go to the city for three days. The sisters looked at him with surprise. He very seldom left home, and just now his practice had been neglected on account of Edward's death. He was a physician.

"How can you leave your patients now?" asked Mrs. Brigham wonderingly.

"I don't know how to, but there is no other way," replied Henry easily. "I have had a telegram from Doctor Mitford."

"Consultation?" inquired Mrs. Brigham.

"I have business," replied Henry.

Doctor Mitford was an old classmate of his who lived in a neighboring city and who occasionally called upon him in the case of a consultation.

After he had gone Mrs. Brigham said to Caroline that after all Henry had not said that he was going to consult with Doctor Mitford, and she thought it very strange.

"Everything is very strange," said Rebecca with a shudder.

"What do you mean?" inquired Caroline sharply.

"Nothing," replied Rebecca.

Nobody entered the library that day, nor the next, nor the next. The third day Henry was expected home, but he did not arrive and the last train from the city had come.

"I call it pretty queer work," said Mrs. Brigham. "The idea of a doctor leaving his patients for three days anyhow, at such a time as this, and I know he has some very sick ones; he said so. And the idea of a consultation lasting three days! There is no sense in it, and *now* he has not come. I don't understand it, for my part."

"I don't either," said Rebecca.

They were all in the south parlor. There was no light in the study opposite, and the door was ajar.

Presently Mrs. Brigham rose—she could not have told why; something seemed to impel her, some will outside her own. She went out of the room, again wrapping her rustling skirts around that she might pass noiselessly, and began pushing at the swollen door of the study.

"She has not got any lamp," said Rebecca in a shaking voice.

Caroline, who was writing letters, rose again, took a lamp (there were two in the room) and followed her sister. Rebecca had risen, but she stood trembling, not venturing to follow.

The doorbell rang, but the others did not hear it; it was on the south door on the other side of the house from the study. Rebecca, after hesitating until the bell rang the second time, went to the door; she remembered that the servant was out.

Caroline and her sister Emma entered the study. Caroline set the lamp on the table. They looked at the wall. "Oh, my God," gasped Mrs. Brigham, "there are—there are *two*—shadows." The sisters stood clutching each other, staring at the awful things on the wall. Then Rebecca came in, staggering, with a telegram in her hand. "Here is—a telegram," she gasped. "Henry is—dead."

THE SOUTHWEST CHAMBER

"That school-teacher from Acton is coming today," said the elder Miss Gill, Sophia.

"So she is," assented the younger Miss Gill, Amanda.

"I have decided to put her in the southwest chamber," said Sophia.

Amanda looked at her sister with an expression of mingled doubt and terror. "You don't suppose she would—" she began hesitatingly.

"Would what?" demanded Sophia, sharply.

She was more incisive than her sister. Both were below the medium height, and stout, but Sophia was firm where Amanda was flabby. Amanda wore a baggy old muslin (it was a hot day), and Sophia was uncompromisingly hooked up in a starched and boned cambric over her high shelving figure.

"I didn't know but she would object to sleeping in that room, as long as Aunt Harriet died there such a little time ago," faltered Amanda.

"Well!" said Sophia, "of all the silly notions! If you are going to pick out rooms in this house where nobody has died, for the boarders, you'll have your hands full. Grandfather Ackley had seven children; four of them died here to my certain knowledge, besides grandfather and grandmother. I think Great-grandmother Ackley, grandfather's mother, died here, too; she must have; and Great-grandfather Ackley, and grandfather's unmarried sister,

Great-aunt Fanny Ackley. I don't believe there's a room nor a bed in this house that somebody hasn't passed away in."

"Well, I suppose I am silly to think of it, and she had better go in there," said Amanda.

"I know she had. The northeast room is small and hot, and she's stout and likely to feel the heat, and she's saved money and is able to board out summers, and maybe she'll come here another year if she's well accommodated," said Sophia. "Now I guess you'd better go in there and see if any dust has settled on anything since it was cleaned, and open the west windows and let the sun in, while I see to that cake."

Amanda went to her task in the southwest chamber while her sister stepped heavily down the back stairs on her way to the kitchen.

"It seems to me you had better open the bed while you air and dust, then make it up again," she called back.

"Yes, sister," Amanda answered, shudderingly.

Nobody knew how this elderly woman with the untrammeled imagination of a child dreaded to enter the southwest chamber, and yet she could not have told why she had the dread. She had entered and occupied rooms which had been once tenanted by persons now dead. The room which had been hers in the little house in which she and her sister had lived before coming here had been her dead mother's. She had never reflected upon the fact with anything but loving awe and reverence. There had never been any fear. But this was different. She entered and her heart beat thickly in her ears. Her hands were cold. The room was a very large one. The four windows, two facing south, two west, were closed, the blinds also. The room was in a film of green gloom. The furniture loomed out vaguely.

The gilt frame of a blurred old engraving on the wall caught a little light. The white counterpane on the bed showed like a blank page.

Amanda crossed the room, opened with a straining motion of her thin back and shoulders one of the west windows, and threw back the blind. Then the room revealed itself an apartment full of an aged and worn but no less valid state. Pieces of old mahogany swelled forth; a peacock-patterned chintz draped the bedstead. This chintz also covered a great easy chair which had been the favorite seat of the former occupant of the room. The closet door stood ajar. Amanda noticed that with wonder. There was a glimpse of purple drapery floating from a peg inside the closet. Amanda went across and took down the garment hanging there. She wondered how her sister had happened to leave it when she cleaned the room. It was an old loose gown which had belonged to her aunt. She took it down, shuddering, and closed the closet door after a fearful glance into its dark depths. It was a long closet with a strong odor of lovage. The Aunt Harriet had had a habit of eating lovage and had carried it constantly in her pocket. There was very likely some of the pleasant root in the pocket of the musty purple gown which Amanda threw over the easy chair.

Amanda perceived the odor with a start as if before an actual presence. Odor seems in a sense a vital part of a personality. It can survive the flesh to which it has clung like a persistent shadow, seeming to have in itself something of the substance of that to which it pertained. Amanda was always conscious of this fragrance of lovage as she tidied the room. She dusted the heavy mahogany pieces punctiliously after she had opened the bed as her sister had directed. She spread fresh towels over the wash-stand and the bureau; she made the bed. Then she thought to take the purple gown from the easy chair and carry it to the garret and put it in the trunk with the other articles of the dead woman's wardrobe which had been packed away there; *but the purple gown was not on the chair!*

Amanda Gill was not a woman of strong convictions even as to her own actions. She directly thought that possibly she had been mistaken and had not removed it from the closet. She glanced at the closet door and saw with surprise that it was open, and she had thought she had closed it, but she instantly was not sure of that. So she entered the closet and looked for the purple gown. *It was not there!*

Amanda Gill went feebly out of the closet and looked at the easy chair again. The purple gown was not there! She looked wildly around the room. She went down on her trembling knees and peered under the bed, she opened the bureau drawers, she looked again in the closet. Then she stood in the middle of the floor and fairly wrung her hands.

"What does it mean?" she said in a shocked whisper.

She had certainly seen that loose purple gown of her dead Aunt Harriet's.

There is a limit at which self-refutation must stop in any sane person. Amanda Gill had reached it. She knew that she had seen that purple gown in that closet; she knew that she had removed it and put it on the easy chair. She also knew that she had not taken it out of the room. She felt a curious sense of being inverted mentally. It was as if all her traditions and laws of life were on their heads. Never in her simple record had any garment not remained where she had placed it unless removed by some palpable human agency.

Then the thought occurred to her that possibly her sister Sophia might have entered the room unobserved while her back was turned and removed the dress. A sensation of relief came over her. Her blood seemed to flow back into its usual channels; the tension of her nerves relaxed.

"How silly I am," she said aloud.

She hurried out and downstairs into the kitchen where Sophia was making cake, stirring with splendid circular sweeps of a wooden spoon a creamy yellow mass. She looked up as her sister entered.

"Have you got it done?" said she.

"Yes," replied Amanda. Then she hesitated. A sudden terror overcame her. It did not seem as if it were at all probable that Sophia had left that foamy cake mixture a second to go to Aunt Harriet's chamber and remove that purple gown.

"Well," said Sophia, "if you have got that done I wish you would take hold and string those beans. The first thing we know there won't be time to boil them for dinner."

Amanda moved toward the pan of beans on the table, then she looked at her sister.

"Did you come up in Aunt Harriet's room while I was there?" she asked weakly.

She knew while she asked what the answer would be.

"Up in Aunt Harriet's room? Of course I didn't. I couldn't leave this cake without having it fall. You know that well enough. Why?"

"Nothing," replied Amanda.

Suddenly she realized that she could not tell her sister what had happened, for before the utter absurdity of the whole thing her belief in her own reason quailed. She knew what Sophia would say if she told her. She could hear her.

"Amanda Gill, have you gone stark staring mad?"

She resolved that she would never tell Sophia. She dropped into a chair and begun shelling the beans with nerveless fingers. Sophia looked at her curiously.

"Amanda Gill, what on earth ails you?" she asked.

"Nothing," replied Amanda. She bent her head very low over the green pods.

"Yes, there is, too! You are as white as a sheet, and your hands are shaking so you can hardly string those beans. I did think you had more sense, Amanda Gill."

"I don't know what you mean, Sophia."

"Yes, you do know what I mean, too; you needn't pretend you don't. Why did you ask me if I had been in that room, and why do you act so queer?"

Amanda hesitated. She had been trained to truth. Then she lied.

"I wondered if you'd noticed how it had leaked in on the paper over by the bureau, that last rain," said she.

"What makes you look so pale then?"

"I don't know. I guess the heat sort of overcame me."

"I shouldn't think it could have been very hot in that room when it had been shut up so long," said Sophia.

She was evidently not satisfied, but then the grocer came to the door and the matter dropped.

For the next hour the two women were very busy. They kept no servant. When they had come into possession of this fine old place by the death of their aunt it had seemed a doubtful blessing. There was not a cent with which to pay for repairs and taxes and insurance, except the twelve hundred dollars which they had obtained from the sale of the little house in which they had been born and lived all their lives. There had been a division in the old Ackley family years before. One of the daughters had married against her mother's wish and had been disinherited. She had married a poor man by the name of Gill, and shared his humble lot in sight of her former home and her sister and mother living in prosperity, until she had borne three daughters; then she died, worn out with overwork and worry.

The mother and the elder sister had been pitiless to the last. Neither had ever spoken to her since she left her home the night of her marriage. They were hard women.

The three daughters of the disinherited sister had lived quiet and poor, but not actually needy lives. Jane, the middle daughter, had married, and died in less than a year. Amanda and Sophia had taken the girl baby she left when the father married again. Sophia had taught a primary school for many years; she had saved enough to buy the little house in which they lived. Amanda had crocheted lace, and embroidered flannel, and made tidies and pincushions, and had earned enough for her clothes and the child's, little Flora Scott.

Their father, William Gill, had died before they were thirty, and now in their late middle life had come the death of the aunt to whom they had never spoken, although they had often seen her, who had lived in solitary state in the old Ackley mansion until she was more than eighty. There had been no will, and they were the only heirs with the exception of young Flora Scott, the daughter of the dead sister.

Sophia and Amanda thought directly of Flora when they knew of the inheritance.

"It will be a splendid thing for her; she will have enough to live on when we are gone," Sophia said.

She had promptly decided what was to be done. The small house was to be sold, and they were to move into the old Ackley house and take boarders to pay for its keeping. She scouted the idea of selling it. She had an enormous family pride. She had always held her head high when she had walked past that fine old mansion, the cradle of her race, which she was forbidden to enter. She was unmoved when the lawyer who was advising her disclosed to her the fact that Harriet Ackley had used every cent of the Ackley money.

"I realize that we have to work," said she, "but my sister and I have determined to keep the place."

That was the end of the discussion. Sophia and Amanda Gill had been living in the old Ackley house a fortnight, and they had three boarders: an elderly widow with a comfortable income, a young Congregationalist clergyman, and the middle-aged single woman who had charge of the village library. Now the school-teacher from Acton, Miss Louisa Stark, was expected for the summer, and would make four.

Sophia considered that they were comfortably provided for. Her wants and her sister's were very few, and even the niece, although a young girl, had small expenses, since her wardrobe was supplied for years to come from that of the deceased aunt. There were stored away in the garret of the Ackley house enough voluminous black silks and satins and bombazines to keep her clad in somber richness for years to come.

Flora was a very gentle girl, with large, serious blue eyes, a seldom-smiling, pretty mouth, and smooth flaxen hair. She was delicate and very young—sixteen on her next birthday.

She came home soon now with her parcels of sugar and tea from the grocer's. She entered the kitchen gravely and deposited them on the table by which her Aunt Amanda was seated stringing beans. Flora wore an obsolete turban-shaped hat of black straw which had belonged to the dead aunt; it set high like a crown, revealing her forehead. Her dress was an ancient purple-and-white print, too long and too large except over the chest, where it held her like a straight waistcoat.

"You had better take off your hat, Flora," said Sophia. She turned suddenly to Amanda. "Did you fill the water-pitcher in that chamber for the school-teacher?" she asked severely. She was quite sure that Amanda had not filled the water-pitcher.

Amanda blushed and started guiltily. "I declare, I don't believe I did," said she.

"I didn't think you had," said her sister with sarcastic emphasis.

"Flora, you go up to the room that was your Great-aunt Harriet's, and take the water-pitcher off the wash-stand and fill it with water. Be real careful, and don't break the pitcher, and don't spill the water."

"In *that* chamber?" asked Flora. She spoke very quietly, but her face changed a little.

"Yes, in that chamber," returned her Aunt Sophia sharply. "Go right along."

Flora went, and her light footstep was heard on the stairs. Very soon she returned with the blue-and-white water-pitcher and filled it carefully at the kitchen sink.

"Now be careful and not spill it," said Sophia as she went out of the room carrying it gingerly.

Amanda gave a timidly curious glance at her; she wondered if she had seen the purple gown.

Then she started, for the village stagecoach was seen driving around to the front of the house. The house stood on a corner.

"Here, Amanda, you look better than I do; you go and meet her," said Sophia. "I'll just put the cake in the pan and get it in the oven and I'll come. Show her right up to her room."

Amanda removed her apron hastily and obeyed. Sophia hurried with her cake, pouring it into the baking-tins. She had just put it in the oven, when the door opened and Flora entered carrying the blue water-pitcher.

"What are you bringing down that pitcher again for?" asked Sophia.

"She wants some water, and Aunt Amanda sent me," replied Flora.

Her pretty pale face had a bewildered expression.

"For the land sake, she hasn't used all that great pitcherful of water so quick?"

"There wasn't any water in it," replied Flora.

Her high, childish forehead was contracted slightly with a puzzled frown as she looked at her aunt.

"Wasn't any water in it?"

"No, ma'am."

"Didn't I see you filling the pitcher with water not ten minutes ago, I want to know?"

"Yes, ma'am."

"What did you do with that water?"

"Nothing."

"Did you carry that pitcherful of water up to that room and set it on the wash-stand?"

"Yes, ma'am."

"Didn't you spill it?"

"No, ma'am."

"Now, Flora Scott, I want the truth! Did you fill that pitcher with water and carry it up there, and wasn't there any there when she came to use it?"

"Yes, ma'am."

"Let me see that pitcher." Sophia examined the pitcher. It was not only perfectly dry from top to bottom, but even a little dusty. She turned severely on the young girl. "That shows," said she, "you did not fill the pitcher at all. You let the water run at the side because you didn't want to carry it upstairs. I am ashamed of you. It's bad enough to be so lazy, but when it comes to not telling the truth—"

The young girl's face broke up suddenly into piteous confusion, and her blue eyes became filmy with tears.

"I did fill the pitcher, honest," she faltered, "I did, Aunt Sophia. You ask Aunt Amanda."

"I'll ask nobody. This pitcher is proof enough. Water don't go off and leave the pitcher dusty on the inside if it was put in ten minutes ago. Now you fill that pitcher full quick, and you carry it upstairs, and if you spill a drop there'll be something besides talk."

Flora filled the pitcher, with the tears falling over her cheeks. She sniveled softly as she went out, balancing it carefully against her slender hip. Sophia followed her.

"Stop crying," said she sharply; "you ought to be ashamed of yourself. What do you suppose Miss Louisa Stark will think. No water in her pitcher in the first place, and then you come back crying as if you didn't want to get it."

In spite of herself, Sophia's voice was soothing. She was very fond of the girl. She followed her up the stairs to the chamber where Miss Louisa Stark was waiting for the water to remove the soil of travel. She had removed her bonnet, and its tuft of red geraniums lightened the obscurity of the mahogany dresser. She had placed her little beaded cape carefully on the bed. She was replying to a tremulous remark of Amanda's, who was nearly fainting from the new mystery of the water-pitcher, that it was warm and she suffered a good deal in warm weather.

Louisa Stark was stout and solidly built. She was much larger than either of the Gill sisters. She was a masterly woman inured to command from years of school-teaching. She carried her swelling bulk with majesty; even her face, moist and red with the heat, lost nothing of its dignity of expression.

She was standing in the middle of the floor with an air which gave the effect of her standing upon an elevation. She turned when Sophia and Flora, carrying the water-pitcher, entered.

"This is my sister Sophia," said Amanda tremulously.

Sophia advanced, shook hands with Miss Louisa Stark and bade her welcome and hoped she would like her room. Then she moved toward the closet. "There is a nice large closet in this room—the best closet in the house. You might have your trunk—" she said, then she stopped short.

The closet door was ajar, and a purple garment seemed suddenly to swing into view as if impelled by some wind.

"Why, here is something left in this closet," Sophia said in a mortified tone. "I thought all those things had been taken away."

She pulled down the garment with a jerk, and as she did so Amanda passed her in a weak rush for the door.

"I am afraid your sister is not well," said the school-teacher from Acton. "She looked very pale when you took that dress down. I noticed it at once. Hadn't you better go and see what the matter is? She may be going to faint."

"She is not subject to fainting spells," replied Sophia, but she followed Amanda.

She found her in the room which they occupied together, lying on the bed, very pale and gasping. She leaned over her.

"Amanda, what is the matter; don't you feel well?" she asked.

"I feel a little faint."

Sophia got a camphor bottle and began rubbing her sister's forehead.

"Do you feel better?" she said.

Amanda nodded.

"I guess it was that green apple pie you ate this noon," said Sophia. "I declare, what did I do with that dress of Aunt Harriet's? I guess if you feel better I'll just run and get it and take it up garret. I'll stop in here again when I come down. You'd better lay still. Flora can bring you up a cup of tea. I wouldn't try to eat any supper."

Sophia's tone as she left the room was full of loving concern. Presently she returned; she looked disturbed, but angrily so. There was not the slightest hint of any fear in her expression.

"I want to know," said she, looking sharply and quickly around, "if I brought that purple dress in here, after all?"

"I didn't see you," replied Amanda.

"I must have. It isn't in that chamber, nor the closet. You aren't lying on it, are you?"

"I lay down before you came in," replied Amanda.

"So you did. Well, I'll go and look again."

Presently Amanda heard her sister's heavy step on the garret stairs. Then she returned with a queer defiant expression on her face.

"I carried it up garret, after all, and put it in the trunk," said she. "I declare, I forgot it. I suppose your being faint sort of put it out of my head. There it was, folded up just as nice, right where I put it."

Sophia's mouth was set; her eyes upon her sister's scared, agitated face were full of hard challenge.

"Yes," murmured Amanda.

"I must go right down and see to that cake," said Sophia, going out of the room. "If you don't feel well, you pound on the floor with the umbrella."

Amanda looked after her. She knew that Sophia had not put that purple dress of her dead Aunt Harriet in the trunk in the garret.

Meantime Miss Louisa Stark was settling herself in the south-west chamber. She unpacked her trunk and hung her dresses carefully in the closet. She filled the bureau drawers with nicely folded linen and small articles of dress. She was a very punc-tilious woman. She put on a black India silk dress with purple flowers. She combed her grayish-blond hair in smooth ridges back from her broad forehead. She pinned her lace at her throat with a brooch, very handsome, although somewhat obsolete—a bunch of pearl grapes on black onyx, set in gold filigree. She had purchased it several years ago with a considerable portion of the stipend from her spring term of school-teaching.

As she surveyed herself in the little swing mirror surmounting the old-fashioned mahogany bureau she suddenly bent forward and looked closely at the brooch. It seemed to her that something was wrong with it. As she looked she became sure. Instead of the familiar bunch of pearl grapes on the black onyx, she saw a knot of blonde and black hair under glass surrounded by a border of twisted gold. She felt a thrill of horror, though she could not tell why. She unpinned the brooch, and it was her own familiar one, the pearl grapes and the onyx. "How very foolish I am," she thought. She thrust the pin in the laces at her throat and again looked at herself in the glass, and there it was again—the knot of blond and black hair and the twisted gold.

Louisa Stark looked at her own large, firm face above the brooch and it was full of terror and dismay which were new to it. She straightway began to wonder if there could be anything wrong with her mind. She remembered that an aunt of her mother's had been insane. A sort of fury with herself possessed her. She stared at the brooch in the glass with eyes at once angry and terrified. Then she removed it again and there was her own old brooch. Finally she thrust the gold pin through the lace again, fastened it and turning a defiant back on the glass, went down to supper.

At the supper table she met the other boarders—the elderly widow, the young clergyman and the middle-aged librarian. She viewed the elderly widow with reserve, the clergyman with respect, the middle-aged librarian with suspicion. The latter wore a very youthful shirt-waist, and her hair in a girlish fashion which the school-teacher, who twisted hers severely from the straining roots at the nape of her neck to the small, smooth coil at the top, condemned as straining after effects no longer hers by right.

The librarian, who had a quick acridness of manner, addressed her, asking what room she had, and asked the second time in spite of the school-teacher's evident reluctance to hear her. She even, since she sat next to her, nudged her familiarly in her rigid black silk side.

"What room are you in, Miss Stark?" said she.

"I am at a loss how to designate the room," replied Miss Stark stiffly.

"Is it the big southwest room?"

"It evidently faces in that direction," said Miss Stark.

The librarian, whose name was Eliza Lippincott, turned abruptly to Miss Amanda Gill, over whose delicate face a curious color compounded of flush and pallor was stealing.

"What room did your aunt die in, Miss Amanda?" asked she abruptly.

Amanda cast a terrified glance at her sister, who was serving a second plate of pudding for the minister.

"That room," she replied feebly.

"That's what I thought," said the librarian with a certain triumph. "I calculated that must be the room she died in, for it's the best room in the house, and you haven't put anybody in it before. Somehow the room that anybody has died in lately is generally the last room that anybody is put in. I suppose *you* are so strong-minded you don't object to sleeping in a room where anybody died a few weeks ago?" she inquired of Louisa Stark with sharp eyes on her face.

"No, I do not," replied Miss Stark with emphasis.

"Nor in the same bed?" persisted Eliza Lippincott with a kittenish reflection.

The young minister looked up from his pudding. He was very spiritual, but he had had poor pickings in his previous boarding place, and he could not help a certain abstract enjoyment over Miss Gill's cooking.

"You would certainly not be afraid, Miss Lippincott?" he remarked, with his gentle, almost caressing inflection of tone. "You do not for a minute believe that a higher power would allow any manifestation on the part of a disembodied spirit—who we trust is in her heavenly home—to harm one of His servants?"

"Oh, Mr. Dunn, of course not," replied Eliza Lippincott with a blush. "Of course not. I never meant to imply—"

"I could not believe you did," said the minister gently. He was very young, but he already had a wrinkle of permanent anxiety between his eyes and a smile of permanent ingratiation on his lips. The lines of the smile were as deeply marked as the wrinkle.

"Of course dear Miss Harriet Gill was a professing Christian," remarked the widow, "and I don't suppose a professing Christian would come back and scare folks if she could. I wouldn't be a mite afraid to sleep in that room; I'd rather have it than the one I've got. If I was afraid to sleep in a room where a good woman died, I wouldn't tell of it. If I saw things or heard things I'd think the fault must be with my own guilty conscience." Then she turned to Miss Stark. "Any time you feel timid in that room I'm ready and willing to change with you," said she.

"Thank you; I have no desire to change. I am perfectly satisfied with my room," replied Miss Stark with freezing dignity, which was thrown away upon the widow.

"Well," said she, "any time, if you should feel timid, you know what to do. I've got a real nice room; it faces east and gets the morning sun, but it isn't so nice as yours, according to my way of thinking. I'd rather take my chances any day in a room anybody had died in than in one that was hot in summer. I'm more afraid of a sunstroke than of spooks, for my part."

Miss Sophia Gill, who had not spoken one word, but whose mouth had become more and more rigidly compressed, suddenly rose from the table, forcing the minister to leave a little pudding, at which he glanced regretfully.

Miss Louisa Stark did not sit down in the parlor with the other boarders. She went straight to her room. She felt tired after her journey, and meditated a loose wrapper and writing a few letters quietly before she went to bed. Then, too, she was conscious of a feeling that if she delayed, the going there at all might assume more terrifying proportions. She was full of defiance against herself and her own lurking weakness.

So she went resolutely and entered the southwest chamber. There was through the room a soft twilight. She could dimly discern everything, the white satin scroll-work on the wall-paper and the white counterpane on the bed being most evident. Consequently both arrested her attention first. She saw against the wall-paper directly facing the door the waist of her best black satin dress hung over a picture.

"That is very strange," she said to herself, and again a thrill of vague horror came over her.

She knew, or thought she knew, that she had put that black satin dress waist away nicely folded between towels in her trunk. She was very choice of her black satin dress.

She took down the black waist and laid it on the bed preparatory to folding it, but when she attempted to do so she discovered that the two sleeves were firmly sewed together. Louisa Stark stared at the sewed sleeves. "What does this mean?" she asked herself. She examined the sewing carefully; the stitches were small, and even, and firm, of black silk.

She looked around the room. On the stand beside the bed was something which she had not noticed before: a little old-fashioned work-box with a picture of a little boy in a pinafore on the top. Beside this work-box lay, as if just laid down by the user, a spool of black silk, a pair of scissors, and a large steel thimble with a hole in the top, after an old style. Louisa stared at these, then at the sleeves of her dress. She moved toward the door. For a moment she thought that this was something legitimate about which she might demand information; then she became doubtful. Suppose that work-box had been there all the time; suppose she had forgotten; suppose she herself had done this absurd thing, or suppose that she had not, what was to hinder the others from thinking so; what was to hinder a doubt being cast upon her own memory and reasoning powers?

Louisa Stark had been on the verge of a nervous breakdown in spite of her iron constitution and her great will power. No woman can teach school for forty years with absolute impunity. She was more credulous as to her own possible failings than she had ever been in her whole life. She was cold with horror and terror, and yet not so much horror and terror of the supernatural as of her own self. The weakness of belief in the supernatural was nearly impossible for this strong nature. She could more easily believe in her own failing powers.

"I don't know but I'm going to be like Aunt Marcia," she said to herself, and her fat face took on a long rigidity of fear.

She started toward the mirror to unfasten her dress, then she remembered the strange circumstance of the brooch and stopped short. Then she straightened herself defiantly and marched up to the bureau and looked in the glass. She saw reflected therein, fastening the lace at her throat, the old-fashioned thing of a large oval, a knot of fair and black hair under glass, set in a rim of twisted gold. She unfastened it with trembling fingers and looked at it. It was her own brooch, the cluster of pearl grapes on black onyx. Louisa Stark placed the trinket in its little box on the nest of pink cotton and put it away in the bureau drawer. Only death could disturb her habit of order.

Her fingers were so cold they felt fairly numb as she unfastened her dress; she staggered when she slipped it over her head. She went to the closet to hang it up and recoiled. A strong smell of lovage came in her nostrils; a purple gown near the door swung softly against her face as if impelled by some wind from within. All the pegs were filled with garments not her own, mostly of somber black, but there were some strange-patterned silk things and satins.

Suddenly Louisa Stark recovered her nerve. This, she told herself, was something distinctly tangible. Somebody had been taking liberties with her wardrobe. Somebody had been hanging some one else's clothes in her closet. She hastily slipped on her dress again and marched straight down to the parlor. The people were seated there; the widow and the minister were playing backgammon. The librarian was watching them. Miss Amanda Gill was mending beside the large lamp on the center table. They all looked up with amazement as Louisa Stark entered. There was something strange in her expression. She noticed none of them except Amanda.

"Where is your sister?" she asked peremptorily of her.

"She's in the kitchen mixing up bread," Amanda quavered; "is there anything—" But the school-teacher was gone.

She found Sophia Gill standing by the kitchen table kneading dough with dignity. The young girl Flora was bringing some flour from the pantry. She stopped and stared at Miss Stark, and her pretty, delicate young face took on an expression of alarm.

Miss Stark opened at once upon the subject in her mind.

"Miss Gill," said she, with her utmost school-teacher manner, "I wish to inquire why you have had my own clothes removed from the closet in my room and others substituted?"

Sophia Gill stood with her hands fast in the dough, regarding her. Her own face paled slowly and reluctantly, her mouth stiffened.

"What? I don't quite understand what you mean, Miss Stark," said she.

"My clothes are not in the closet in my room and it is full of things which do not belong to me," said Louisa Stark.

"Bring me that flour," said Sophia sharply to the young girl, who obeyed, casting timid, startled glances at Miss Stark as she passed her. Sophia Gill began rubbing her hands clear of the dough. "I am sure I know nothing about it," she said with a certain tempered asperity. "Do you know anything about it, Flora?"

"Oh, no, I don't know anything about it, Aunt Sophia," answered the young girl, fluttering.

Then Sophia turned to Miss Stark. "I'll go upstairs with you, Miss Stark," said she, "and see what the trouble is. There must be some mistake." She spoke stiffly with constrained civility.

"Very well," said Miss Stark with dignity. Then she and Miss Sophia went upstairs. Flora stood staring after them.

Sophia and Louisa Stark went up to the southwest chamber. The closet door was shut. Sophia threw it open, then she looked at Miss Stark. On the pegs hung the school-teacher's own garments in ordinary array.

"I can't see that there is anything wrong," remarked Sophia grimly.

Miss Stark strove to speak but she could not. She sank down on the nearest chair. She did not even attempt to defend herself. She saw her own clothes in the closet. She knew there had been no time for any human being to remove those which she thought she had seen and put hers in their places. She knew it was impossible. Again the awful horror of herself overwhelmed her.

"You must have been mistaken," she heard Sophia say.

She muttered something, she scarcely knew what. Sophia then went out of the room. Presently she undressed and went to bed. In the morning she did not go down to breakfast, and when Sophia came to inquire, requested that the stage be ordered for the noon train. She said that she was sorry, but was ill, and feared lest she might be worse, and she felt that she must return home at once. She looked ill, and could not take even the toast and tea which Sophia had prepared for her. Sophia felt a certain pity for her, but it was largely mixed with indignation. She felt that she knew the true reason for the school-teacher's illness and sudden departure, and it incensed her.

"If folks are going to act like fools we shall never be able to keep this house," she said to Amanda after Miss Stark had gone; and Amanda knew what she meant.

Directly the widow, Mrs. Elvira Simmons, knew that the school-teacher had gone and the southwest room was vacant, she begged to have it in exchange for her own. Sophia hesitated a moment; she eyed the widow sharply. There was something about the large, roseate face worn in firm lines of humor and decision which reassured her.

"I have no objection, Mrs. Simmons," said she, "if—"

"If what?" asked the widow.

"If you have common sense enough not to keep fussing because the room happens to be the one my aunt died in," said Sophia bluntly.

"Fiddlesticks!" said the widow, Mrs. Elvira Simmons.

That very afternoon she moved into the southwest chamber. The young girl Flora assisted her, though much against her will.

"Now I want you to carry Mrs. Simmons' dresses into the closet in that room and hang them up nicely, and see that she has everything she wants," said Sophia Gill. "And you can change the bed and put on fresh sheets. What are you looking at me that way for?"

"Oh, Aunt Sophia, can't I do something else?"

"What do you want to do something else for?"

"I am afraid."

"Afraid of what? I should think you'd hang your head. No; you go right in there and do what I tell you."

Pretty soon Flora came running into the sitting-room where Sophia was, as pale as death, and in her hand she held a queer, old-fashioned frilled nightcap.

"What's that?" demanded Sophia.

"I found it under the pillow."

"What pillow?"

"In the southwest room."

Sophia took it and looked at it sternly.

"It's Great-aunt Harriet's," said Flora faintly.

"You run down street and do that errand at the grocer's for me and I'll see that room," said Sophia with dignity. She carried the nightcap away and put it in the trunk in the garret where she had supposed it stored with the rest of the dead woman's belongings. Then she went into the southwest chamber and made the bed and assisted Mrs. Simmons to move, and there was no further incident.

The widow was openly triumphant over her new room. She talked a deal about it at the dinner-table.

"It is the best room in the house, and I expect you all to be envious of me," said she.

"And you are sure you don't feel afraid of ghosts?" said the librarian.

"Ghosts!" repeated the widow with scorn. "If a ghost comes I'll send her over to you. You are just across the hall from the southwest room."

"You needn't," returned Eliza Lippincott with a shudder. "I wouldn't sleep in that room, after—" she checked herself with an eye on the minister.

"After what?" asked the widow.

"Nothing," replied Eliza Lippincott in an embarrassed fashion.

"I trust Miss Lippincott has too good sense and too great faith to believe in anything of that sort," said the minister.

"I trust so, too," replied Eliza hurriedly.

"You did see or hear something—now what was it, I want to know?" said the widow that evening when they were alone in the parlor. The minister had gone to make a call.

Eliza hesitated.

"What was it?" insisted the widow.

"Well," said Eliza hesitatingly, "if you'll promise not to tell."

"Yes, I promise; what was it?"

"Well, one day last week, just before the school-teacher came, I went in that room to see if there were any clouds. I wanted to wear my gray dress, and I was afraid it was going to rain, so I wanted to look at the sky at all points, so I went in there, and—"

"And what?"

"Well, you know that chintz over the bed, and the valance, and the easy chair; what pattern should you say it was?"

"Why, peacocks on a blue ground. Good land, I shouldn't think any one who had ever seen that would forget it."

"Peacocks on a blue ground, you are sure?"

"Of course I am. Why?"

"Only when I went in there that afternoon it was not peacocks on a blue ground; it was great red roses on a yellow
ground."

"Why, what do you mean?"

"What I say."

"Did Miss Sophia have it changed?"

"No. I went in there again an hour later and the peacocks
were there."

"You didn't see straight the first time."

"I expected you would say that."

"The peacocks are there now; I saw them just now."

"Yes, I suppose so; I suppose they flew back."

"But they couldn't."

"Looks as if they did."

"Why, how could such a thing be? It couldn't be."

"Well, all I know is those peacocks were gone for an hour
that afternoon and the red roses on the yellow ground were
there instead."

The widow stared at her a moment, then she began to laugh
rather hysterically.

"Well," said she, "I guess I sha'n't give up my nice room for
any such tomfoolery as that. I guess I would just as soon have red
roses on a yellow ground as peacocks on a blue; but there's no
use talking, you couldn't have seen straight. How could such a
thing have happened?"

"I don't know," said Eliza Lippincott; "but I know I wouldn't
sleep in that room if you'd give me a thousand dollars."

"Well, I would," said the widow, "and I'm going to."

When Mrs. Simmons went to the southwest chamber that night
she cast a glance at the bed-hanging and the easy chair. There

208

were the peacocks on the blue ground. She gave a contemptuous thought to Eliza Lippincott.

"I don't believe but she's getting nervous," she thought. "I wonder if any of her family have been out at all."

But just before Mrs. Simmons was ready to get into bed she looked again at the hangings and the easy chair, and there were the red roses on the yellow ground instead of the peacocks on the blue. She looked long and sharply. Then she shut her eyes, and then opened them and looked. She still saw the red roses. Then she crossed the room, turned her back to the bed, and looked out at the night from the south window. It was clear and the full moon was shining. She watched it a moment sailing over the dark blue in its nimbus of gold. Then she looked around at the bed hangings. She still saw the red roses on the yellow ground.

Mrs. Simmons was struck in her most venerable point. This apparent contradiction of the reasonable as manifested in such a commonplace thing as chintz of a bed-hanging affected this ordinarily unimaginative woman as no ghostly appearance could have done. Those red roses on the yellow ground were to her much more ghostly than any strange figure clad in the white robes of the grave entering the room.

She took a step toward the door, then she turned with a resolute air. "As for going downstairs and owning up I'm scared and having that Lippincott girl crowing over me, I won't for any red roses instead of peacocks. I guess they can't hurt me, and as long as we've both of us seen 'em I guess we can't both be getting loony," she said.

Mrs. Elvira Simmons blew out her light and got into bed and lay staring out between the chintz hangings at the moon-lit room. She said her prayers in bed always as being more comfortable, and presumably just as acceptable in the case of a faithful servant with a stout habit of body. Then after a little she fell asleep; she was of too practical a nature to be kept long awake by anything which had no power of actual bodily effect upon her. No stress of the spirit had ever disturbed her slumbers. So she slumbered between the red roses, or the peacocks, she did not know which.

But she was awakened about midnight by a strange sensation in her throat. She had dreamed that some one with long white fingers was strangling her, and she saw bending over her the face of an old woman in a white cap. When she waked there was no old woman, the room was almost as light as day in the full moonlight, and looked very peaceful; but the strangling sensation at her throat continued, and besides that, her face and ears felt muffled. She put up her hand and felt that her head was covered with a ruffled nightcap tied under her chin so tightly that it was exceedingly uncomfortable. A great qualm of horror shot over her. She tore the thing off frantically and flung it from her with a convulsive effort as if it had been a spider. She gave, as she did so, a quick, short scream of terror. She sprang out of bed and was going toward the door, when she stopped.

It had suddenly occurred to her that Eliza Lippincott might have entered the room and tied on the cap while she was asleep. She had not locked her door. She looked in the closet, under the bed; there was no one there. Then she tried to open the door, but to her astonishment found that it was locked—bolted on the inside. "I must have locked it, after all," she reflected with wonder, for she never locked her door. Then she could scarcely conceal from herself that there was something out of the usual about it all. Certainly no one could have entered the room and departed locking the door on the inside. She could not control the long shiver of horror that crept over her, but she was still resolute. She resolved that she would throw the cap out of the window. "I'll see if I have tricks like that played on me, I don't care who does it," said she quite aloud. She was still unable to believe wholly in the supernatural. The idea of some human agency was still in her mind, filling her with anger.

She went toward the spot where she had thrown the cap— she had stepped over it on her way to the door—but it was not there. She searched the whole room, lighting her lamp, but she could not find the cap. Finally she gave it up. She extinguished her lamp and went back to bed. She fell asleep again, to be again awakened in the same fashion. That time she tore off the cap as before, but she did not fling it on the floor as before. Instead she held to it with a fierce grip. Her blood was up.

Holding fast to the white flimsy thing, she sprang out of bed, ran to the window which was open, slipped the screen, and flung it out; but a sudden gust of wind, though the night was calm, arose and it floated back in her face. She brushed it aside like a cobweb and she clutched at it. She was actually furious. It eluded her clutching fingers. Then she did not see it at all. She examined the floor, she lighted her lamp again and searched, but there was no sign of it.

Mrs. Simmons was then in such a rage that all terror had disappeared for the time. She did not know with what she was angry, but she had a sense of some mocking presence which was silently proving too strong against her weakness, and she was aroused to the utmost power of resistance. To be baffled like this and resisted by something which was as nothing to her straining senses filled her with intensest resentment.

Finally she got back into bed again; she did not go to sleep. She felt strangely drowsy, but she fought against it. She was wide awake, staring at the moonlight, when she suddenly felt the soft white strings of the thing tighten around her throat and realized that her enemy was again upon her. She seized the strings, untied them, twitched off the cap, ran with it to the table where her scissors lay and furiously cut it into small bits. She cut and tore, feeling an insane fury of gratification.

"There!" said she quite aloud. "I guess I sha'n't have any more trouble with this old cap."

She tossed the bits of muslin into a basket and went back to bed. Almost immediately she felt the soft strings tighten around her throat. Then at last she yielded, vanquished. This new refutal of all laws of reason by which she had learned, as it were, to spell her theory of life, was too much for her equilibrium. She pulled off the clinging strings feebly, drew the thing from her head, slid weakly out of bed, caught up her wrapper and hastened out of the room. She went noiselessly along the hall to her own old room: she entered, got into her familiar bed, and lay there the rest of the night shuddering and listening, and if she dozed, waking with a start at the feeling of the pressure upon her throat to find that it was not there, yet still to be unable to shake off entirely the horror.

When daylight came she crept back to the southwest chamber and hurriedly got some clothes in which to dress herself. It took all her resolution to enter the room, but nothing unusual happened while she was there. She hastened back to her old chamber, dressed herself and went down to breakfast with an imperturbable face. Her color had not faded. When asked by Eliza Lippincott how she had slept, she replied with an appearance of calmness which was bewildering that she had not slept very well. She never did sleep very well in a new bed, and she thought she would go back to her old room.

Eliza Lippincott was not deceived, however, neither were the Gill sisters, nor the young girl, Flora. Eliza Lippincott spoke out bluntly.

"You needn't talk to me about sleeping well," said she. "I know something queer happened in that room last night by the way you act."

They all looked at Mrs. Simmons, inquiringly—the librarian with malicious curiosity and triumph, the minister with sad incredulity, Sophia Gill with fear and indignation, Amanda and the young girl with unmixed terror. The widow bore herself with dignity.

"I saw nothing nor heard nothing which I trust could not have been accounted for in some rational manner," said she.

"What was it?" persisted Eliza Lippincott.

"I do not wish to discuss the matter any further," replied Mrs. Simmons shortly. Then she passed her plate for more creamed potato. She felt that she would die before she confessed to the ghastly absurdity of that nightcap, or to having been disturbed by the flight of peacocks off a blue field of chintz after she had scoffed at the possibility of such a thing. She left the whole matter so vague that in a fashion she came off the mistress of the situation. She at all events impressed everybody by her coolness in the face of no one knew what nightly terror.

After breakfast, with the assistance of Amanda and Flora, she moved back into her old room. Scarcely a word was spoken during the process of moving, but they all worked with trembling haste and looked guilty when they met one another's eyes, as if conscious of betraying a common fear.

That afternoon the young minister, John Dunn, went to Sophia Gill and requested permission to occupy the southwest chamber that night.

"I don't ask to have my effects moved there," said he, "for I could scarcely afford a room so much superior to the one I now occupy, but I would like, if you please, to sleep there tonight for the purpose of refuting in my own person any unfortunate superstition which may have obtained root here."

Sophia Gill thanked the minister gratefully and eagerly accepted his offer.

"How anybody with common sense can believe for a minute in any such nonsense passes my comprehension," said she.

"It certainly passes mine how anybody with Christian faith can believe in ghosts," said the minister gently, and Sophia Gill felt a certain feminine contentment in hearing him. The minister was a child to her; she regarded him with no tincture of sentiment, and yet she loved to hear two other women covertly condemned by him and she herself thereby exalted.

That night about twelve o'clock the Reverend John Dunn essayed to go to his nightly slumber in the southwest chamber. He had been sitting up until that hour preparing his sermon.

He traversed the hall with a little night-lamp in his hand, opened the door of the southwest chamber, and essayed to enter. He might as well have essayed to enter the solid side of a house. He could not believe his senses. The door was certainly open; he could look into the room full of soft lights and shadows under the moonlight which streamed into the windows. He could see the bed in which he had expected to pass the night, but he could not enter. Whenever he strove to do so he had a curious sensation as if he were trying to press against an invisible person who met him with a force of opposition impossible to overcome. The minister was not an athletic man, yet he had considerable strength. He squared his elbows, set his mouth hard, and strove to push his way through into the room. The opposition which he met was as sternly and mutely terrible as the rocky fastness of a mountain in his way.

For a half hour John Dunn, doubting, raging, overwhelmed with spiritual agony as to the state of his own soul rather than fear, strove to enter that southwest chamber. He was simply powerless against this uncanny obstacle. Finally a great horror as of evil itself came over him. He was a nervous man and very young. He fairly fled to his own chamber and locked himself in like a terror-stricken girl.

The next morning he went to Miss Gill and told her frankly what had happened, and begged her to say nothing about it lest he should have injured the cause by the betrayal of such weakness, for he actually had come to believe that there was something wrong with the room.

"What it is I know not, Miss Sophia," said he, "but I firmly believe, against my will, that there is in that room some accursed evil power at work, of which modern faith and modern science know nothing."

Miss Sophia Gill listened with grimly lowering face. She had an inborn respect for the clergy, but she was bound to hold that southwest chamber in the dearly beloved old house of her fathers free of blame.

"I think I will sleep in that room myself tonight," she said, when the minister had finished.

He looked at her in doubt and dismay.

"I have great admiration for your faith and courage, Miss Sophia," he said, "but are you wise?"

"I am fully resolved to sleep in that room tonight," said she conclusively. There were occasions when Miss Sophia Gill could put on a manner of majesty, and she did now.

It was ten o'clock that night when Sophia Gill entered the southwest chamber. She had told her sister what she intended doing and had been proof against her tearful entreaties. Amanda was charged not to tell the young girl, Flora.

"There is no use in frightening that child over nothing," said Sophia.

Sophia, when she entered the southwest chamber, set the lamp which she carried on the bureau, and began moving about the room, pulling down the curtains, taking off the nice white counterpane of the bed, and preparing generally for the night.

As she did so, moving with great coolness and deliberation, she became conscious that she was thinking some thoughts that were foreign to her. She began remembering what she could not have remembered, since she was not then born: the trouble over her mother's marriage, the bitter opposition, the shutting the door upon her, the ostracizing her from heart and home. She became aware of a most singular sensation as of bitter resentment herself, and not against the mother and sister who had so treated her own mother, but against her own mother, and then she became aware of a like bitterness extended to her own self. She felt malignant toward her mother as a young girl whom she remembered, though she could not have remembered, and she felt malignant toward her own self, and her sister Amanda, and Flora. Evil suggestions surged in her brain—suggestions which turned her heart to stone and which still fascinated her. And all the time by a sort of double consciousness she knew that what she thought was strange and not due to her own volition. She knew that she was thinking the thoughts of some other person, and she knew who. She felt herself possessed.

But there was tremendous strength in the woman's nature. She had inherited strength for good and righteous self-assertion, from the evil strength of her ancestors. They had turned their own weapons against themselves. She made an effort which seemed almost mortal, but was conscious that the hideous thing was gone from her. She thought her own thoughts. Then she scouted to herself the idea of anything supernatural about the terrific experience. "I am imagining everything," she told herself. She went on with her preparations; she went to the bureau to take down her hair. She looked in the glass and saw, instead of her softly parted waves of hair, harsh lines of iron-gray under the black borders of an old-fashioned head-dress. She saw instead of her smooth, broad forehead, a high one wrinkled with the intensest concentration of selfish reflections of a long life; she saw instead of her steady blue eyes, black ones with depths of malignant reserve, behind a broad meaning of ill will; she saw instead of her firm, benevolent mouth one with a hard, thin line, a network of melancholic wrinkles. She saw instead of her own face, middle-aged and good to see, the expression of a life of honesty and good will to others and patience under trials, the face of a very old woman scowling forever with unceasing hatred and misery at herself and all others, at life, and death, at that which had been and that which was to come. She saw instead of her own face in the glass, the face of her dead Aunt Harriet, topping her own shoulders in her own well-known dress!

Sophia Gill left the room. She went into the one which she shared with her sister Amanda. Amanda looked up and saw her standing there. She had set the lamp on a table, and she stood holding a handkerchief over her face. Amanda looked at her with terror.

"What is it? What is it, Sophia?" she gasped.

Sophia still stood with the handkerchief pressed to her face.

"Oh, Sophia, let me call somebody. Is your face hurt? Sophia, what is the matter with your face?" fairly shrieked Amanda.

Suddenly Sophia took the handkerchief from her face.

"Look at me, Amanda Gill," she said in an awful voice.

Amanda looked, shrinking.

"What is it? Oh, what is it? You don't look hurt. What is it, Sophia?"

"What do you see?"

"Why, I see you."

"Me?"

"Yes, you. What did you think I would see?"

Sophia Gill looked at her sister.

"Never as long as I live will I tell you what I thought you would see, and you must never ask me," said she.

"Well, I never will, Sophia," replied Amanda, half weeping with terror.

"You won't try to sleep in that room again, Sophia?"

"No," said Sophia; "and I am going to sell this house."

THE LOST GHOST

rs. John Emerson, sitting with her needlework beside the window, looked out and saw Mrs. Rhoda Meserve coming down the street, and knew at once by the trend of her steps and the cant of her head that she meditated turning in at her gate. She also knew by a certain something about her general carriage—a thrusting forward of the neck, a bustling hitch of the shoulders—that she had important news. Rhoda Meserve always had the news as soon as the news was in being, and generally Mrs. John Emerson was the first to whom she imparted it. The two women had been friends ever since Mrs. Meserve had married Simon Meserve and come to the village to live.

Mrs. Meserve was a pretty woman, moving with graceful flirts of ruffling skirts; her clear-cut, nervous face, as delicately tinted as a shell, looked brightly from the plumy brim of a black hat at Mrs. Emerson in the window. Mrs. Emerson was glad to see her coming. She returned the greeting with enthusiasm, then rose hurriedly, ran into the cold parlor and brought out one of the best rocking-chairs. She was just in time, after drawing it up beside the opposite window, to greet her friend at the door.

"Good-afternoon," said she. "I declare, I'm real glad to see you. I've been alone all day. John went to the city this morning. I thought of coming over to your house this afternoon, but I couldn't bring my sewing very well. I am putting the ruffles on my new black dress skirt."

"Well, I didn't have a thing on hand except my crochet work," responded Mrs. Meserve, "and I thought I'd just run over a few minutes."

"I'm real glad you did," repeated Mrs. Emerson. "Take your things right off. Here, I'll put them on my bed in the bedroom. Take the rocking-chair."

Mrs. Meserve settled herself in the parlor rocking-chair, while Mrs. Emerson carried her shawl and hat into the little adjoining bedroom. When she returned Mrs. Meserve was rocking peacefully and was already at work hooking blue wool in and out.

"That's real pretty," said Mrs. Emerson.

"Yes, I think it's pretty," replied Mrs. Meserve.

"I suppose it's for the church fair?"

"Yes. I don't suppose it'll bring enough to pay for the worsted, let alone the work, but I suppose I've got to make something."

"How much did that one you made for the fair last year bring?"

"Twenty-five cents."

"It's wicked, ain't it?"

"I rather guess it is. It takes me a week every minute I can get to make one. I wish those that bought such things for twenty-five cents had to make them. Guess they'd sing another song. Well, I suppose I oughtn't to complain as long as it is for the Lord, but sometimes it does seem as if the Lord didn't get much out of it."

"Well, it's pretty work," said Mrs. Emerson, sitting down at the opposite window and taking up her dress skirt.

"Yes, it is real pretty work. I just *love* to crochet."

The two women rocked and sewed and crocheted in silence for two or three minutes. They were both waiting. Mrs. Meserve waited for the other's curiosity to develop in order that her news might have, as it were, a befitting stage entrance. Mrs. Emerson waited for the news. Finally she could wait no longer.

"Well, what's the news?" said she.

"Well, I don't know as there's anything very particular," hedged the other woman, prolonging the situation.

"Yes, there is; you can't cheat me," replied Mrs. Emerson.

"Now, how do you know?"

"By the way you look."

Mrs. Meserve laughed consciously and rather vainly.

"Well, Simon says my face is so expressive I can't hide anything more than five minutes no matter how hard I try," said she. "Well, there is some news. Simon came home with it this noon. He heard it in South Dayton. He had some business over there this morning. The old Sargent place is let."

Mrs. Emerson dropped her sewing and stared.

"You don't say so!"

"Yes, it is."

"Who to?"

"Why, some folks from Boston that moved to South Dayton last year. They haven't been satisfied with the house they had there—it wasn't large enough. The man has got considerable property and can afford to live pretty well. He's got a wife and his unmarried sister in the family. The sister's got money, too. He does business in Boston and it's just as easy to get to Boston from here as from South Dayton, and so they're coming here. You know the old Sargent house is a splendid place."

"Yes, it's the handsomest house in town, but—"

"Oh, Simon said they told him about that and he just laughed. Said he wasn't afraid and neither was his wife and sister. Said he'd risk ghosts rather than little tucked-up sleeping-rooms without any sun, like they've had in the Dayton house. Said he'd rather risk *seeing* ghosts, than risk being ghosts themselves. Simon said they said he was a great hand to joke."

"Oh, well," said Mrs. Emerson, "it is a beautiful house, and maybe there isn't anything in those stories. It never seemed to me they came very straight anyway. I never took much stock in them. All I thought was—if his wife was nervous."

"Nothing in creation would hire me to go into a house that I'd ever heard a word against of that kind," declared Mrs. Meserve with emphasis. "I wouldn't go into that house if they would give me the rent. I've seen enough of haunted houses to last me as long as I live."

Mrs. Emerson's face acquired the expression of a hunting hound.

"Have you?" she asked in an intense whisper.

"Yes, I have. I don't want any more of it."

"Before you came here?"

"Yes; before I was married—when I was quite a girl."

Mrs. Meserve had not married young. Mrs. Emerson had mental calculations when she heard that.

"Did you really live in a house that was—" she whispered fearfully.

Mrs. Meserve nodded solemnly.

"Did you really ever—see—anything—"

Mrs. Meserve nodded.

"You didn't see anything that did you any harm?"

"No, I didn't see anything that did me harm looking at it in one way, but it don't do anybody in this world any good to see things that haven't any business to be seen in it. You never get over it."

There was a moment's silence. Mrs. Emerson's features seemed to sharpen.

"Well, of course I don't want to urge you," said she, "if you don't feel like talking about it; but maybe it might do you good to tell it out, if it's on your mind, worrying you."

"I try to put it out of my mind," said Mrs. Meserve.

"Well, it's just as you feel."

"I never told anybody but Simon," said Mrs. Meserve. "I never felt as if it was wise perhaps. I didn't know what folks might think. So many don't believe in anything they can't understand, that they might think my mind wasn't right. Simon advised me not to talk about it. He said he didn't believe it was anything supernatural, but he had to own up that he couldn't give any explanation for it to save his life. He had to own up that he didn't believe anybody could. Then he said he wouldn't talk about it. He said lots of folks would sooner tell folks my head wasn't right than to own up they couldn't see through it."

"I'm sure I wouldn't say so," returned Mrs. Emerson reproachfully. "You know better than that, I hope."

"Yes, I do," replied Mrs. Meserve. "I know you wouldn't say so."

"And I wouldn't tell it to a soul if you didn't want me to."

"Well, I'd rather you wouldn't."

"I won't speak of it even to Mr. Emerson."

"I'd rather you wouldn't even to him."

"I won't."

Mrs. Emerson took up her dress skirt again; Mrs. Meserve hooked up another loop of blue wool. Then she begun:

"Of course," said she, "I ain't going to say positively that I believe or disbelieve in ghosts, but all I tell you is what I saw. I can't explain it. I don't pretend I can, for I can't. If you can, well and good; I shall be glad, for it will stop tormenting me as it has done and always will otherwise. There hasn't been a day nor a night since it happened that I haven't thought of it, and always I have felt the shivers go down my back when I did."

"That's an awful feeling," Mrs. Emerson said.

"Ain't it? Well, it happened before I was married, when I was a girl and lived in East Wilmington. It was the first year I lived there. You know my family all died five years before that. I told you."

Mrs. Emerson nodded.

"Well, I went there to teach school, and I went to board with a Mrs. Amelia Dennison and her sister, Mrs. Bird. Abby, her name was—Abby Bird. She was a widow; she had never had any children. She had a little money—Mrs. Dennison didn't have any—and she had come to East Wilmington and bought the house they lived in. It was a real pretty house, though it was very old and run down. It had cost Mrs. Bird a good deal to put it in order. I guess that was the reason they took me to board. I guess they thought it would help along a little. I guess what I paid for my board about kept us all in victuals. Mrs. Bird had enough to live on if they were careful, but she had spent so much fixing up the old house that they must have been a little pinched for awhile.

"Anyhow, they took me to board, and I thought I was pretty lucky to get in there. I had a nice room, big and sunny and furnished pretty, the paper and paint all new, and everything as neat as wax. Mrs. Dennison was one of the best cooks I ever saw, and I had a little stove in my room, and there was always a nice fire there when I got home from school. I thought I hadn't been in such a nice place since I lost my own home, until I had been there about three weeks.

"I had been there about three weeks before I found it out, though I guess it had been going on ever since they had been in the house, and that was most four months. They hadn't said anything about it, and I didn't wonder, for there they had just bought the house and been to so much expense and trouble fixing it up.

"Well, I went there in September. I begun my school the first Monday. I remember it was a real cold fall, there was a frost the middle of September, and I had to put on my winter coat. I remember when I came home that night (let me see, I began school on a Monday, and that was two weeks from the next Thursday), I took off my coat downstairs and laid it on the table in the front entry. It was a real nice coat—heavy black broadcloth trimmed with fur; I had had it the winter before. Mrs. Bird called after me as I went upstairs that I ought not to leave it in the front entry for fear somebody might come in and take it, but I only laughed and called back to her that I wasn't afraid. I never was much afraid of burglars.

"Well, though it was hardly the middle of September, it was a real cold night. I remember my room faced west, and the sun was getting low, and the sky was a pale yellow and purple, just as you see it sometimes in the winter when there is going to be a cold snap. I rather think that was the night the frost came the first time. I know Mrs. Dennison covered up some flowers she had in the front yard, anyhow. I remember looking out and seeing an old green plaid shawl of hers over the verbena bed. There was a fire in my little wood-stove. Mrs. Bird made it, I know. She was a real motherly sort of woman; she always seemed to be the happiest when she was doing something to make other folks happy and comfortable. Mrs. Dennison told me she had always been so. She said she had coddled her husband within an inch of his life. 'It's lucky Abby never had any children,' she said, 'for she would have spoilt them.'

"Well, that night I sat down beside my nice little fire and ate an apple. There was a plate of nice apples on my table. Mrs. Bird put them there. I was always very fond of apples. Well, I sat down and ate an apple, and was having a beautiful time, and thinking how lucky I was to have got board in such a place with such nice folks, when I heard a queer little sound at my door. It was such a little hesitating sort of sound that it sounded more like a fumble than a knock, as if some one very timid, with very little hands, was feeling along the door, not quite daring to knock. For a minute I thought it was a mouse. But I waited and it came again, and then I made up my mind it was a knock, but a very little scared one, so I said, 'Come in.'

"But nobody came in, and then presently I heard the knock again. Then I got up and opened the door, thinking it was very queer, and I had a frightened feeling without knowing why.

"Well, I opened the door, and the first thing I noticed was a draft of cold air, as if the front door downstairs was open, but there was a strange close smell about the cold draft. It smelled more like a cellar that had been shut up for years, than out-of-doors. Then I saw something. I saw my coat first. The thing that held it was so small that I couldn't see much of anything else. Then I saw a little white face with eyes so scared and wishful that they seemed as if they might eat a hole in anybody's heart. It was a dreadful little face, with something about it which made it different from any other face on earth, but it was so pitiful that somehow it did away a good deal with the dreadfulness. And there were two little hands spotted purple with the cold, holding up my winter coat, and a strange little far-away voice said: 'I can't find my mother.'

"'For Heaven's sake,' I said, 'who are you?'

"Then the little voice said again: 'I can't find my mother.'

"All the time I could smell the cold and I saw that it was about the child; that cold was clinging to her as if she had come out of some deadly cold place. Well, I took my coat, I did not know what else to do, and the cold was clinging to that. It was as cold as if it had come off ice. When I had the coat I could see the child more plainly. She was dressed in one little white garment made very simply. It was a nightgown, only very long, quite covering her feet, and I could see dimly through it her little thin body mottled purple with the cold. Her face did not look so cold; that was a clear waxen white. Her hair was dark, but it looked as if it might be dark only because it was so damp, almost wet, and might really be light hair. It clung very close to her forehead, which was round and white. She would have been very beautiful if she had not been so dreadful.

"'Who are you?' says I again, looking at her.

"She looked at me with her terrible pleading eyes and did not say anything.

"'What are you?' says I. Then she went away. She did not seem to run or walk like other children. She flitted, like one of those little filmy white butterflies, that don't seem like real ones they are so light, and move as if they had no weight. But she looked back from the head of the stairs. 'I can't find my mother,' said she, and I never heard such a voice.

"'Who is your mother?' says I, but she was gone.

"Well, I thought for a moment I should faint away. The room got dark and I heard a singing in my ears. Then I flung my coat onto the bed. My hands were as cold as ice from holding it, and I stood in my door, and called first Mrs. Bird and then Mrs.

Dennison. I didn't dare go down over the stairs where that had gone. It seemed to me I should go mad if I didn't see somebody or something like other folks on the face of the earth. I thought I should never make anybody hear, but I could hear them stepping about downstairs, and I could smell biscuits baking for supper. Somehow the smell of those biscuits seemed the only natural thing left to keep me in my right mind. I didn't dare go over those stairs. I just stood there and called, and finally I heard the entry door open and Mrs. Bird called back:

"'What is it? Did you call, Miss Arms?'

"'Come up here; come up here as quick as you can, both of you,' I screamed out; 'quick, quick, quick!'

"I heard Mrs. Bird tell Mrs. Dennison: 'Come quick, Amelia, something is the matter in Miss Arms' room.' It struck me even then that she expressed herself rather queerly, and it struck me as very queer, indeed, when they both got upstairs and I saw that they knew what had happened, or that they knew of what nature the happening was.

"'What is it, dear?' asked Mrs. Bird, and her pretty, loving voice had a strained sound. I saw her look at Mrs. Dennison and I saw Mrs. Dennison look back at her.

"'For God's sake,' says I, and I never spoke so before—'for God's sake, what was it brought my coat upstairs?'

"'What was it like?' asked Mrs. Dennison in a sort of failing voice, and she looked at her sister again and her sister looked back at her.

"'It was a child I have never seen here before. It looked like a child,' says I, 'but I never saw a child so dreadful, and it had on a nightgown, and said she couldn't find her mother. Who was it? What was it?'

"I thought for a minute Mrs. Dennison was going to faint, but Mrs. Bird hung onto her and rubbed her hands, and whispered in her ear (she had the cooingest kind of voice), and I ran and got her a glass of cold water. I tell you it took considerable courage to go downstairs alone, but they had set a lamp on the entry table so I could see. I don't believe I could have spunked up enough to have gone downstairs in the dark, thinking every second that child might be close to me. The lamp and the smell of the biscuits baking seemed to sort of keep my courage up, but I tell you I didn't waste much time going down those stairs and out into the kitchen for a glass of water. I pumped as if the house was afire, and I grabbed the first thing I came across in the shape of a tumbler: it was a painted one that Mrs. Dennison's Sunday school class gave her, and it was meant for a flower vase.

"Well, I filled it and then ran upstairs. I felt every minute as if something would catch my feet, and I held the glass to Mrs. Dennison's lips, while Mrs. Bird held her head up, and she took a good long swallow, then she looked hard at the tumbler.

"'Yes,' says I, 'I know I got this one, but I took the first I came across, and it isn't hurt a mite.'

"'Don't get the painted flowers wet,' says Mrs. Dennison very feebly, 'they'll wash off if you do.'

"'I'll be real careful,' says I. I knew she set a sight by that painted tumbler.

"The water seemed to do Mrs. Dennison good, for presently she pushed Mrs. Bird away and sat up. She had been laying down on my bed.

"'I'm all over it now,' says she, but she was terribly white, and her eyes looked as if they saw something outside things. Mrs. Bird wasn't much better, but she always had a sort of settled sweet, good look that nothing could disturb to any great extent. I knew I looked dreadful, for I caught a glimpse of myself in the glass, and I would hardly have known who it was.

"Mrs. Dennison, she slid off the bed and walked sort of tottery to a chair. 'I was silly to give way so,' says she.

"'No, you wasn't silly, sister,' says Mrs. Bird. 'I don't know what this means any more than you do, but whatever it is, no one ought to be called silly for being overcome by anything so different from other things which we have known all our lives.'

"Mrs. Dennison looked at her sister, then she looked at me, then back at her sister again, and Mrs. Bird spoke as if she had been asked a question.

"'Yes,' says she, 'I do think Miss Arms ought to be told—that is, I think she ought to be told all we know ourselves.'

"'That isn't much,' said Mrs. Dennison with a dying-away sort of sigh. She looked as if she might faint away again any minute. She was a real delicate-looking woman, but it turned out she was a good deal stronger than poor Mrs. Bird.

"'No, there isn't much we do know,' says Mrs. Bird, 'but what little there is she ought to know. I felt as if she ought to when she first came here.'

"'Well, I didn't feel quite right about it,' said Mrs. Dennison, 'but I kept hoping it might stop, and any way, that it might never trouble her, and you had put so much in the house, and we needed the money, and I didn't know but she might be nervous and think she couldn't come, and I didn't want to take a man boarder.'

"'And aside from the money, we were very anxious to have you come, my dear,' says Mrs. Bird.

"'Yes,' says Mrs. Dennison, 'we wanted the young company in the house; we were lonesome, and we both of us took a great liking to you the minute we set eyes on you.'

"And I guess they meant what they said, both of them. They were beautiful women, and nobody could be any kinder to me than they were, and I never blamed them for not telling me before, and, as they said, there wasn't really much to tell.

"They hadn't any sooner fairly bought the house, and moved into it, than they began to see and hear things. Mrs. Bird said they were sitting together in the sitting-room one evening when they heard it the first time. She said her sister was knitting lace (Mrs. Dennison made beautiful knitted lace) and she was reading the *Missionary Herald* (Mrs. Bird was very much interested in mission work), when all of a sudden they heard something. She heard it first and she laid down her *Missionary Herald* and listened, and then Mrs. Dennison she saw her listening and she drops her lace. 'What is it you are listening to, Abby?' says she. Then it came again and they both heard, and the cold shivers went down their backs to hear it, though they didn't know why. 'It's the cat, isn't it?' says Mrs. Bird.

"'It isn't any cat,' says Mrs. Dennison.

"'Oh, I guess it *must* be the cat; maybe she's got a mouse,' says Mrs. Bird, real cheerful, to calm down Mrs. Dennison, for she saw she was 'most scared to death, and she was always afraid of her fainting away. Then she opens the door and calls, 'Kitty, kitty, kitty!' They had brought their cat with them in a basket when they came to East Wilmington to live. It was a real handsome tiger cat, a tommy, and he knew a lot.

"Well, she called 'Kitty, kitty, kitty!' and sure enough the kitty came, and when he came in the door he gave a big yawl that didn't sound unlike what they had heard.

"'There, sister, here he is; you see it was the cat,' says Mrs. Bird. 'Poor kitty!'

"But Mrs. Dennison she eyed the cat, and she give a great screech.

"'What's that? What's that?' says she.

"'What's what?' says Mrs. Bird, pretending to herself that she didn't see what her sister meant.

"'Something's got hold of that cat's tail,' says Mrs. Dennison. 'Somethin's got hold of his tail. It's pulled straight out, an' he can't get away. Just hear him yawl!'

"'It isn't anything,' says Mrs. Bird, but even as she said that she could see a little hand holding fast to that cat's tail, and then the child seemed to sort of clear out of the dimness behind the hand, and the child was sort of laughing then, instead of looking sad, and she said that was a great deal worse. She said that laugh was the most awful and the saddest thing she ever heard.

"Well, she was so dumbfounded that she didn't know what to do, and she couldn't sense at first that it was anything supernatural. She thought it must be one of the neighbor's children who had run away and was making free of their house, and was teasing their cat, and that they must be just nervous to feel so upset by it. So she speaks up sort of sharp.

"'Don't you know that you mustn't pull the kitty's tail?' says she. 'Don't you know you hurt the poor kitty, and she'll scratch you if you don't take care. Poor kitty, you mustn't hurt her.'

"And with that she said the child stopped pulling that cat's tail and went to stroking her just as soft and pitiful, and the cat put his back up and rubbed and purred as if he liked it. The cat never seemed a mite afraid, and that seemed queer, for I had always heard that animals were dreadfully afraid of ghosts; but then, that was a pretty harmless little sort of ghost.

"Well, Mrs. Bird said the child stroked that cat, while she and Mrs. Dennison stood watching it, and holding onto each other, for, no matter how hard they tried to think it was all right, it didn't look right. Finally Mrs. Dennison she spoke.

"'What's your name, little girl?' says she.

"Then the child looks up and stops stroking the cat, and says she can't find her mother, just the way she said it to me. Then Mrs. Dennison she gave such a gasp that Mrs. Bird thought she was going to faint away, but she didn't. 'Well, who is your mother?' says she. But the child just says again 'I can't find my mother—I can't find my mother.'

"'Where do you live, dear?' says Mrs. Bird.

"'I can't find my mother,' says the child.

"Well, that was the way it was. Nothing happened. Those two women stood there hanging onto each other, and the child stood in front of them, and they asked her questions, and everything she would say was: 'I can't find my mother.'

"Then Mrs. Bird tried to catch hold of the child, for she thought in spite of what she saw that perhaps she was nervous and it was a real child, only perhaps not quite right in its head, that had run away in her little nightgown after she had been put to bed.

"She tried to catch the child. She had an idea of putting a shawl around it and going out—she was such a little thing she could have carried her easy enough—and trying to find out to which of the neighbors she belonged. But the minute she moved toward the child there wasn't any child there; there was only that little voice seeming to come from nothing, saying 'I can't find my mother,' and presently that died away.

"Well, that same thing kept happening, or something very much the same. Once in awhile Mrs. Bird would be washing dishes, and all at once the child would be standing beside her with the dish-towel, wiping them. Of course, that was terrible. Mrs. Bird would wash the dishes all over. Sometimes she didn't tell Mrs. Dennison, it made her so nervous. Sometimes when they were making cake they would find the raisins all picked over, and sometimes little sticks of kindling-wood would be found laying beside the kitchen stove. They never knew when they would come across that child, and always she kept saying over and over that she couldn't find her mother. They never tried talking to her, except once in awhile Mrs. Bird would get desperate and ask her something, but the child never seemed to hear it; she always kept right on saying that she couldn't find her mother.

"After they had told me all they had to tell about their experience with the child, they told me about the house and the people that had lived there before they did. It seemed something dreadful had happened in that house. And the land agent had never let on to them. I don't think they would have bought it if he had, no matter how cheap it was, for even if folks aren't really afraid of anything, they don't want to live in houses where such dreadful things have happened that you keep thinking about them. I know after they told me I should never have stayed there another night, if I hadn't thought so much of them, no matter how comfortable I was made; and I never was nervous, either. But I stayed. Of course, it didn't happen in my room. If it had I could not have stayed."

"What was it?" asked Mrs. Emerson in an awed voice.

"It was an awful thing. That child had lived in the house with her father and mother two years before. They had come—or the father had—from a real good family. He had a good situation:

he was a drummer for a big leather house in the city, and they lived real pretty, with plenty to do with. But the mother was a real wicked woman. She was as handsome as a picture, and they said she came from good sort of people enough in Boston, but she was bad clean through, though she was real pretty spoken and most everybody liked her. She used to dress out and make a great show, and she never seemed to take much interest in the child, and folks began to say she wasn't treated right.

"The woman had a hard time keeping a girl. For some reason one wouldn't stay. They would leave and then talk about her awfully, telling all kinds of things. People didn't believe it at first; then they began to. They said that the woman made that little thing, though she wasn't much over five years old, and small and babyish for her age, do most of the work, what there was done; they said the house used to look like a pig-sty when she didn't have help. They said the little thing used to stand on a chair and wash dishes, and they'd seen her carrying in sticks of wood most as big as she was many a time, and they'd heard her mother scolding her. The woman was a fine singer, and had a voice like a screech-owl when she scolded.

"The father was away most of the time, and when that happened he had been away out West for some weeks. There had been a married man hanging about the mother for some time, and folks had talked some; but they weren't sure there was anything wrong, and he was a man very high up, with money, so they kept pretty still for fear he would hear of it and make trouble for them, and of course nobody was sure, though folks did say afterward that the father of the child had ought to have been told.

"But that was very easy to say; it wouldn't have been so easy to find anybody who would have been willing to tell him such a thing as that, especially when they weren't any too sure. He set his eyes by his wife, too. They said all he seemed to think of was to earn money to buy things to deck her out in. And he about worshiped the child, too. They said he was a real nice man. The men that are treated so bad mostly are real nice men. I've always noticed that.

"Well, one morning that man that there had been whispers about was missing. He had been gone quite a while, though, before they really knew that he was missing, because he had gone away and told his wife that he had to go to New York on business and might be gone a week, and not to worry if he didn't get home, and not to worry if he didn't write, because he should be thinking from day to day that he might take the next train home and there would be no use in writing. So the wife waited, and she tried not to worry until it was two days over the week, then she run into a neighbor's and fainted dead away on the floor; and then they made inquiries and found out that he had skipped—with some money that didn't belong to him, too.

"Then folks began to ask where was that woman, and they found out by comparing notes that nobody had seen her since the man went away; but three or four women remembered that she had told them that she thought of taking the child and going to Boston to visit her folks, so when they hadn't seen her around, and the house shut, they jumped to the conclusion that was where she was. They were the neighbors that lived right around her, but they didn't have much to do with her, and she'd gone out of her way to tell them about her Boston plan, and they didn't make much reply when she did.

"Well, there was this house shut up, and the man and woman missing and the child. Then all of a sudden one of the women that lived the nearest remembered something. She remembered that she had waked up three nights running, thinking she heard a child crying somewhere, and once she waked up her husband, but he said it must be the Bisbees' little girl, and she thought it must be. The child wasn't well and was always crying. It used to have colic spells, especially at night. So she didn't think any more about it until this came up, then all of a sudden she did think of it. She told what she had heard, and finally folks began to think they had better enter that house and see if there was anything wrong.

"Well, they did enter it, and they found that child dead, locked in one of the rooms. (Mrs. Dennison and Mrs. Bird never used that room; it was a back bedroom on the second floor.)

"Yes, they found that poor child there, starved to death, and frozen, though they weren't sure she had frozen to death, for she was in bed with clothes enough to keep her pretty warm when she was alive. But she had been there a week, and she was nothing but skin and bone. It looked as if the mother had locked her into the house when she went away, and told her not to make any noise for fear the neighbors would hear her and find out that she herself had gone.

"Mrs. Dennison said she couldn't really believe that the woman had meant to have her own child starved to death. Probably she thought the little thing would raise somebody, or folks would try to get in the house and find her. Well, whatever she thought, there the child was, dead.

"But that wasn't all. The father came home, right in the midst of it; the child was just buried, and he was beside himself. And—he went on the track of his wife, and he found her, and he shot her dead; it was in all the papers at the time; then he disappeared.

Nothing had been seen of him since. Mrs. Dennison said that she thought he had either made way with himself or got out of the country, nobody knew, but they did know there was something wrong with the house.

"'I knew folks acted queer when they asked me how I liked it when we first came here,' says Mrs. Dennison, 'but I never dreamed why till we saw the child that night.'"

"I never heard anything like it in my life," said Mrs. Emerson, staring at the other woman with awestruck eyes.

"I thought you'd say so," said Mrs. Meserve. "You don't wonder that I ain't disposed to speak light when I hear there is anything queer about a house, do you?"

"No, I don't, after that," Mrs. Emerson said.

"But that ain't all," said Mrs. Meserve.

"Did you see it again?" Mrs. Emerson asked.

"Yes, I saw it a number of times before the last time. It was lucky I wasn't nervous, or I never could have stayed there, much as I liked the place and much as I thought of those two women; they were beautiful women, and no mistake. I loved those women. I hope Mrs. Dennison will come and see me sometime.

"Well, I stayed, and I never knew when I'd see that child. I got so I was very careful to bring everything of mine upstairs, and not leave any little thing in my room that needed doing, for fear she would come lugging up my coat or hat or gloves or I'd find things done when there'd been no live being in the room to do them. I can't tell you how I dreaded seeing her; and worse than the seeing her was the hearing her say, 'I can't find my mother.' It was enough to make your blood run cold. I never heard a living child cry for its mother that was anything so pitiful as that dead one. It was enough to break your heart.

"She used to come and say that to Mrs. Bird oftener than to any one else. Once I heard Mrs. Bird say she wondered if it was possible that the poor little thing couldn't really find her mother in the other world, she had been such a wicked woman.

"But Mrs. Dennison told her she didn't think she ought to speak so nor even think so, and Mrs. Bird said she shouldn't wonder if she was right. Mrs. Bird was always very easy to put in the wrong. She was a good woman, and one that couldn't do things enough for other folks. It seemed as if that was what she lived on. I don't think she was ever so scared by that poor little ghost, as much as she pitied it, and she was 'most heartbroken because she couldn't do anything for it, as she could have done for a live child.

"'It seems to me sometimes as if I should die if I can't get that awful little white robe off that child and get her in some clothes and feed her and stop her looking for her mother,' I heard her say once, and she was in earnest. She cried when she said it. That wasn't long before she died.

"Now I am coming to the strangest part of it all. Mrs. Bird died very sudden. One morning—it was Saturday, and there wasn't any school—I went downstairs to breakfast, and Mrs. Bird wasn't there; there was nobody but Mrs. Dennison. She was pouring out the coffee when I came in. 'Why, where's Mrs. Bird?' says I.

"'Abby ain't feeling very well this morning,' says she; 'there isn't much the matter, I guess, but she didn't sleep very well, and her head aches, and she's sort of chilly, and I told her I thought she'd better stay in bed till the house gets warm.' It was a very cold morning.

"'Maybe she's got cold,' says I.

"'Yes, I guess she has,' says Mrs. Dennison. 'I guess she's got cold. She'll be up before long. Abby ain't one to stay in bed a minute longer than she can help.'

"Well, we went on eating our breakfast, and all at once a shadow flickered across one wall of the room and over the ceiling the way a shadow will sometimes when somebody passes the window outside. Mrs. Dennison and I both looked up, then out of the window; then Mrs. Dennison she gives a scream.

"'Why, Abby's crazy!' says she. 'There she is out this bitter cold morning, and—and—' She didn't finish, but she meant the child. For we were both looking out, and we saw, as plain as we ever saw anything in our lives, Mrs. Abby Bird walking off over the white snow-path with that child holding fast to her hand, nestling close to her as if she had found her own mother.

"'She's dead,' says Mrs. Dennison, clutching hold of me hard. 'She's dead; my sister is dead!'

"She was. We hurried upstairs as fast as we could go, and she was dead in her bed, and smiling as if she was dreaming, and one arm and hand was stretched out as if something had hold of it; and it couldn't be straightened even at the last—it lay out over her casket at the funeral."

"Was the child ever seen again?" asked Mrs. Emerson in a shaking voice.

"No," replied Mrs. Meserve; "that child was never seen again after she went out of the yard with Mrs. Bird."

SWEET-FLOWERING PERENNIAL

rs. Clara Woods was in the bank, standing in front of the paying-teller's little window, having one of her modest dividend checks cashed. She was folding the crisp notes carefully when she was startled by the voice of a man who stood next in the waiting line behind her.

"May I speak to you a moment when I leave the window?" queried the voice.

Mrs. Woods, turning, recognized the man as the notable fixture of humanity in Mrs. Noble's very select boarding-house where she herself lived. The gentleman was wealthy, aged, and privileged, since for countless seasons he had been a feature of Noble's. The fact that Mr. Allston boarded there was Noble's best asset.

"Certainly, Mr. Allston," replied Mrs. Woods almost inaudibly, but emphasizing her agreement with a nod. She was a middle-aged woman, with nothing to distinguish her from a thousand other middle-aged women.

She stepped aside and stood by the high circular structure fitted out with paper, pens, and bank literature generally, and almost at once Mr. Allston joined her. At a slightly perceptible gesture—Mr. Allston, of course, never actually beckoned a lady to follow his lead—she went behind him toward the rotary door of the bank, where they were almost out of hearing. Mr. Allston, in his guarded voice, spoke at once.

"May I ask at what hour you left the house, Mrs. Woods?" said he.

Mrs. Woods, catching a vague alarm from his manner, replied that she had left quite early. She had been shopping, and was now about to return to the house for luncheon.

"I advise you not to do so," cautioned the old gentleman. Mrs. Woods gazed at him. She was frankly alarmed.

"Why?" she began.

"Noble's was quarantined an hour ago," said the old man. "One of the Sims children has scarlet-fever. They don't dare move it in this weather, so they have nurses, and the sign is up on the front door. Mrs. Noble is distressed, but she can't help it. You had better not return for luncheon, or you will be quarantined."

"I have not seen the Sims children for days and days," declared Mrs. Woods with an air of relief. "I have not even seen Mrs. Sims. Mrs. Noble told me yesterday that little Muriel was ailing and her mother was staying with her. It must have been the fever coming on."

"Of course," replied Allston. "I got out, luckily, just before the notice was put up. Then I met Dr. Vane, and he told me. He advised me not to go into the house, as it might mean being a prisoner there for some time. So I got away as fast as possible. I am going to a hotel. It is very inconvenient, but it would be more so being shut up at Noble's for days, perhaps weeks."

"I think perhaps I had better not return," said Mrs. Woods, hesitatingly. She was casting about in her mind exactly what she could do. Then Mr. Allston inquired if he could be of any service, and she thanked him and said no. He remarked that it would of course be very annoying and inconvenient for both of them, and went forth from the bank, while she went into the ladies' waiting-room. She sat down and remained quiet, but inwardly she was aware of precisely the sensations of a wandering, homeless cat.

It was, of course, rather obvious that she would either have to go to a hotel—a quiet hotel for those of her ilk—or return to Noble's and remain in quarantine. She was even inclined toward the latter course, as involving less trouble. She considered that probably the period of isolation would be limited, and that she would not seriously object to remaining housed in her own nest rather than settle even temporarily in a new one.

Then she suddenly reflected that little Muriel Sims was not the only child at Noble's. There were the two Dexter boys. She was almost sure that they had never had scarlet fever. There was the Willis baby. There was little Annabel Ames. Suppose all these came down with scarlet fever? Why, that might mean quarantine for months. Then, also, there was the noise of so many children confined to the house. Probably none of them had escaped quarantine. The little Dexter boys were very boisterous children. They would probably slide down the banisters all day. Mrs. Woods again vibrated mentally toward the hotel.

Then Miss Selma Windsor entered. She did not notice Mrs. Woods. That was Selma's way. She was not apt to notice people unless she almost collided with them.

Selma entered and seated herself at one of the little writing-tables, took some papers from her black-leather bag, and began to examine them with as complete an air of detachment as if she were entirely alone in the world.

Mrs. Woods made an involuntary movement. She half rose; then she settled back. She was still entirely unnoticed by the other woman, who continued to examine her papers. She was probably about Mrs. Woods's own age. Mrs. Woods reflected upon that.

"We went to Miss Waters's school, but Selma was in a higher class," she told herself. She wondered, quite impartially, whether that proved superior wits or superior age on the part of Selma.

She was not astute enough to realize that Selma had very few of her own ravages of time. Selma deceived people, though not intentionally. She had no desire to look older than she need. A woman who does that is almost monstrous. Selma simply considered that certain clothes were suitable for a woman of her age, and she wore them. She also considered that a certain invariable style of hair-dressing must be adopted. She adopted it. The result was that to most people she did look as old as she was.

Casual observers did not recognize the fact that there were no lines in her face; that her skin was smooth, with the ready change of color of youth; that her facial contours remained very nearly intact; that her hair had not lost its youthful thickness and warm color. Selma was regarded by most people, as she was regarded by Mrs. Woods that morning, as a woman over the middle-age line of life.

She generally wore black, and her clothes had always a slightly hesitant note as to the last mode. She wore small black hats, and her fair hair was brushed very smoothly away from her temples. None of it could be seen under the prim brim of her hat. She had removed her gloves. Mrs. Woods did not notice that the hands were as smooth as a girl's, and displayed no prominent veins. She did notice the flash of a great white diamond on one finger, as Selma handled the papers in a tidy, delicate fashion.

She reflected that Selma was a rich woman, and how very fortunate that was, since she had never married. She remembered that Selma lived in the suburbs, in a very wealthy town. She had never visited her there. She had seen but little of her—and that little had been through chance meetings—for years. They always exchanged cards at Christmas. They were on an even level of friendship which both acknowledged, but there was no intimacy.

Mrs. Woods did not feel at liberty to interrupt the other woman in her scrutiny of her papers. Selma scrutinized very leisurely. Evidently something was perplexing her a little, but she did not frown at all. She simply examined and considered, with a serenity which was imperturbable. At last she seemed contented. She refolded the papers, slipped the elastic band around them, put them in her leather bag, fastened it, and began to put on her gloves.

Then, for the first time, she glanced about her as if she were capable of sensing anything or anybody outside her own individuality. She saw Mrs. Woods. Evidently not expecting to see her in that particular place, she did not at once recognize her. However, she was aware that here was a woman whom she knew. She calmly regarded the other's large, rather good-looking, obvious face. Then she rose. She extended her right hand, upon which the glove was now smoothed and buttoned. "How do you do, Clara?" she said, composedly, addressing Mrs. Woods by her Christian name.

Then the two women sat down together on the little leather-covered divan and exchanged confidences—or rather, Clara Woods volunteered them. There was scarcely an exchange, except for the trifling inevitabilities of health and weather. Clara Woods told Selma Windsor about the scarlet fever at Noble's, and how she was as one ship-wrecked without the necessities of life, or compelled to return to indefinite isolation of quarantine.

Selma disposed of the situation pleasantly and gracefully, and finally. "You will, of course, return with me to Laurelville this afternoon," she said. "I can supply you with everything you need. I shall be glad to have you with me until the quarantine is raised."

Clara Woods made only a faint demur. The proposition seemed to her fairly providential. She had not known how to afford that quiet, exclusive hotel. Her income was very limited. Then, too, there had been the apparently insurmountable problem of her belongings quarantined at Noble's.

Clara Woods was a pious woman, and humbly inclined to a conviction of the personal charge of the Deity over her. Visions of shorn lambs, and sparrows fluttering in search of suitable sites for nests, floated through her mind, which was really that of an innocent, simple child in spite of her ponderousness of middle-age. There was something rather lovely in her expression as she looked up into Selma's face. Clara's eyes were shining with vistas of gratitude. Selma, who was imaginative, realized it. She smiled charmingly.

"I am so glad I happened to come in here today," she said.

"It seems like a special providence," returned Clara, ardently; and Selma heard herself practically called a special providence, and rose above her own sense of humor because she understood what was passing in her friend's mentality.

The two lunched together; then Selma had some shopping to do in one of the big stores before they took the four-thirty train to Laurelville. It was probably that little shopping expedition which started queer after-events. At least, Clara Woods always considered them queer, although sometimes she was divided between the queerness of the events and the possible queerness of herself for so estimating them.

Whenever she met Selma, after what happened, she looked at her with a question in her eyes which, if Selma understood, she did not attempt to answer. Whenever Clara Woods endeavored dizzily to understand, she always got back to the ready-made frocks displayed in that great store on the day of her meeting Selma in the bank.

Clara Woods, when she stood with her friend in one of the departments, had something of the sensations which one might have had in the company of royalty—if royalty ever went shopping for ready-made clothes! There was something about Selma Windsor— It was difficult—in fact, impossible—to say what that something was. She was well and expensively clad, though with that slight flatting of the fashion key; but there were hundreds of women as well clad. She had a perfect poise of manner; so had other women by the score. Clara decided that it was impossible to say what it was that awoke to alert life and attention the groups of saleswomen. Selma had no need to stand for a second hesitating, as Clara always did in such places, feeling herself in the rôle of an uninvited guest at some stately function.

Selma was approached at once. There was, apparently, even some rivalry between the trim saleswomen. Clara wondered if Selma was known to any of these. She afterward learned that it was the first time in her life that Selma had entered that department of the store.

"Anything I can show you today, madam?" inquired a voice, and the other women fell back.

Selma expressed her wishes. She and Clara were deferentially shown to seats among the grove of dummies, clad in the latest modes, and resembling a perfectly inanimate afternoon-tea style. Clara felt a reflected glory, as one thing after another was displayed to her friend, not with obsequiousness, but with really fine deference to that mysterious something. Finally the purchase was made, and then Selma and Clara were in a taxicab on their way to the station.

They reached the suburban town where Selma lived about five o'clock. Selma had a limousine waiting for her. Clara experienced an almost childish sense of delight when she sank into the depths of its luxurious padding. Again the innocent, if perhaps absurd, conviction of the special providence which had her in charge that day illumined her whole soul.

"Well, I must say I never dreamed this morning that tonight I would be here," she remarked, happily.

Selma laughed softly. "We are both encountering the very delightfully unexpected," she replied.

"But when I think of coming entirely without baggage!"

"My clothes will fit you perfectly," said Selma. "I have a new black chiffon which I have never worn, which you can wear at dinner tonight."

"You dress for dinner?" asked Clara with an accession of childish pleasure.

"Sometimes. When I am entirely alone I make no change," said Selma, "but tonight I am entertaining—a very unusual thing for me—two guests, my lawyer and his cousin. We have some business to discuss, and I thought we might combine a little festive occasion with it. Mr. Wheeler is a charming gentleman. His cousin I have never met. This cousin is a Southerner, visiting him, and I included him in the invitation. I wished at the time I had another lady, and here she is, provided most providentially."

"Are they young men?"

"Mr. Wheeler is not. He is of our age. He has an invalid wife. I suppose his cousin is also middle-aged. I did not inquire."

By some law of sequence not evident on the surface, Selma immediately began to talk about the costumes which they had seen that afternoon. "It is very strange how the fashions have turned to antebellum days," said she. "How much at home the few survivors of the Civil War would have felt in that crowd of dummies dressed in flounces and fichus and full petticoats!"

"Yes; they even wore plaids," agreed Clara. Then she added that she supposed there must be many wardrobes in which hung duplicates of those very gowns which they had seen that afternoon. "I remember my aunt Clara showing me one exactly like that flounced plaid taffeta, except hers was a purple-and-green plaid, and the one in the store was blue and brown," said she.

Clara noticed a queer expression on the other woman's face, which in the light of after-events she remembered. Selma nodded.

"Yes," she replied. "I dare say you are right."

Her blue eyes were fixed upon the leafless trees against the sky. They had such a curiously childish expression that the other woman laughed softly. Selma looked at her inquiringly.

"You had a look in your eyes which carried me back to our school-days, then," said Clara.

"A look in my eyes?"

"Yes; there was a sparkle in them."

Selma herself laughed. "I wonder sometimes if the sparkle of life is really all over for me," she said. "I cannot accustom myself to being old."

Then the limousine drew up in front of Selma's rather splendid house, set back from the road in a lawn full of straw-clad rose-trees. Clara looked about her with enthusiastic interest.

"What a beautiful place! And you still like roses as much as when you were a girl," she exclaimed.

"Yes, I think the place pretty good. I did not hesitate much about buying it. I had always planned some day to have a country place for the sake of the roses."

When Clara entered the house her delight was increased. Had it not been sinful, she could have blessed the Lord for the disease of scarlet fever which had been the cause of her coming. Clara had, although she was commonplace, a love for the beautiful amenities of life, whose lack had irritated her. She was not a woman to say much concerning her emotions. Fairly hugging herself while gazing about at the soft richness and loveliness, she thought, "After Noble's!"

Selma gave her a beautiful room at the front of the house. Its great windows commanded a view of the drive and the road behind the rose-trees. Clara thought afterward that Selma could have had nothing planned at that time, or she would not have given her that room, from whose windows she could see—well, what she did see.

Clara Woods took a bath, with a secret awe before such luxury. The bath-room belonged to her room, and was all pink and white and silver. Clara had for years been obliged to watch her chance to sneak into the one repulsively shabby, although clean, bathroom at Noble's, and she had always an uneasy impression of publicity in using it. Here it was perfect. Everything was perfect. Her room was done in dark blue with pink roses. She had a long mirror in which she could survey herself when arrayed in Selma's black chiffon.

Selma's maid assisted her to don the gown, and, although she was stouter than her hostess, it fitted her well, because Selma's gowns were always very loose. Clara Woods fairly peacocked before the mirror. The maid surveyed her approvingly. She appreciated the guest's attitude. She had not entirely approved of the loan of the elegant black chiffon which her mistress had never worn; but, once the deed was done, she gloried in it.

Selma's maid had been with her for years, and fairly worshiped her. She gazed at the commonplace guest's reflection in the mirror, made for the time uncommonplace by the elegant costume and a little touch which she, the maid, had given her hair, and beamed with admiration at the effect of her mistress's kindness.

After Clara had gone downstairs she hung up the visitor's street gown, and considered within herself how Miss Selma was too good to live, almost. How many women in the world would despoil themselves of their fine feathers to deck another poor feminine fowl who lacked them? However, Jane triumphed in the knowledge that not all the fine feathers could make another such lady-bird as her own mistress.

That evening Selma in black and silver was adorable. She had failed to make as little of her natural advantages as she had innocently attempted. What if her fair hair were brushed so severely back? Her delicate temples were worth revealing. The high collar concealed her long, graceful throat, but did not deform it. Selma, in a high collar of silver, with a silver band around her head, was really lovely.

The two gentlemen evidently admired their hostess. The cousin, Ross Wheeler, from Kentucky, did not meet the expectations of either Selma or Clara. He was much the junior of his cousin, William B. Wheeler, who had charge of Selma's affairs. However, he had been recently made a partner in business by William B., and in spite of his almost boyish look and manner he was supposed to be taken quite seriously.

The dinner, which was perfect, passed off triumphantly. Even poor old Clara Woods, in her elegant black chiffon, shone in her own estimation. Years ago dinners like that had not been infrequent for her. She felt as if she were taking a blissful little trip back to her own youth.

When it was all over, and the gentlemen had gone, and Selma was bidding her good night in her own room, Clara waxed fairly ecstatic.

"Oh, my dear," she exclaimed, fervently, "if you knew what this means to me after my years in a boarding-house since my little fortune was lost and my poor husband passed away!"

Selma regarded her with self-reproach. She reflected how easy it would have been for her to give the poor soul the little change and pleasure before. It was true, though, that she had not lived long in Laurelville—only since her mother had died, some three years before.

"I am glad, Clara," Selma replied. "Now that you have found the way, there is no reason why you should not come often."

"Oh, thank you," responded Clara. "I am enjoying myself as I never thought to enjoy myself this side of heaven." She sighed romantically and reminiscently. "What a very charming gentleman Mr. Wheeler—the elder Mr. Wheeler—is!" said she.

"Yes, I like him," agreed Selma. "I have never regretted employing him. He forgot some papers tonight, though, and we could not settle a little matter of business for which he really came out. The dinner was hardly more than incidental, although he did wish to introduce his cousin."

"His cousin is a beautiful young man," declared Clara.

"Yes; and he must be clever in spite of his youth, or Mr. Wheeler would not have taken him into partnership," replied Selma.

Suddenly a change came over her face. Clara started.

"What is the matter?" asked Selma. The change had vanished.

"Nothing, only you—looked suddenly—not like yourself."

"Did I?" responded Selma, absently. She said good night, hoped Clara would sleep well, and trailed her sparkling black and silver draperies out of the room.

Clara Woods stood still a moment after the door was closed, thinking. "She looked exactly as she did when she was a girl, for a minute," said Clara Woods to herself.

Clara was almost asleep when she heard the ring of the telephone, the upstairs one, in Selma's room. She heard Selma's voice, but could not distinguish a word. She did not try to. Clara Woods had a scorn for curiosity. She felt herself above it, and her high position was about to be sorely attacked.

At breakfast the next morning Selma announced that she was very sorry, but she would be obliged to go to New York on business on the noon train. Mr. Wheeler had telephoned, she said.

"I heard the telephone ring," returned Clara.

Selma started. "I fear the talk kept you awake," she said. "I held the wire quite a time."

"Oh no," said Clara; "I could only distinguish a soft murmur of voices. It did not disturb me at all. I fell asleep while you were talking."

Selma appeared strangely relieved. Clara noticed with wonder that the look at which she had started the night before was again upon Selma's face. Selma, in her pale-blue house dress, was rather amazing that morning. It was not so much that she looked young in color and contour, but the very essence of youth was in her carriage and her glance. She looked alive, as only living things which have been a short time upon the earth look alive.

Her blue eyes were full of challenge; her chin had the lift of a conqueror; her very hair sprang from its restraining pins with the lustiness of childhood.

Selma and Clara sat together lingeringly over their breakfast, then Selma excused herself, and Clara settled herself happily in the library with newspapers and magazines. She was conscious, half fearfully, of being in a state of jubilation that she distrusted. She was of New England parentage, and involuntarily stiffened her spiritual back to bear reverses when in the midst of unusual delights. It did not seem to Clara Woods that this could last long. It seemed to her entirely too good to be true.

It was not a great while before her perturbation of soul began. It was, in fact, that very noon. Selma had told her that she was going to New York on the noon train, and had apologized for the necessity of leaving her guest to lunch alone. Clara was in her room about fifteen minutes before train-time, when she heard the whir of Selma's car in the drive. She saw a figure step lightly into the car, and she gave a little gasp.

That was surely not Selma Windsor! That was a lightly stepping girl, with a toss of fair hair under a blue hat, over which floated a blue chiffon veil. The girl was clad in ultra style. She was a companion, as far as clothes went, of that notable company of dummies in the New York store where they had been yesterday. Wide blue skirts floated around that slender figure. A loose coat of black velvet, of the antebellum fashion, was worn over the blue gown.

The girl seated herself. Clara could not distinguish anything of her face under the loose wave of her veil, except a vague fairness of color and grace of outline. The car whirred, and Adam, smart in his chauffeur's costume, drove rapidly around the curve of the drive. In a second Clara saw the car in the road. Then it was out of sight. She wondered who that girl was. She looked at her watch and wondered how Selma could make her train, since she was so delayed by a visitor. Clara never doubted that the girl was a visitor whom Selma had sent home in her car. Selma must know some people in Laurelville, although she had heard her remark that she had made few acquaintances, and no friends, there. This girl must be one of the acquaintances.

Clara watched very idly beside her window for the return of the car and Selma's departure for her train. Presently the car returned. Adam drove directly past the curve of the drive to the garage. Clara looked at her watch. There were now only three minutes before the train was due.

When Clara heard the broken, hollow music of the Japanese bells which announced luncheon, she went downstairs, expecting, of course, to find Selma in the dining-room, and hear her announce the change of program which had kept her at home. There was one plate laid in Clara's place on the table, and Jane stood there ready to wait. She had, somehow, the air of a sentinel on duty when Clara entered.

Clara Woods was in one respect rather a remarkable woman. In spite of what she had seen, she said nothing. She ate her dainty luncheon, with not as much appetite as she had eaten her breakfast. She asked nothing. She said nothing, except to make the usual remarks due from guest to servant. Then she returned to her room. Therein she sat down and looked rather pale.

"Who," demanded Mrs. Clara Woods of her own stuttering intelligence, "was that girl?"

For some cause Clara Woods avoided her front windows that afternoon. She remained in her own room for some time, writing letters at the inlaid desk between the other windows which did not command the road. Then she heard the telephone-bell in Selma's room, and Jane tapped at the door and informed her that Miss Selma wished to speak to her on the long-distance from New York.

Selma's room was beautiful, but rather strangely furnished for a woman of Selma's apparent character. It was something between a young girl's room and a bachelor apartment. One surveying it—knowing nothing of its occupant—might easily have conceived that either a young girl had married a bachelor settled in his habits, and brought him home to live with her people, or that the old bachelor had yielded to a young wife's girlish preferences. Certainly, white-silk curtains strewn with violets, looped back with that particular shade of blue which suits the flowers, white walls with a frieze of violets tied with blue ribbons, and a marvel of a dressing-table decked with silver and crystal were fairly absurd combined with a great lion-skin in front of the fireplace, a polar-bear skin in the center of the great room, and heavy, leather-covered divan and easy chairs.

"What a queer room!" thought Clara. The telephone was on a little table beside Selma's bed. The bed had a leopard skin flung over the foot, and the counterpane and pillows were of heavy yellow satin.

Selma's voice came clearly over the wire. "I am so sorry, Clara," said Selma, "but I find I am detained. I cannot be home in time for dinner. I probably cannot be home until the ten-thirty train. Jane will take care of you. I am sorry, but you will not mind."

Clara replied that of course she would not mind, assured her that she was being very well cared for, bade her good-by, and hung up the receiver. She kept on her own dress, which was a good one, for her solitary dinner. Jane waited on her, as at luncheon, and she made no attempt at satisfying any wonder or curiosity which she might have felt. Jane at times cast an apprehensive glance at her. Clara felt the glance, but never met it.

After dinner she sat in the library and read the evening paper. Then she found a book which interested her, although she felt nervous and uneasy, and from time to time thought of her own humble nest at Noble's. The hours passed. She heard the automobile go out of the yard, and at the same time Jane entered the room. She asked Mrs. Woods if she could do anything for her, and looked so disturbed that Clara understood. "She wishes me to go upstairs," she told herself. With a stiff subservience to all wishes of that kind, she rose and went. She realized that it was not judged by Jane as advisable that she should be downstairs when that motor-car returned from the station.

She heard it as she sat in the dressing-gown which Selma had provided, continuing her letter-writing (Clara had a large circle of feminine correspondents). She expected to hear voices. She heard none. She wondered if Selma had not returned on the ten-thirty train, then dismissed the wonder as unworthy. It was none of her business.

She waited a long time before she returned to the library for the book which she had been reading. She considered that there had been time enough for all mysteries with which she had no concern to settle themselves, when she stole downstairs and got the book. Some of the lights had been turned off, but many were on. It was quite evident that Selma had not returned. Jane looked in at the library door and asked if she could do anything. Clara replied, in an almost apologetic voice, that she had come down for a book. Then she heard a car speeding up the drive.

Jane's face became almost agonized. Clara sped out of the library. It was years since her middle-aged feet had moved as swiftly as they did along the hall and up the stairs. She gained her own room, opened the door, turned to close it, and saw the face of the girl coming upstairs. Clara could not help that one glimpse, but it was so fleeting that nobody on the stairs—Jane came after the blue-clad figure—saw anything but the flirt of the closing door.

Clara sat down helplessly. Always before her eyes was the face she had seen, the face of the blue-clad girl ascending the stairs. The face was fair and sweet, so sweet of expression that it compelled admiration for that alone. It was smiling radiantly. Soft, fair hair tossed over the forehead, as innocently and boldly round at the temples as a baby's.

Clara Woods remembered Selma Windsor when she looked like that, exactly like that. The likeness was uncanny. Clara had little imagination or she would then have gone far in imaginative fields. She did tell herself that the girl looked enough like Selma to be her own daughter. She went no further.

Clara went to bed. She could not sleep. She rose early, and after dressing sat in her room waiting for sounds in the house to denote that other people were astir. At the breakfast-hour she went downstairs. She was aware of a queer unsteadiness. She could not analyze her perturbation, but felt helpless before it.

When Clara entered the breakfast-room Selma greeted her from a little conservatory beyond. She had been tending a few blooming plants which she kept there. Selma said, "Good morning," and there was nothing unusual in her manner. There was nothing unusual in Clara's, although she looked pale. Breakfast was served, and she and Selma partook of it, and the mysterious girl did not appear, and was not mentioned.

Selma said nothing about her trip to New York, except to express regrets that Clara had been left to dine alone. Selma, eating breakfast, did not look in the least tired. On the contrary, Clara thought she looked, in some strange, intangible fashion, younger and fresher. Her voice rang silvery. She laughed easily and delightfully.

"You seem just as you did when we were girls together at school," Clara exclaimed, involuntarily. Then Selma gave a quick start, but recovered herself directly.

"Those were the happiest days of my youth, those days at school," she said, and there was a sad note in her voice.

Clara did not reply. She had known very little about Selma, except through those days at school. Selma began to talk more freely than she had ever done. She told how her home life had been saddened, even embittered, by an older sister who was an invalid; one of those kickers against the pricks who drag all who love them into their own abyss of misery. Selma and her father and mother had been as beaten slaves under that sore tyranny, which had endured until the sister died, long after Selma's youth had passed.

"I never," she said, "could have company of my own age. I never could go like other young girls." She flushed slightly. "I could not have a lover on account of poor Esther," she said. Then she added, with a curious naïveté, "I have always wondered what it would be like."

Jane brought in hot waffles, and the personal conversation ceased. After breakfast the two women went upstairs. It was a windy morning. Selma's door was blown open as they reached it, and a sudden puff of wind caused a skirt to flash out with a sudden surprise of blue, like a bird of spring, from an open closet door. Selma did not act as if she saw it. Clara again felt shaken, and proceeded to her own room, telling Selma she had some letters to write.

In her room she sat down and pondered. She might not own to curiosity—other people's affairs might be sacred in her estimation—but she could not ignore, in the privacy of her own consciousness, the blue flirt of that skirt. After a while, however, she gained command over herself, with her usual incontrovertible argument that it was none of her business. She went downstairs, and Selma provided her with some fancy-work, and the two visited serenely all the forenoon.

After luncheon they separated. Clara had a habit of lying down for an hour. This afternoon she fell asleep—the effect of her wakeful night. She started up about four o'clock. She had heard a motor in the drive. Against her own will she slipped down from the divan and peered out of a window. There was a great touring-car and a magnificent chauffeur, and Mr. William B. Wheeler's handsome young cousin was assisting into the tonneau the girl—*the girl*—clad this time in fawn-color, ruffling to her waist, with a quaint velvet mantle to match, fitch furs, and a fawn-colored poke bonnet with a long feather curling to her shoulder.

The car sped away. Clara really felt faint. She lay down again on the divan. It crossed her mind that she might go in search of Selma and see if she were in the house; then she dismissed the thought as unworthy. A very soul of small honor had Clara Woods. She immolated herself upon that little shrine, which most women would not have considered a shrine at all.

Clara finally dressed herself and then hurried downstairs to the library, whose windows did not command the drive. There she read conscientiously. Finally Selma came in smiling. Clara noticed guiltily that her cheeks were flushed as if by coming in contact with cold, outdoor air. It was curious that Clara was the one who felt guilty before all this. Selma seemed entirely unruffled until Clara inquired if they were to dress for dinner that night, if guests were expected. Suddenly Selma flushed. She looked for one second like a young girl trapped with some love-secret, then she answered composedly that she expected nobody, and it was not necessary to dress.

There was a tap on the door, and Adam entered. He wished to see his mistress with regard to preparing a new garden-patch. Selma excused herself. When she returned she was smiling happily.

"I shall have a lovely new garden this year," she said. "I have bought half an acre at the left of the house, and I am to have a flower-garden—a flower-garden with a stone wall around it, a wonderful flower-garden!"

"What kind of flowers?" inquired Clara, and was surprised at the intensity and readiness of her friend's reply.

"Perennials," she exclaimed with force. "Always perennials. Always the flowers which return every year of their own accord. I like no other flowers. Always the returning flowers—roses and lilies and hyacinths and narcissi and hollyhocks. There are plenty of them. No need for us to trouble ourselves with flowers which demand taking up and gathering and replanting. It is always a perennial flower for me! I love a rose which has returned to its own garden-home year after year. There is faithfulness and true love and unconquerable youth about a flower like that!"

Clara stared at her. "I suppose so," she assented rather vaguely. Selma puzzled her in more ways than one. However, a perfectly pleasant little conversation ensued. Selma asked about some old school friends of whom Clara had kept track through the years.

The solitary dinner passed off happily. The two separated rather early. Selma owned to having a slight headache. Clara read awhile, then went to bed. She was just beginning to feel drowsy when she heard a motor in the drive, and simultaneously she noticed a thin line of light across her floor. She had not quite closed her door. Somebody had turned on all the hall lights, and they shone through the crack. It was too much for Clara Woods. Curiosity raged and would not be subdued.

She slid noiselessly out of bed and stood behind the door. She peered through that slight opening and saw—the girl, all clad in rose-color, a full skirt blossoming around her, ribbons and laces fluttering. She beheld the girl fairly dancing on slim, pointed feet along the hall toward the stairs. At the same time the fragrance of roses came to her, and she remembered how fond Selma used to be of that perfume, and how the other girls used to make fun of her for using it in such quantities. All the hall was now scented with roses. There might have been a garden of them.

Clara closed her door noiselessly and went back to bed. That night she was so tired that she slept. The next morning she wondered if the girl would appear at the breakfast-table, but there was only Selma in a lavender morning gown, sweet and dignified and serene as ever.

Whatever there was to conceal, Selma was careless, for again when Clara went upstairs—Selma had gone out with her gardener to give directions for her garden of perennials—Selma's door was open, and over a chair lay a fluff of rose-pink and lace and ribbons.

Clara shook her head. She went into her own room, and she thought of Noble's. She had lived there over ten years, and nothing in the least mysterious had happened. She wished herself safely back, but again she stifled her curiosity. She stifled it, and in fact never quite knew if it had been gratified—if she ever found out the truth of the case. Clara had always a mild wonder if a cleverer woman than she might not have known exactly what had happened, what did happen. For the climax of the happening came very soon. And it came in an absurd sort of fashion.

Selma had been busy in her own room all the afternoon. Clara had not seen her since luncheon. Finally she dressed in one of the costumes which had been placed at her disposal—a pretty black net trimmed with jet—and went downstairs to the library. After trying a book which did not especially interest her, she settled herself comfortably in a long lounging-chair beside a window. Although the day was far spent, it was not dark.

Clara lay back, gazed out of the window at the grounds, and reflected. Where she sat she could see, mirrored in a picture facing the large drawing-room into which the library opened, the two actors in the little drama of mystery. She could not help seeing them unless she moved, which was quite out of the question.

Clara stared at the reflecting surface of the picture facing the interior of the drawing-room, and she saw Mr. William B. Wheeler's cousin—that charming young man from the South— enter and seat himself. She saw in the picture that he was very pale and evidently ill at ease. Then Selma entered. To Clara she looked much older than usual. Her black-satin gown was very plain; her fair hair was strained back very severely from her temples. She also looked pale and worn.

Clara saw Selma and the young man shake hands; then, with no preamble—he was hardly more than a boy—he sank down on his knees before the woman, buried his face in her black-satin lap, and his great, boyish frame shook. Then Clara heard the boy say, chokingly: "Forgive me, Miss Windsor. I am—hard hit."

Clara saw Selma's face bent over the bowed, fair head pityingly, like the face of a mother. The young man went on:

"You must know that I understand how very odd this may all seem to you. I have only seen her those few times. But from the very first minute she entered Cousin William's office that morning after we dined here—when he had telephoned you, and you had sent your niece to represent you because you were ill—from that very first minute it was all over with me. She was so sweet and kind. She stayed and went to that concert with me, although I know she feared lest you think she ought not. Everything happened so very quickly. She was not at fault. She never encouraged me, led me on, you know. You surely don't think I am such a cad as to imply that, Miss Windsor?"

Clara heard Selma's reply, "No, I certainly do not think you mean to imply that."

The boy went on. "I know I was terribly headlong. I have always been headlong. It is in my blood; and I was so sure of myself. She was so wonderful. Then I wrote her that note. Did you see it? She showed it to you, didn't she? I expected of course she would."

Clara saw Selma bow her head in assent.

"Then she sent that special-delivery note of refusal. You saw that?"

Selma again bowed her head.

"Do you think it was—final? Will there never be any hope?" cried the young fellow with a great gasp.

Clara heard Selma say "No," in a strange voice.

"There is no use in my asking to see her?" pleaded the boy, pitifully.

"She has—gone," replied Selma.

"And she is not coming back?"

"I doubt if she ever comes back."

Clara saw the fair head of the young man on Selma's black-satin lap. She saw the broad young shoulders heave. She saw Selma Windsor put her hand lovingly on the fair hair and stroke it, and murmur something which she did not catch. But soon the young man stood up, and his white face was lit by a brave smile.

"Oh, of course, Miss Windsor," he said, "it is all the fortune of life and love and war. Of course I have courage enough to take what comes. Of course I am not beaten. Of course I am young, and shall get over it. I am not a coward. I simply did love her so, and it is the first time I was ever so hard hit. It is all right. I am sorry that I have troubled you. It is all right, but—I am going back to Kentucky tonight. I am going into business with a fellow of my own age. I have told Cousin William. He was upset, and I did not tell him why I was backing out of the partnership so soon. He did not like it very well. I am sorry, for he is a mighty good sort. But I have to go. I have plenty of fight in me for everything, but a fellow has to choose his own battle-field sometimes. I am ashamed of myself, to tell you the truth, Miss Windsor. Your niece is wonderful, but I never thought any girl living could settle me as soon as this. She is wonderful, though."

Clara saw in the picture the young man gazing intently at Selma Windsor. "You must have looked much like her when you were a girl," he said.

"Yes, I think I did," replied Selma.

Then Clara saw the two make what was apparently an involuntary movement, and Selma had kissed the young man, and he had held her for a second like a lover.

Then Clara did close her eyes. She remembered when it was all over except the fervent good-byes and kind wishes which the two exchanged. Clara heard the door close behind the boy. She heard Selma leave the drawing-room, and soon, in the now fast-fading light, she saw her talking with Adam over the flower-garden in which she was to have her perennial blooms when spring and summer came again.

Clara seized her opportunity. She made her retreat, all unseen, to her own room. When later she and Selma met at dinner everything was as usual. After dinner they had a pleasant evening. The two ladies played a game of Patience.

Nothing more which savored of the mysterious happened during Clara's visit. She remained until the quarantine at Noble's was lifted. She enjoyed herself thoroughly.

She visited Selma again rather often, spending week-ends. They were closer friends than they had ever been, and Clara never knew the explanation of what she had unwittingly seen and heard. It suited her obvious mind better to believe that a niece of Selma's had really been in the house and had a love-affair, and for some unexplainable reason had been concealed from her. She had not the imagination to conceive of the other possibility—that some characters, like some flowers, may have within themselves the power of perennial bloom, if only for an hour or a day, and may revisit, with such rapture of tenderness that it hardly belongs to earth, their own youth and spring-time, in the never-dying garden of love and sweet romance.

THE JADE BRACELET

awrence Evarts was on his way home from his law-office in Somerset when he caught sight of the inexplicable circle in the snow. The snow was hard and smooth, and the circle immediately arrested his attention. It was just outside the compact snow of the sidewalk, in what would have been the gutter had there been any gutters in Somerset.

Lawrence carried a neatly-folded umbrella. He was exceedingly punctilious in all his personal habits. It had threatened snow earlier in the day, although now the sky was brilliantly clear, and the stars were shining out, one by one, in the ineffable rose, violet and yellow tints of the horizon.

Lawrence poked with the steel point of his umbrella at the circle, and struck something hard. He endeavored to lift whatever it was with the umbrella-point, but was unable to do so. Then, frowning a little, he removed his English glove, plunged his hand into the snow and drew it up again with the jade bracelet. It was beautiful, cabbage-green jade, cut out of the solid stone and very large—a man's bracelet, and rather large for his own hand. Evarts had a small hand.

He stood staring at it. He immediately remembered having seen somewhere, in a Chinese laundry, a Chinaman wearing a bracelet of a similar design. But there was no Chinese laundry in Somerset; he could not remember that there was one in Lloyds, which was the only other village for miles large enough to support a laundry.

Once a Chinaman had penetrated to Somerset, but the hoodlum element, which was large and flourishing, had routed him out. He had disappeared, presumably for more peaceable fields of cleanliness, although there had been dark rumors which had died away, both for lack of substantiation, and of interest in the uncanny heathen—as most of the citizens adjudged him.

Lawrence stood gazing at the thing with wonder; then obeying some unaccountable impulse, he slipped it over his right hand, the one from which he had removed the glove. Immediately the horror was upon him. He realized, although fighting hard against the realization, that there was another hand beside his own in the jade bracelet. He gave his hand a sharp jerk to rid himself of the sensation, but it remained. He could feel the other hand and wrist, although he could see absolutely nothing. Only his sense of touch was reached, and one other, his sense of smell. Overpowering the clear, frosty atmosphere came the strange pungency of opium and sandalwood. But worse than the uncanny assailing of the senses—far worse—was something else. Into his clear Western mind, trained from infancy to logical inferences, Christian belief, and right estimates of things, stole something foreign and antagonistic. Strange memories, strange outlooks, seemed misting over his own familiar ones, as smoke mists a window.

Evarts snatched the bracelet from his wrist and gave it a fling back into the snow. Then something worse happened. He still had the feel of the thing on his wrist, but the pull of the other hand and wrist became stronger, he fairly choked with the opium smoke, and the strange cloud dimmed his own personality with greater force. He drew on his glove, but unmistakably it would not go on over the invisible bracelet.

"What the devil!" Evarts said quite aloud. He could see in the snow the clearly-cut circle where the bracelet had fallen. He withdrew his glove, picked up the thing again, put it on and walked along, shaking the snow from his hand. It was unmistakably better on than off. The strange sensations were not so pronounced. Still, it was bad enough, in all conscience.

Presently, as he walked along, Evarts met a friend, who stared at him after he had said good-evening.

"What is the matter? Are you ill?" he asked, turning back.

"No," replied Evarts shortly.

"You look like the deuce," his friend remarked wonderingly. Evarts was conscious that the man stood still a moment staring at him, but he did not turn. He walked on, feeling as if he were in handcuffs with the devil. It became more and more horrible.

When he reached his boarding-house he went straight to his room, and did not go down to dinner. No one came to ask why he did not. He had not any intimates in the house, and, indeed, was one who was apt to keep himself to himself, regulate his own actions and resent questions concerning them.

He turned on his electric light and tried to write a letter. He was able to do that, as far as the mere mechanical action was concerned. The other hand moved in accordance with his. But what he wrote—! Evarts stared incredulously at the end of the first page. What he had written was in a language unfamiliar to him, both in words and characters, and yet the meaning was horribly clear. He could not conceive of the possibility of his writing things of such hideous significance, and, moreover, of a significance hitherto unknown to him.

He tore up the sheet and threw it into the waste-paper basket; then he lit his pipe and tried to smoke, but the scent of opium came in his nostrils instead of tobacco. He flung his pipe aside and took up the evening paper, but to his horror he read in a twofold fashion, as one may see double. There were horrors enough, as usual, but there were horrors besides, which dimmed them.

He tossed the paper to the floor, and sat for a few moments looking about him. He had rather luxurious apartments: a large sitting-room, bedroom and bath; and he had gathered together some choice things in the way of furniture and bric-a-brac. He had rather a leaning to Oriental treasures, and there were some good things in the way of Persian rugs and hangings. Just before his chair was a fine prayer-rug, with its graceful triangle which should point toward the Holy City.

Suddenly he seemed to see, kneeling there, not a Moslem but a small figure in a richly-wrought robe, with a long slimy braid, and before it sat a squat, grinning bronze god. That was too much.

"Good God!" Evarts muttered to himself, and sprang up. He got his coat and hat, put them on hurriedly and rushed out of the room and the house, all the time with that never-ceasing sensation of the other hand and wrist in the jade bracelet. He hurried down the street until he reached the office of a physician, a friend of his, perhaps the closest he had in Somerset. There was a light in the office, and Evarts entered without ceremony.

Dr. Van Brunt was alone. He had just finished his dinner and was having his usual smoke, leaning back luxuriously in a very old Morris chair, well-worn to all the needs of his figure. He was a short man, heavily blond-bearded.

"Thank God, I smell tobacco instead of that cursed other thing!" was Evarts' first salutation. Van Brunt looked at him, then he jumped up with heavy alacrity. "For Heaven's sake, what's to pay, old man?" he said.

"The devil, I rather guess," answered Evarts, settling himself in a forlorn hunch on the nearest chair.

Dr. Van Brunt remained standing, looking at him with consternation.

"You look like the devil," he remarked finally.

"I feel like him, I reckon," responded Evarts gloomily. Now that he was there, he shrank from confidence. He felt a decided tug at his wrist, and hardly seemed to realize himself at all, because of the cloud of another personality before his mental vision.

Dr. Van Brunt stood before him, scowling with perplexity, his fuming pipe in hand. Then he said suddenly: "What in thunder is that thing you've got on your wrist?"

"Some token from hell, I begin to think," answered Evarts.

"Where did you get it?"

"I found it in the snow near the corner of State Street, and I was fool enough to put the infernal thing on."

"Why on earth don't you take it off, if it bothers you?"

"I have tried it, and the second state is worse than the first. Look here—"

"What is it?"

"You know I never drink, except an occasional glass of wine at a dinner, and an occasional pint of beer, mostly to keep you company."

"Of course I do. What—?"

"You know I am not in any sense a drinking man."

"Of course I know it. Why?"

"Why?" Evarts faced him fiercely. "Why, then, do I see things that nobody, except men who have sold their souls and wits for drink, see?"

"You don't."

"Yes, I do. I must be mad. For God's sake, Van Brunt, tell me if I am mad, and do something for me if you can!"

Van Brunt sat down again in his chair and took a whiff of his pipe, but he did not remove his great blue eyes from Evarts.

"Mad, nothing!" he said. "Don't you suppose I know a maniac when I see him? What on earth are you ranting about, anyway? And what is it about that green thing on your arm, and why don't you take it off?"

"I tell you I am in the innermost circles of hell when it is off!" cried Evarts.

"What made you put the thing on, anyway?"

"I don't know. My evil angel, I reckon."

Dr. Van Brunt leaned forward and looked closely at the jade bracelet. "It is a fine specimen," he said. "I have never seen anything like it, except"—he hesitated a moment, and was evidently endeavoring to recall something. "I know where I saw one like it," he said suddenly. "That poor devil of a Chinaman who started a laundry here five years ago, and was routed out of town, had its facsimile. I remember noticing it one day, just before he was run out. Don't you remember?"

"I don't know what I remember," replied Evarts. He jerked the bracelet angrily as he spoke, then gave a great start of horror, for the invisible thing which he felt had seemed to come closer at the jerk.

"Why on earth don't you take that thing off?" asked Van Brunt again. He continued to smoke and to watch his friend closely.

"Didn't I tell you it was worse off than on? Then he gets so close, ugh!"

"He? Who?"

"Don't ask me. How do I know? The devil, I think, or one of his friends."

"Rot!"

"It's so."

"Sit down, Evarts, and have a pipe, and put that nonsense out of your head."

"Put it out of my head?" repeated Evarts bitterly. Suddenly a thought struck him. "See here; you don't believe that I am talking rationally," he said.

"I think something has happened to upset you," replied Van Brunt guardedly.

"I see. Well, try the thing yourself."

Evarts as he spoke withdrew the bracelet with a jerk. He paled perceptibly as he did so, and set his mouth hard, as if with pain or disgust. He extended the shining green circle toward Van Brunt, who took it, laughing, although there was an anxious gleam in his eyes.

Van Brunt, oddly enough, since he was a large man, had small hands. The bracelet slipped on his wrist as easily as it had done on Evarts'. He sat quite still for a second. He gave one more puff at his pipe, then he laid it on the table. His great blond face changed. He looked at Evarts.

"What is this infernal thing, anyhow?" he said.

"Don't ask me. I am as wise as yourself. But now you know what torment I am in." Evarts spoke with a feeble triumph.

"You don't mean you feel it without the bracelet?"

"Try it."

Van Brunt took off the bracelet and laid it on the table beside his pipe. His face contracted. "My God!" he ejaculated.

"Now you know."

"Good Lord! I am remembering devilish things which never happened. I am going backward like a crab."

Evarts nodded.

"You mean you feel the same thing?"

"Don't I?"

"As if some infernal thing was handcuffed to you?"

Evarts nodded.

"Well," said Van Brunt slowly. "I did not think I believed in much of anything, but now I believe in the devil." He took up the bracelet. Evarts made a sudden gesture of remonstrance. "For the love of God! let me have it on again," he said hoarsely. "I don't think I can stand this much longer."

Van Brunt gave the bracelet to Evarts, who slipped it over his hand; immediately an expression of something like relief came over his face.

"You don't feel quite so—with it on?" asked Van Brunt.

"No, but it is bad enough anyway. And you?"

Van Brunt grimaced. "As for me, I am handcuffed to a fiend," he said.

Evarts sat down, with the bracelet still on his wrist. "Van Brunt, what does it mean?" he asked helplessly.

"Ask me what is on the other side of the moon."

"You honestly don't know?"

"I can't diagnose the case, or cases, unless you are crazy and the microbe has hit me, too, for I am as crazy as you are."

Evarts looked down at the shining green circle on his wrist.

"I wish I'd let the thing alone," said he.

"So do I."

Suddenly Van Brunt arose. He was a man of a less sensitive nervous organization than the other, and his mouth was set hard, and even his hands clenched, as for a fight. "See here, old fellow," he said, "we've had enough of this. It is time to put a stop to it. Have you had any dinner?"

"Do you think—?" began Evarts.

"Well, you've got to eat dinner, whether you want to or not. This is nonsense!"

Van Brunt struck the call-bell on his table violently and his man entered. A look of surprise overspread his face as he looked at his master and Evarts, but he said nothing.

"Tell Hannah, if there was any soup left over from dinner to warm it immediately, and send up whatever else was left. Mr. Evarts has not dined. Tell her to be as quick as possible."

"Yes, sir," replied the man.

"And, Thomas."

"Yes, sir."

"Get a bottle of that old port, and open it."

"Yes, sir."

After the man had gone Evarts and Van Brunt sat in a moody silence. Both were pale, and both had expressions of suffering and disgust, as if from the contact of some loathsome thing, but Van Brunt still kept his mouth set hard. He even resumed his pipe.

It was not long before dinner was announced and he sprang to his feet, and laid his hand on Evarts' shoulder. "Now, come, old man," he said. "When you've got some good roast beef and old port in your stomach the mists will leave your brain."

"The mists are on your brain, and you have the good roast beef in your stomach," returned Evarts bitterly, but he arose.

"But I haven't the old port," said Van Brunt with an attempt at jocularity, as the two men entered the dining-room. Van Brunt kept bachelor's hall, and a neat maid was in attendance.

Her master saw her quick glance of amazement at their altered faces.

"You may go, Katie," said Van Brunt. "Mr. Evarts and I will wait upon ourselves."

After the maid had left Evarts leaned his elbows on the table and bent his head forward with a despairing gesture. "I can't eat," he almost moaned.

"You can and will!" replied Van Brunt, and ladled out the smoking soup. Evarts did eat mechanically, and both men drank of the old port. They sat side by side at the table, for the greater convenience of serving.

After Evarts had finished his dinner, and the two men had despatched the wine, they looked at each other. Evarts gave a glance of horror at the green thing on his wrist. "Well?" he said, with a kind of interrogative bitterness.

Van Brunt tried to laugh. "Take that confounded thing off and put it out of your mind," he said.

"You want to wear it yourself," Evarts returned almost savagely.

Van Brunt laughed. "No, I don't. I can stand it," he said, "but I'll be hanged if I believe I could suffer much more in hell. The devilish thing is converting me, paradoxically."

"What does it mean?" asked Evarts again.

"Don't know. If it keeps up much longer I'll try a narcotic for both of us."

"Not"—Evarts shuddered.

"No, not opium, if I know myself."

As he spoke, Van Brunt had his eyes fixed upon a spot directly in front of the fireplace, and Evarts knew that he saw what he himself saw—the horrible, prostrate figure covered with embroideries, and the grinning idol.

"You see?" he gasped.

"Yes, I do see, confound it! I'll do something before long."

"You feel as if—"

"Yes."

"—there is something between us?"

"Yes. Don't talk about it. I'll do something soon, if it keeps up."

Evarts made a quick gesture. He grasped the tableknife beside him.

"I'll do something now!" he cried, and made a thrust.

Van Brunt's face whitened. Almost simultaneously he grasped another knife and did the same thing. Then the two men drew long breaths and looked at each other.

"It's gone," said Evarts, and he almost sobbed.

Van Brunt was still pale, but he recovered his equilibrium more quickly.

"What was it?" gasped Evarts. "Oh! what was it? Am I going mad?"

"Going mad? No."

"There's a reason why I ask. It concerns someone very dear to me. I have not said much about Agnes Leeds to you; in fact, I have not said much to her; but sometimes I think that she—I have thought that I—when my practice was a little better. Good God! Van Brunt, I am not mad, am I? That would make marriage impossible for us."

"You are no more mad than I am," said Van Brunt. He gazed at his friend scrutinizingly. "What case have you on hand now?" he asked.

"The Day girl's; the murder case, you know."

Van Brunt nodded. "Just so. You have had that horrible murder thing on your mind, and—say, old fellow, your collar looks somewhat the worse for wear—"

"Yes, my laundress failed me this week, and I have been so horribly busy today that I have not had time to buy some fresh ones before the stores closed."

"Just so. And you wished that there was a Chinese laundry here, I'll be bound!"

"I don't know but I did," admitted Evarts, with a dawning expression of relief. Then his face fell again. "But what of the jade bracelet?" he said. He glanced at his wrist and gave a great start, "Good God! it's gone," he cried.

"Of course it is gone," said Van Brunt coolly. "It never was there."

"But you—saw it?"

"Thought I saw it. My dear fellow, the whole thing is a clear case of hypnotism; something for the Psychical Research. You were all overwrought with your work, nerves in a devil of a state, and you hypnotized yourself, and then—you hypnotized me."

Evarts sat staring at Van Brunt, with the look of one who is trying to turn a corner of mentality. Then the door was flung open violently, and Van Brunt's man rushed in, pale and breathless.

"Doctor!" he gasped.

"What is it?"

"Oh, Dr. Van Brunt, there's a Chinaman dead right out in front of the office door, and he's got two stabs in his side, and he's got a green bracelet on his wrist!"

Dr. Van Brunt turned ashy white. "Nonsense!" he said.

"It's so, doctor."

"Well, I'll come," said Van Brunt in a voice which he kept steady. "You run and get the police, Thomas. Maybe he isn't dead. I'll come."

"He's stone dead!" said the man in a shocked voice as he hurried out.

"Oh, my God!" said Evarts. "If we—if I—killed him, what about Agnes?"

"I can tell quickly enough which of us killed him," said Van Brunt rising. Both men hurried out of the room.

There was already a crowd around the ghastly thing, and police uniforms glittered among them. The fact that the dead Chinaman happened to be in front of his office had no significance for anybody present. There was no question of suspicion for either himself or Evarts. Some men held lanterns while Van Brunt examined the dead Chinaman. It was soon done, and the body was carried away in an undertaker's wagon, with the crowd in tow.

Then Van Brunt and Evarts entered the office. Evarts looked at his friend, and he was as white as the dead man himself.

"Well?" he stammered.

Van Brunt laughed, and clasped him on the shoulder. "It's all right, old man," he said. "My knife did the deed."

"But"—stammered Evarts, "I was on the heart side."

"What if you were? Your knife went nowhere near the heart. Mine cut the heart clean. I lunged around to the front of the thing. Don't you remember?"

"Are you sure?"

"I know it. You can rest easy now."

"But—you?" said Evarts in a voice from which, for very shame, he tried to suppress the joy.

Van Brunt laughed again. "It was a poisonous thing," he said. "Did you see his face?" he shuddered in spite of himself. "Men kill snakes of a right," he added.

"But how do you explain—?"

280

"I don't explain. All you have to consider is that you did not do it; and all I have to consider is that I have set my heel on something which would have bruised it."

As he spoke he was preparing a powder, which he presently handed to Evarts. "Now, go home, old man," he said. "Take a warm bath, and this, and go to bed and dream of Agnes Leeds."

After Evarts was gone Van Brunt stood still for a moment. His face had suddenly turned ghastly, and all the assumed lightness had vanished. He struck the bell and told his man to bring up another bottle of the old port. When it came he poured out a glass for himself and gave one to the man. "You've got a turn, too, Thomas," he said.

The man, who was shivering from head to foot, looked at his master.

"Did you see its face, sir?" he whispered.

"Better put it out of your mind."

"He looked like a fiend. I doubt if I can ever stop seeing him," said the man. Then he swallowed the wine and went out.

Van Brunt settled himself again in his old Morris chair, and lit his pipe. He gave a few whiffs, then stopped and gazed straight ahead of him with horror. The face of the dead Chinaman was vividly before his eyes again.

"Thank God, he does not know he did it!" he whispered, and a good smile came over his great blond face.

THE WHITE SHAWL

"usy?"

"Yes, Willy."

"Where are you?"

"Right here, Willy."

"Sort of dark."

"Yes, it is rather dark."

"Don't light the lamp yet."

"Don't worry. I won't light the lamp till you want it."

"I—can't see out of the window. I bet I ought to stand the other way. Want—to see out the window facing the tracks."

"You'd be right in a draft then. I'll see out the window for you."

"Can you see the signals?"

"Course I can."

"See the gates?"

"You know I can." The old woman laughed sweetly, even gayly. She was spent and sad, yet there was a ring of real humor in her laugh.

Susy Dunn had a gallant soul. All her life that gay acceptance of adversity as well as joy had cheered her on like a soldier. Always before her mental vision was something like the wave of a captain's hand, the flash of a flag.

"See 'em without glasses, too," she added, "spite of all the doctors telling me I ought to put 'em on years ago."

"Susy, little tired," the broken-hearted woman laughed again.

She knew what she knew about the track, but kept her knowledge to herself.

He did not dream of the real seriousness of the situation, this old dying keeper of the crossing-gates.

That morning the doctor who was attending him had told Susy that the man who had charge of the signal tower had died suddenly. There was not a man in the village who could fill his place, and there was the worst north-easter of the winter raging.

One of the directors of the railroad lived in the village and Doctor Evarts had just seen him. "Little Sloane girl has tonsilities, and I was in there this morning," he told Susy. "And Sloane was near out of his mind about this signal tower here. He says it's one of the nastiest little danger spots on the road with those tracks crossing the way they do. The Corporation ought to fix it. Sloane says it has been brought up time and time again, and he's said and voted all he can, but some of them are waiting for an accident to get a move on. Sloane had wired to Oxbridge for a man and got a reply that he'd come. I guess it's all right if he can get here. It is one of the worst storms I was ever out in, and that road to Oxbridge drifts enough to stall a train when every other road is clear."

Susy looked at him with quick anxiety. "Willy knows about the signals as well as the gates. If he knew he would be out there if he was dying," she said.

"Mustn't let him know, whatever you tell him."

Susy watched the doctor's car hump and slide out of the yard and down the road. "He can't get here again today," she thought.

Then she had begun to watch the signal tower and the gates from the window. She had not seen one signal; the gates had not gone down. Only two trains had gone through after the doctor left, a passenger and a short freight.

Every moment which she could snatch, she had spent in watching the signal-tower seeming to veer and slant before the fierce drive of the snow-packed gale. She knew that the boy who had taken Willy's place at the gates was not there. She had wondered if possibly the boy might not have taught him. But she knew, as the hours wore on, that there was no man for the tower, no boy for the gates, and the earth like an ocean in a hurricane, heaving up mountains of deadly fury, in gulfs of despair.

Willy questioned her continually and she lied those lies which the unselfish lie to spare pain.

"Jimmy tending the gates?"

"Yes, Willy."

"See him?"

"Yes, Willy."

"Hope he holds out. He ain't anything but a boy. It would be pretty hard for Tom minding the tower and the gates too. Hope he holds out."

"Don't you worry. He'll hold out."

"The snow ain't drifted, is it?"

Susy laughed her gallant laugh in the face of a dreadful world. "I guess a canary bird could hop over all the drifts I see."

"Tom tending the signals all right?"

"Didn't you see the green light yourself on the wall at the foot of your bed when the last train went through?"

"I don't know. My eyes seem sort of dim."

"I guess you forget seeing it."

"My eyes are dim. Susy, is the wind blowing just as hard?"

"Wind must be going down."

"I can't hear any too well. Half the time can't tell whether a noise is in my head or outside it," Willy sighed wearily.

"You hear all right."

"I wish I could go out and see for myself that the signals and the gates are being tended to."

"Now Willy, you stop worrying. You'll get so you can't get out to tend the gates for a month if you worry. You'll make yourself worse. You must stop it. It's wearing on you, and it's sort of wearing on me too."

"I don't mean to tire you all out, Susy."

"Of course you don't. You're my blessed old man. I speak so just on your own account. The signals will be tended and the gates kept. I promise you that and you know I never promise you anything that don't come true."

"You mustn't try to go out, Susy. You are too lame."

"Who said anything about my going out? There's the three fifty-seven now; it is almost fifteen minutes late. Hear it?"

"I can't seem to," the old man replied patiently. "Gates and signals all right?"

"See the green light show up on the wall there and winking in the looking glass over the shelf?"

"Mebbe I do see it."

Willy lay in his bed, very flatly, the patchwork quilt drawn up under his sharp, bristling old chin. Through his beard-stubble his skin gleamed ghastly white. His eyes were still bright with a strange questioning brightness, seeming to demand information concerning the destination of a little unimportant, unknown old man. Old Willy Dunn's eyes, as he lay there dying, asked terrible questions.

Susy seemed to hear them. They shouted, unanswered in her own heart, stirring it to rebellion, because of the love of an old wife, which passes the love of a mother, for her old man, as the time of parting drew near.

The angry love and pity, which filled her heart, as she watched over her dying husband, expanded it to almost breaking point. Her small old face was beautiful with fadeless romance and endurance of youth.

Willy had always thought his wife very beautiful, never dreaming that it was the love for him shining from her whole face which made her seem so. Always when a man sees himself reflected as a god in the eyes of a woman, he sees the mystery of beauty and does not understand.

Before the day quite faded Susy prepared Willy's supper. The light in the room was now ghastly, a snow-light streaming through the windows like the effulgence from a corpse. The wind blew fiercely, many miles an hour. Great waves of snow sprayed against the windows, with every departing gust leaving always a delicately frozen spume.

Susy was thankful that her husband could not hear the roar of the wind, could not see with his failing eyes the up-toss of the storm. Now and then she drew the quilt over his face, opened the window giving on the railroad crossing, and brushed away the snow. She kept that one window clear enough to enable her to see the gates and the tower.

Susy placed Willy's little meal before him and tugged at his sinking shoulders with her skinny arms. "Try and lift yourself up a little mite, pa," she said. Ever since they had lost their one child years ago, she had sometimes called Willy "pa." It pleased him.

Poor old Willy tried, but he was very feeble. His thin shoulders heaved upward then sank down helplessly. "I—don't—seem to—want anything to—eat," he gasped.

"Just take a swaller of this nice hot tea and a mouthful of this milk toast."

Susy kept her arm under Willy's neck and fed him. His mouth gaped like a sick bird's. He swallowed pitifully obedient, but with great difficulty.

When Susy took the tray away, tears were streaming over her face. "You shan't be pestered any longer, pa," she said.

She carried the tray into the kitchen and set it on the table. She leaned her head against the wall, and shook with great sobs. "Sometimes being deaf is a blessing for them that can't hear," she wailed out.

All her little body was racked with terrible grief. The black and white cat came rubbing against her, as animals will do when their beloved humans are in grief. His back arched, his tail waved. He made little affectionate leaps against her knees. Susy caught him up and wept into his soft fur until it was sodden.

Suddenly she heard Willy call. She put the cat down softly and hurried into the next room.

"Is it—time for—the express?" Willy gasped wildly.

"Wait a minute. I'll see." Susy went close to the loud-ticking clock on the shelf. "Not quite time."

"How long?"

"Oh, a good twenty-five minutes."

"Has it stopped snowing?"

Susy gazed out at the gray drifting violence of the snow and lied again. "Yes, Willy."

"Has it drifted? I wonder if Jimmy will have grit enough to stay all night with Tom if the snow is deep on the tracks and he has to be extra watching. Pretty hard on Tom to see to the tower and gates both on a bad night. Wonder if—Jimmy has got—grit enough."

"Course he has. Boys always have more grit than grown men. Don't know enough to be scared."

As Susy spoke, she knew in the depths of her agonized heart that Jimmy, little fair-haired, mother's boy, had not had grit enough even to face the elemental odds of the day, for his coming, much less for staying. She knew that the Oxbridge train had been stalled, that the man for whom Mr. Sloane had wired had not arrived. She knew of Tom, stark and dead, released from all tasks of earth. She knew that not a human being, man or boy was there to tend signals or gates. A night of awful storm was closing in. It was nearly time for the express; another train, a local, was due seven minutes later. If either or both was off schedule! Off schedule in that blinding fury of white storm, what then?

Susy said she would go down cellar for more coal before it got darker. When she was down cellar she began to pray. Susy came of a God-fearing race. All her life, she had read the Bible, she had attended church, she had prayed—now she *prayed*. For the first time in her life in the cold, gloomy cellar, knees on stones, prostrate before a mighty conception of a higher Power, cut off from all human aid, she realized some Presence while she prayed. Great waves of love and awe, also a terrible defiance born of despair, swept over her.

"God Almighty," prayed Susy in her wild voice of accusation and terror, and the greatest love of Humanity, the love for its Creator, despite the awful suffering of enforced life. "God Almighty, show me how to keep the gates. You sent the storm. You call Tom from this world. You know. Lives will be lost, lives not finished. Help me to keep the gates."

Susy carried the scuttle of coal upstairs. As she entered the room Willy stirred. "The express."

Susy heard a swiftly swelling roar. She ran to the window. A green light flashed out, a slanting shaft of green light; the gates clanged down.

"The express has gone through," she proclaimed in a loud, strangely clear voice.

"The signals? The gates?"

"The green light came on; the gates went down."

A gasp of relief came from the little mound of humanity in the bed. "Tom—Jimmy, there?"

Susy said nothing. She was trying to light the lamp. Her hands were cold and stiff.

"Why don't you speak, ma?"

"Everything was all right, pa."

"Both there," Willy murmured peacefully. The shadow of a smile was over his gray face.

After the lamp was lighted, Susy looked at the clock. It was time for the local, overtime by two minutes. The express had been late. Susy stood out of sight of Willy. She seemed as if in a closet of sacredly isolated self, alone with her new conception of God.

She prayed again with a terrible silent shout of her whole being. "The gates, the signals. God, show me how to keep them."

"Susy."

"Yes, pa."

"Blow out the lamp and watch for the next train."

"Yes, pa."

Susy blew out the light and sat down beside the window. It seemed to her that the whole room was vocal with her prayer. It drowned the roar of the storm for her.

The man in the bed breathed heavily. She knew that his dying eyes were strained toward the window.

Susy saw or thought she saw the green light flash out like a living emerald; the gates swing majestically down. Then the train labored past after a short stop. No one got off the train. "No passengers tonight, pa," she called out loudly.

The engineer was visible leaning sidewise from the cab in a cloud of rosy smoke. The gates reared up, the train chugged out of sight, the red light disappearing through the drive of the snow.

"All right, pa. There was the green light, then the gates went down, the train came and stopped, no passengers; saw Mike Kelly leaning out the engine. Then the train went on, now the gates are up. Don't you worry one mite more pa. A higher Power than us looks out for things sometimes."

"Jimmy is an awful smart boy to be tugging at the gates such a night as this," the old man said, almost sobbing.

"He wouldn't be so smart if there wasn't some higher Power back of him." Susy's voice had a noble quality, also a curiously shamed one. She could not show even to her dying husband more than a glimpse of her stunned faith.

"Light the lamp now, Susy."

Susy lighted the lamp. It stood on the table in the center of the room, the table with a fringed cover. Susy looked at the old man in the bed. He was changing rapidly. He was so sunken upon himself that he seemed disappearing. His face was sharped out with the death-rigor. His mouth was open ready to gasp.

"How do you feel, pa?"

"I—don't know, ma."

"You'll be better in the morning."

Willy made a slight movement with his head. A ghost of a smile, half sweet, half sardonic, widened his face. He said something which Susy did not catch.

"Anything you want, pa?"

Susy placed her ear close to the poor gaping mouth, struggling into speech. She heard one word and understood.

It was Sunday night, and always on Sunday night, she and Willy had been accustomed to a chapter in the Bible, which Willy read, and he afterward repeated the Lord's Prayer. Susy got the Bible from the center table, put on her spectacles, and read the Twenty-third Psalm. Willy could not hear at first. Finally she raised her voice to a shout. Then she knelt beside the bed and said the Lord's Prayer, also in a very loud voice.

After the Amen, she did not rise. She still knelt, her face buried in the bed-clothes. She was then praying her own terrible, almost blasphemous prayer about the signals and the gates. Susy felt a feeble touch on her bowed head, an inquiring, wondering touch. She rose.

"I didn't hear the—Amen."

"I said it."

"Blow out the light and look at the tower and the—gates—ma."

"They will be all right."

As Susy rose a red light shone out on the opposite wall. The old man raised himself in bed with an awful cry.

"Danger!" cried old Willy, whose dying body kept his faithful soul from duty. "The red light! Danger!"

Susy sobbed dryly. She ran across the red light, laying like a flag over the floor, into her bedroom. It was icy cold. The room was not quite dark because of the dreadful corpse-like pallor of the storm, driving in full fury against the one window.

Susy sank on her knees beside the white-mounded bed, hearing as she did so, poor Willy's feeble cry of "Danger!" Susy prayed again. She was there only a second, but in that second was concentrated the mighty impulse of a human heart toward the Greatness from which it came, toward which it went.

Susy hastened back to the other room. It was full of golden light. "Tom's onto it," whispered Willy, "Tom and Jimmy. That light's caution. They're lookin' out. Yellow light—Caution."

Suddenly instead of the yellow light flashed the splendid green.

"Track clear!" Willy shouted with incredible strength. "Susy! Window!"

Susy looked out of the window, shading her eyes from the light in the room with her curved hand.

"Green light," she said in her voice of strange awe and triumph. "Green light, train through."

Willy lay still.

"Hear the train, pa?"

Willy did not reply.

Susy left the window and bent over her husband. He seemed fairly melting into the bed so complete was his collapse. Obviously nothing had kept him alive so long except his anxiety over his unfulfilled duty, acting like a stimulant to his passing soul.

Susy sobbed, a little meek, dry sob. Her husband paid no heed. She went again into the freezing bedroom. When she came out, her face was pitiful but stern. She brought clothing and sheets, and laid them in neat piles on a sofa.

It was time for Willy's medicine. She held the spoon to his ashy parted lips. "Try and swaller, pa."

Willy moved his head slightly in meek protest. He rolled his eyes pitifully at his wife. He could not swallow.

"You shan't be pestered any more, pa," Susy said.

She put away the medicine. Then she sat beside the bed and waited. Her stern, pitying, loving eyes never swerved from her husband's face. She saw him in the past, the present. She saw him obediently dying there, an old spent man; she saw him in his strong middle-age when he had held a responsible position in connection with the railroad. Mr. Sloane had obtained it for him. He had always been a good friend of Willy's.

After Willy's fever which had prematurely aged him, Mr. Sloane had placed him in the only post for which his strength was fitted, gate-keeper, and paid him liberally. She saw Willy in his youth when he had come courting her. He had been a gay, laughing, handsome boy. All the girls had envied her.

The old wife, sitting beside her dying man, loved him with a comprehension and memory of the fullness of love as she had never loved him before. Through the hours the storm howled and drifted, the signals never failed, and the crossing-gates clanged up and down amid the chugging roar of the laboring trains, and no disaster befell.

When the weak new day was born, the storm was over, and the man in the bed had begun his dreadful stertorous last breathings of mortal life. Susy raised his lopping head in an effort to ease him. She had seen people die. She knew that Willy was dying.

It was past three o'clock. She thought dully that Doctor Evarts would not come now until daylight. "Most likely his car got stalled trying to get here," her thoughts spelled out. Susy was anxious about the doctor. He was not young, he was overworked, and such a storm was a man-killer like a beast of the jungle. She reflected that his coming could do no good here. Her poor old man was past medical science. Doctor Evarts was to have brought the district nurse with him on this call. The nurse would have been a comfort, a good, middle-aged woman who had buried her own husband.

Susy hoped the nurse, if she were with the doctor in the stalled car, was well wrapped. It was clearing cold. Willy continued to breathe those shocking breaths which mark the passing of a soul from its body of earth. Susy spoke to him now and then, but he did not seem to hear her.

She sat still and watched. The breaths seemed to shake the house. Suddenly they stopped. It was still, and the stillness seemed to smite the ears like a cannonade.

Susy was stunned for a few moments. Then she rose and went about her last duty to her husband, her little wiry body and frail arms doing apparently superhuman tasks. She was lame, too. She had fallen and injured her knee the winter before and had never fully recovered.

She limped about, performing her last duties to her husband slowly and painfully, but thoroughly. At last the little dead man lay peacefully in his clean smooth bed, his upturned face wearing an expression of calm rapture.

Susy crept across to the window. The storm was over. At the last it had rained and frozen. The earth looked like a white ocean suddenly petrified at the height of the storm. The trees were bent stiffly to the icy snow and fastened there. The telegraph wires sagged in rigid loops. Everything gave out blinding lights as from sheets of silver and gold with sudden flashes of jewels. Susy gazed out dumbly for a few minutes. Then she collapsed. She lay quite still on the floor, a little helpless bundle, until Doctor Evarts and the nurse found her.

Following them was a tall, fur-coated man, Sloane the railroad director. His high-powered car had made it possible for the doctor's small one to get through the drifts, had in fact towed it.

The doctor and the nurse lifted little Susy, carried her into the bedroom, and worked over her.

Sloane bent over the dead man, his face very grave. He had been Willy's friend. The two had been boys in school together. Sloane sat down beside the window which gave on the station. He looked both sad and puzzled.

The doctor and the nurse went back and forth between the bedroom and the warm kitchen. The fragrance of coffee filled the air. Sloane stopped the doctor. "How is she?"

"All right. Little determined women like her have terrible tenacity of life. She only dropped because for the moment she was down and out."

"Who laid him out?"

"She."

"How?"

The doctor laughed grimly. "I don't know, suppose I might say reserve strength. No mortal, man or woman, knows how much is owned, until a test comes."

"I cannot understand."

"Neither can I. It is physically impossible apparently of course, but there you are, no one else was here. She did it. Women of her sort are almost terrible when a demand is made on their love and strength, and there is no one else. Sometimes it has seemed to me they can work miracles."

"She is a good little woman. I shall see that she is provided for all the rest of her life in comfort."

"Glad to hear that. Come out in the kitchen and have some coffee. Wait a minute. Come to the door with me first."

The men stood in the doorway looking out at the blinding, glittering morning. The crossing gates upreared, splendid slant of ice. There was a little chimney in the tower. It was plumed with violet and rosy smoke.

"The line to that tower there, the telephone line was open all night," Sloane said in a curious, dry voice.

The doctor turned sharply on him. "Open? Thought the telephone lines were all out. Mine was and is."

"That line to the tower, special line, was open all night. Kept calling up, always got an answer."

"Who answered?"

"I don't know. Didn't know the voice. It was thin and low, but very clear, almost like singing."

"You see there is not one foot print to that tower. Foot prints would show in the crust."

The doctor nodded.

"Wait a bit. I am going over there."

The doctor stood waiting while Sloane went crunching through the frozen snow-crust. He was not gone long.

The nurse came and told the doctor about Susy. "She is coming to," she said softly. "She wants her little white shawl. I can't find it."

"Well, put something else over her, I will be in directly."

Sloane returned, a fluffy mass over his arm. He was obviously agitated.

"What is it?" asked the doctor.

"Looks to me like a woman's shawl, found it right beside the telephone."

The doctor paled slowly. "It is Susy's shawl. Have seen her wearing it dozens of times. She has just asked for it. The nurse told me."

The doctor took the shawl into the house.

"Coming out all right," he said to Sloane when he returned. "That was her shawl."

"Did she remember?"

"No, and she must not be told. She is cast on simple lines."

The men stood staring at each other in a sort of horror.

"How in Heaven's name do you account for it?" Sloane gasped.

"Don't account for it. This is not the first time I have been at a loss to account for them. Maybe there is a thinner wall and a door into the next dimension for loving women that men never find. Love like that woman's is an invincible Power."

DEATH

here is a little garden full of white flowers before this house, before this little house, which is sunken in a green hillock to the lintel of its door. The white flowers are full of honey; yellow butterflies and bees suck at them. The unseen wind comes rushing like a presence and a power which the heart feels only. The white flowers press together before it in a soft tumult, and shake out fragrance like censers; but the bees and the butterflies cling to them blowing. The crickets chirp in the green roof of the house unceasingly, like clocks which have told off the past, and will tell off the future.

I pray you, friend, who dwells in this little house sunken in the green hillock, with the white flower-garden before the door?

A dead man.

Passes he ever out of his little dwelling and down the path between his white flower-bushes?

He never passes out.

There is no chimney in that grassy roof. How fares he when the white flowers are gone and the white storm drives?

He feels it not.

Had he happiness?

His heart broke for it.

Does his heart pain him in there?

He has forgot.

Comes ever anybody here to visit him?

298

His widow comes in her black veil, and weeps here, and sometimes his old mother, wavering out in the sun like a black shadow.

And he knows it not?

He knows it not.

He knows not of his little prison-house in the green hillock, of his white flower-garden, of the winter storm, of his broken heart, and his beloved who yet bear the pain of it, and send out their thoughts to watch with him in the wintry nights?

He knows it not.

Only the living know?

Only the living.

Then, then the tombs be not for the dead, but the living! I would, I would, I would that I were dead, that I might be free from the tomb, and sorrow, and death!

STORY SOURCES

"In the Marsh-land" and "Death" first published as part of "Pastels in Prose" in *Harper's New Monthly Magazine*, December 1892. Not previously collected.

"The Shadows on the Wall" first published in *Everybody's Magazine*, March 1903 and collected in *The Wind in the Rose-Bush* (Doubleday Page, 1903).

"A Far-Away Melody" first published in *Harper's Bazar*, 22 September 1883 and collected in *A Humble Romance* (Harper, 1887) and in *Collected Ghost Stories* (Arkham House, 1974).

"The Wind in the Rose-Bush" first published in *Everybody's Magazine*, February 1902 and collected in *The Wind in the Rose-Bush* (Doubleday Page, 1903).

"A Gentle Ghost" first published in *Harper's New Monthly Magazine*, August 1889 and collected in *A New England Nun* (Harper, 1891).

"Silence" first published in *Harper's New Monthly Magazine*, July 1893 and collected in *Silence and Other Stories* (Harper, 1898).

"The School-Teacher's Story" first published in *Romance*, February 1894 and collected in *Lost Ghosts* (Hippocampus Press, 2018).

"The Vacant Lot" first published in *Everybody's Magazine*, September 1902 and collected in *The Wind in the Rose-Bush* (Doubleday Page, 1903).

"Luella Miller" first published in *Everybody's Magazine*, December 1902 and collected in *The Wind in the Rose-Bush* (Doubleday Page, 1903).

"The Southwest Chamber" first published in *Everybody's Magazine*, April 1903 and collected in *The Wind in the Rose-Bush* (Doubleday Page, 1903).

"The Lost Ghost" first published in *Everybody's Magazine*, May 1903 and collected in *The Wind in the Rose-Bush* (Doubleday Page, 1903).

"Sweet-Flowering Perennial" first published in *Harper's New Monthly Magazine*, July 1915 and collected in *The Uncollected Stories* (University of Mississippi, 1992).

"The Jade Bracelet" first published in *The Forum*, April 1918 and collected in *Collected Ghost Stories* (Arkham House, 1974).

"The White Shawl", unpublished at the time of her death and collected in *The Uncollected Stories* (University of Mississippi, 1992).